Deal with the Fae King

Bride of the Fae King

Silya Barakat

Copyright © 2023 Silya Barakat

All rights reserved

The characters and events portrayed in this book are fictitious. Any similarity to real persons, living or dead, is coincidental and not intended by the author.

No part of this book may be reproduced, or stored in a retrieval system, or transmitted in any form or by any means, electronic, mechanical, photocopying, recording, or otherwise, without express written permission of the publisher.

ISBN (paperback): 9798376547724

Cover design by: Silya Barakat

To all the fictional men lovers out there:

I feel the need to take a moment and give a special dedication to you all. You know who you are—the readers who swoon over the heroes in our stories, who get lost in their fantasies of passionate encounters and happy endings.

This book is for you. May it provide all the seductive thrills and unforgettable moments you could ever hope for.

PS: Sorry mom, but I wrote this book instead of giving you grandkids.

Contents

Title Page
Copyright
Dedication
Chapter 1   1
Chapter 2   14
Chapter 3   28
Chapter 4   40
Chapter 5   51
Chapter 6   65
Chapter 7   80
Chapter 8   93
Chapter 9   104
Chapter 10   120
Chapter 11   135
Chapter 12   150
Chapter 13   163

Chapter 14	176
Chapter 15	193
Chapter 16	209
Chapter 17	220
Chapter 18	233
Chapter 19	248
Chapter 20	261
Chapter 21	275
Chapter 22	285
Chapter 23	300
Chapter 24	309
Chapter 25	321
Chapter 26	337
Chapter 27	349
Chapter 28	361
Chapter 29	369
Chapter 30	377
Chapter 31	386
Chapter 32	395
Chapter 33	404
Chapter 34	418
Thanks you so much for reading!	429
About The Author	431
Books By This Author	433

Chapter 1

A Fae deal

Warm blood sprayed against my cheek, and I knew I just made an irrevocable mistake.

Whenever anyone tried to make a deal with the Fae, misfortune always followed it.

Always.

Connor's body crumpled to the ground. His eyes were wide open, but the glimmer of life was slowly fading.

A sickening feeling welled up inside me as deep crimson stains spread across the roots of the ancient oak trees.

My hand clenched around the hilt of my dagger as I looked around.

No one was here.

Not to mortal senses, anyway.

I looked towards Isra, and my heart ached to hear her muffled sobs reverberating through the trees.

Her hands trembled as she covered her face, hiding the tears that were streaming down her cheeks.

I'd made a mistake.

I promised Isra that there would be no deaths in this deal, but now I had failed her.

I wanted to say something, to offer some kind of comfort or hope, but I knew it wouldn't be enough.

She had trusted me, and I had let her down.

I placed my arm around her shoulder, drawing her close. "It's okay," I whispered. But the words felt hollow and meaningless. I should have listened to my gut and stayed hidden away in the palace. "Can you be brave for me?"

Isra nodded, her tears glistening in the moonlight.

Only one person could have done this.

The Winter King.

Sweat beaded on my forehead as I stepped into the clearing.

All I had to do was make this deal—and pray he wouldn't ask for more than I could offer him. And I was willing to give up a lot to achieve my goal.

Everyone feared the Winter King.

Everyone.

His reputation for being sly and cruel was known far and wide in his dealings. A monster with no mercy or remorse.

His people held him in high regard and I knew he could be just, even if he wasn't particularly generous.

The leaves crackled and snapped as I stepped forward, the sound echoing through the air.

It was time to be brave.

Frost spread across the ground, and the cold seeped into my bones. I glanced around at the trees.

Their trunks were tall and ancient.

A shadow moved in the corner of my eye. It moved closer and closer with each step.

Connor's body was reduced to a pile of gray ash and dust. As the particles drifted through the air, they sparkled like stars.

My stomach dropped. My fingers tightened

around the hilt of my dagger.

The Winter King had arrived.

Power radiated around me, and I slowly looked up.

My eyes met the gaze of the Winter King, his icy stare piercing my soul.

He stepped into the clearing, his metallic armor clanking with each step.

He was dressed all in black, his cape billowing behind him.

I noticed the fur trimming, a deep, blood-red hue, stained from his past dealings, standing out in stark contrast.

His cape was embroidered with jewels, and a silver mask concealed his face.

The eerie, haunting howl of a wolf echoed in the night.

I stepped closer, my hand never leaving my dagger's hilt. "Greetings Winter King. I seek an audience."

My voice was loud and assured as I lowered my head in respect.

He stepped forward, his boots sinking into the soft earth beneath him.

A gloved finger gently caressed my cheek, smearing the blood that stained it.

"It suits you." His voice was like liquid ice, cold and calculating. "The blood caresses your skin like a lover."

It felt like he could see through me as he stepped back.

"He intended to sell you out to the Selwyn queen, a helpless victim ready for slaughter. He was ready to betray you for a bar of gold. But I saved you."

I believed him.

My stepmother's every thought and action was centered on securing the throne. She had total control over my father and was now determined to have her son ascend to the throne.

As long as she lived, my life would be at risk.

I swallowed hard, my throat dry. "A bar of gold? That doesn't even come close to my true value."

The Winter King nodded, his eyes glittering in the moonlight. "I'm sure it's true for some people." He gave Isra a fleeting glance before his gaze fell on me. "You have my undivided attention. What is it you yearn for?"

Isra shook her head, her voice trembling. "We need your aid to shield the kingdom from the Selwyn queen's ambitions."

No, Isra! That's not what we discussed! I wanted to yell, but bit my lip and stayed silent.

The Winter King fixed his gaze on me. "Is that so?"

His voice was like a whisper, but I could feel the power behind it.

"Thank you for saving me from certain death. I'm greatly indebted to you."

"Debts are to be repaid." He stepped closer, the heat of his breath washing over my cheeks. "But I'm feeling incredibly benevolent today. What do you desire of me?"

From the corner of my eye, I saw Isra's eyes on me; her fear was palpable in the air.

My heart beat quickly in my chest, the thudding echoing in my ears.

I was painfully aware of the cost, but I knew I had to do it.

It was the only way I could ensure the security of my kingdom.

To protect myself.

He was the only one that I could turn to for help.

"We seem to have started off on a sour note. Allow me to formally introduce myself." He stepped back, his hands spread wide and still.

"You may call me Doran. And you are?"

His name? Not a title, but a name. A fake name, perhaps? That wouldn't shock me in the least.

What did I know about the Fae? People often embellished stories about them, making them sound more fantastic than they actually were.

Legends and tales of old paled compared to what I was experiencing - this was real.

How could I identify the truth from lies?

"Aleyna," I said, my voice barely above a whisper. "My name is Aleyna."

"Aleyna." He rolled the name on his tongue as if savoring the taste of it. "Your name is as enchanting as you are."

Charming words. His flattery fell on deaf ears; I was not convinced.

I was playing a dangerous game and one misstep could mean my doom. He wasn't a man to cross, but a man to negotiate with.

"I may call you Doran?" I paused, my eyes scanning the area as I considered my next move. "Is that really your name?"

"You may call me whatever you like, princess." He took a step closer, invading my personal space again. From behind his mask, his eyes bored into mine. Her gray eyes were like a winter sky, bleak and cold with a hint of something wild. "Why don't we continue this conversation elsewhere?"

He gestured towards the trees, and Isra stepped forward, grabbing my arm. "Forgive me, princess," she said, her fingers twitching nervously, "but I can't help but feel this isn't safe."

My dearest lady-in-waiting was right, of course.

His plans and ambitions were a mystery to me, leaving me to speculate about what he was capable of.

"I accept your offer. Unfortunately, I cannot accept your invitation. We can talk here and now."

"Do you not trust me?" He held out his hand, his palm outstretched in a silent invitation for me to accept. "You have questions and I have answers."

Someone with good sense would utter a firm "no".

I considered myself to be sensible.

Desperation made one do dangerous, foolhardy things.

A sudden wave of energy rushed through

me when I took his hand. "Very well." I took a deep breath. "Lead the way."

At that moment, I knew two things: Doran was not to be trusted, and we were going to have a discussion that would decide my fate. A deal with the Fae King that could save my kingdom - or doom it forever.

Nobody knew what would happen, and the stakes were incredibly high. I only hoped the results wouldn't be too catastrophic.

He led me into the darkness of the forest. His gloved hand stayed firmly in mine, as if he was goading me into taking this risk.

My heartbeat quickened, but I didn't pull away.

Fools rush in, they say. Every now and then, a bit of foolishness can be the smartest thing to do.

As we traveled through the forest, the light of the clearing faded away, replaced by the darkness of the trees.

Animals scurried around our feet and the wind rustled through the leaves.

We made a strange pair, walking hand in hand through the darkness. A giant of a Fae king and a desperate mortal princess.

"Where are we going?" I asked, my voice barely rising above the silence.

He stopped and turned to me, his masked face inches away from mine. "You'll see soon enough."

We continued to walk in silence, the only sound being the crunch of leaves beneath our feet.

Finally, we reached a clearing. We stepped into a glade of shimmering ice, the stars shimmering and radiating a bright, icy light.

In the center of the glade, I spotted a dining table, two chairs, and a tray with refreshments.

His hand enveloped mine, squeezing gently, as if to caution me to remain silent.

From the darkness, a wolf emerged, its eyes shining in the pale moonlight.

As the wolf approached, its paw steps were heavy, thudding against the ground.

Its fur was a deep shade of white, with a slight sheen to it like fresh-fallen snow.

It stopped next to the Fae king, who placed his hand on its fur.

The wolf's fur brushed against my feet as it curled up in a small ball.

Its eyes held a wisdom beyond its years.

Doran gestured towards the chairs,

inviting me to sit down.

I sat down opposite him, my eyes drawn to the glistening stream winding through the glade.

This was his domain, and I was only a guest.

"I prefer to do business civilly," he said, filling two glasses with a bright red grenadine. "Let us make a deal."

I took a sip and heard the clink of ice cubes against the glass.

The grenadine was sweet and calming, and it tasted of ripe berries on my tongue.

I tried to read his expression, looking for the slightest hint of emotion. But the mask made it impossible.

"What do you propose?"

He leaned in close to me, his hands lightly touching mine, as if he were about to reveal something.

I leaned forward, the sudden movement causing a creak in the chair.

"Most people would have been too frightened to stay, yet here you stand, surrounded by the darkness."

"Most people would have run." I leaned

back and enjoyed the sound of the grenadine swishing around in my glass. "Everyone knows a deal isn't really a deal unless you pay for it."

I refused to be intimidated by him. I was desperate, but not foolish.

I was prepared to negotiate, and I knew that any deal he proposed would come with its own risks.

"What do you offer that is worth my time?" I said, lifting my chin and meeting his gaze.

His eyes glimmered with a hint of amusement. "What I offer is far greater than what you can imagine."

He paused, letting the silence hang in the air as if to emphasize his words.

"Take my deal and you'll be rewarded - you will have a peaceful kingdom and receive the answers you seek."

A shiver ran down my spine.

The sweetest of offers, and if accepted, I would be bound by the Fae King's word.

Now I needed to know his terms.

"I don't care for foolish mortals who make rash decisions." He waved his hand, and the glade turned brighter, as if it was lit by a thousand stars. "But I sense something special in you. That's why I chose you."

For a moment, I felt like the most powerful person in this realm.

I straightened my back and met his gaze. "I approached you."

"And I don't answer all calls," he said, his voice low. "But there was something special about you. You had the courage to come looking for me, and the boldness to remain when you found me."

The light caught the intricate patterns on his silver mask.

"So here we are, Aleyna. It's time we discuss the terms of our agreement."

My knuckles turned white as I grasped my hands together, struggling to keep my composure.

"What do you want from me?"

Chapter 2

His price

"The question is." Doran mimicked me, perfectly recreating the same intonation I had used. "What do you want from me?" He spread his hands. "I will give you what your heart desires. Power, wealth, immortality. Whatever you long for, it can be yours."

And all of that was in his power to give. I knew it, and he did too. We both knew the stakes of this deal.

All I had to do was decide.

"And in exchange?" I asked, already knowing the answer.

"In exchange for my gifts," Doran replied, his voice softening. "You will give me what I want."

I leaned back in my chair, my head spinning with ideas, my heart racing.

What could he possibly want me to offer him?

Did he want my soul?

I took a deep breath and met his gaze. "What is it you desire from me?"

"Your response will determine the outcome."

I glanced away, avoiding eye contact.

His wolf watched us, the air around us filled with its low, rumbling growl.

I sensed he was testing me, and I knew that if I wanted whatever he was offering, I'd have to pay the cost.

We both knew why I approached him. But he wanted me to say the words out loud, to accept my fate.

I glanced back up at him and mustered the courage to say the words that would forever alter my destiny. "The throne of Ilanya shall be mine."

I didn't hesitate in my answer. Everything I had done up to that point had been leading up to that moment.

It was my birthright.

"If it is the crown you seek, I will bestow it upon you and make you queen."

Doran leaned forward again, his eyes boring into mine. Black smoke swirled within their depths as if a part of him was trying to escape.

"I require something in return for this. Are you willing to make the sacrifice?"

I remembered the way my stepmother's eyes glinted when she warned me of the Fae. Her childhood was filled with stories of their strength - and the price they expected in return.

I knew that I needed to be precise with my wording.

Otherwise, the consequence *would* be dire.

I looked him in the eye. "I'm willing to make this sacrifice if you give me what I want." My head was filled with a sense of determination. "When my father passes away, I will take my rightful place as the sovereign ruler of Ilanya."

Each word was spoken slowly and deliberately, leaving no doubt I was claiming my birthright.

"The kingdom of Ilanya will be mine, and I will be its sole ruler. That is my one and only demand."

"And you wish for me to kill your brother so that you may take his place?"

When I heard his words, my eyebrows rose in disbelief.

Did he really have the audacity to ask me if I wanted my brother dead? I heard tales of the Fae king's cruelness, but what I saw today was far more sinister.

Could I make a deal with him? Could I stomach doing that to my brother?

Every cell in my body was telling me to say no.

"No, absolutely not. His place? No," I replied firmly, my voice unwavering. "I want nothing more than what is rightfully mine by birthright. I refuse to watch my brother suffer, unless it is absolutely vital for me to take the throne."

Even if there wasn't a close bond between us, Artur was my brother, and I was determined to protect him no matter what. His death would wreck me.

I didn't want to be remembered as the kin slayer.

I held my breath, waiting for Doran's verdict.

He studied me in silence, his expression

unreadable.

"He's your father's firstborn son."

"Foreign succession laws have no bearing over Ilanya. I am the rightful heir."

"You will have your throne. Your brother will be taken care of, and you will ascend to the throne of Ilanya, the cheers of your people echoing in the air."

"What do you want in exchange for that?"

I held my breath as my heart fluttered in anticipation of his answer. I will go to any lengths to get what I want. Even if it meant making a deal with the devil himself.

"This is a favorable outcome for both of us. The last thing you want is a Selwyn, even if he's only half, sitting on the throne."

The Selwyn family were unwavering in their loyalty to the Summer Court, and their loathing of the Winter Court and its king was undeniable.

Doran was looking to leverage this opportunity to not only become stronger, but also gain more authority in the mortal realms.

A clever move, and it was the main reason I approached him.

"Are you familiar with the Fae courts?"

The basics and nothing extra.

But my lack of knowledge wouldn't stop me from striking a bargain with Doran.

"I know enough. A loyal friend in the mortal realm will benefit you."

Power shifted in the air as if the sun and moon collided.

The frosty chill of the Fae king's presence seeped through my veins, freezing all emotion from my body.

I swallowed hard and forced my chin up. "What is it that you want from me?"

He leaned in closer, and a knot of fear tightened in my stomach. "And what do you, *friend*, think is a fair price for what you are offering?" he drawled.

I sat in silence, ruminating on how I could craft the perfect offer. It had to be something that would benefit us both.

What could I possibly offer the Winter King?

"The choice is yours," I concluded finally. He was too powerful to accidentally insult. "What is your price?"

He stared intently at me, his gaze carefully studying my features.

He spoke with a certain detachment, his words carefully chosen, "Your firstborn child."

No.

No matter the terms of this deal, I could not bring myself to sacrifice the life of my future child.

I opened my mouth to protest, but he silenced me with a dismissive gesture.

"That is my price. You decide whether or not you accept it. I'm the only one who can help you achieve your goal."

"That is your price?"

"That is my price."

He spoke in a flat, emotionless tone, but the gravity of his words seemed to linger in the air.

My child?

My insides churned and I felt nauseous.

I wanted to turn it down, but the feeling of desperation was too powerful to ignore.

There was no other choice - this was the only way for me to take the throne.

Think. Aleyna. Think.

What if he fathered this child? A husband, a father, and a Fae with extraordinary strength and magical abilities?

Yes, that would be the ideal option.

I could keep my child safe and still abide by the terms of this bargain.

The sound of my heartbeat echoed in my head as I reluctantly looked into his eyes.

I expected a high price - and I will pay it. But I would do it my way, no matter what.

"Agreed," I said. "You can father my firstborn child. When will we get wed?"

"You wish to have a child with me?" Doran's voice was suddenly husky, the need clear in his eyes.

Checkmate.

The corner of my mouth quirked up in a half-smile, and I nodded. "Yes. That is part of our agreement. Or did I misunderstand the terms?"

His eyes flashed, and a cold mist descended upon the bottle of grenadine on the table, leaving a thin layer of frost.

My head tilted, and I raised my chin in a silent challenge. "Do you wish me to marry another?"

"No," he spoke in a low, hushed voice, his gaze never shifting away from me. "I will take you as my wife and father my child. And you will be my queen."

I inhaled, my nostrils flaring. "No, I will take full control of my kingdom, and be its queen," I corrected him. "You will simply be the father of my child. You will not be the King of Ilanya. *Or* have any power. You will only be my husband."

A powerful husband I could rely on to protect my child and I. A husband who would help me secure the throne of Ilanya.

But I would not be his queen - I would be Ilanya's.

He laughed softly, and the tension dissipated. "Very well."

He took off his mask, revealing his face for the first time.

I swallowed hard.

His face was a masterpiece, more beautiful than I ever would have thought possible.

High cheekbones, full lips, and eyes that seemed to shimmer like ice. His shoulder-length, pitch-black hair fell around his face like a curtain.

For a moment, I almost forgot about our bargain.

He was breathtaking.

And dangerous.

He flashed me a knowing smirk, his lips curved in a sly smile.

The tales about the beauty and cunning of the Fae were true. What else was true?

"Your beauty has not been exaggerated, Winter King. I accept your terms."

He chuckled softly; the sound sent a shiver down my spine. "And you are bolder than I expected."

"A woman must be bold to survive in this world." I forced a smile. "But now, I believe we have a wedding to plan."

He removed his gloves and placed them on the table. "That she must. But I suggest you be careful with your boldness, my queen. It can lead you to places you may not want to go."

"Marrying a king is not a terrible destination," I retorted, my voice resolute.

He laughed again; the sound echoing through the glade. "Trust me, my queen. You will not regret this alliance. It pleases me that my wife finds me attractive."

I bit my lip and averted my gaze, my face feeling hot and my heart pounding.

Now that I made the deal, I needed to act

more like a ruler than an apprehensive princess.

"Your wife?"

"Yes." He leaned backward, and his eyes glimmered in the light. "You belong to me now. My queen. My wife."

His.

I couldn't deny that the thought of being his queen sent a thrill through me, but I knew better than to let my guard down.

I expected a powerful alliance - but not this. I refused to be controlled by him - I was the master of my own fate.

I squared my shoulders and met his gaze with a steady one of my own. "I'm not your wife. Yet."

He placed his hands on the table. "But you will be. Today."

The sweet smell of my glass of grenadine filled my nostrils as my fingers tightened around it. "I will be a formidable ally, and I demand the same from you. But not today."

He smiled, a strange glint in his eyes. Frost and fire combined to create a beautiful, yet dangerous, force. "You wish to rescind our deal?"

I shook my head. "No. If we are going to do this, we are doing this the proper way. A wedding ceremony is necessary for a true union."

His eyebrow quirked. "You are surprisingly traditional for a Winter Queen."

What did he expect? That I'd be a passive pawn in his game?

"I may not have been born into Fae nobility, but I know how to rule like one. A proper wedding ceremony and union between us is the only way to ensure I will become queen."

In Ilanya, rumors spread quickly and were more destructive than any sword. Playing this by the rules was essential.

He nodded, a hint of admiration in his gaze. "Very well. We shall have our mortal wedding. Who would have thought?"

He smiled a genuine, warm smile that lit up his face.

For a moment, I was mesmerized by him, forgetting he was the dangerous Fae king and instead imagining him as my future husband.

But then he blinked, and it was gone, the illusion broken.

I nodded slowly. "Yes, a mortal wedding is necessary to make this union true."

He stood up and reached out his hand to me. "I accept your terms."

I hesitated for a second, then reached out

and took his hand. His fingers were stiff, the chill of winter crawling up my spine.

He leaned in, and I felt the warmth of his breath on my skin before his lips gently grazed my cheek. My skin prickled with goosebumps.

"Until our wedding day then, my queen," he murmured in a low voice, his breath an icy whisper on my skin.

I tried to pull away, but he held me tight, his grip unyielding.

"I make a solemn vow to you, my queen. If you attempt to fool me, you will live to regret it."

I shivered as he spoke, and his icy words made me trust every word he said.

I swallowed hard, my mouth unable to form a reply, so I just nodded.

He stepped back, and I felt a slight tug as his fingers reluctantly left mine, his smile still beaming with pleasure. "You wouldn't be foolish enough to do that, would you?"

Weakness flooded my body, and I stumbled back. Now was no time to give in to fear or doubt.

"I warn you, Winter King." My voice was crisp. "Don't try to trick me. I'm mortal, but I am a queen. And queens have power."

He chuckled softly, the sound sending a

chill down my spine. "I'm sure they do,"

He faded into the shadows, leaving me alone in the murky night.

I heard the creak of the chair as I stumbled back into my seat.

What had I done?

Chapter 3

Priestess

Snowflakes fluttered down from the sky, lightly landing on the white sand of the beach. The sun was scorching, but I welcomed its warmth as the mist from the waves sprayed against my veil.

In the distance, I saw a figure approaching; it was him — my soon-to-be husband, Doran.

His gray eyes sparkled in the sunlight, and his powerful frame shimmered like ice.

His silver armor clinked as he moved, and his furs were thick and luxurious.

His face was as otherworldly as ever, but it held something else - authority and power.

Today, I would marry a man whose face

I had memorized, but whose name was still a mystery.

Princess Aleyna, wife of the Winter King.

I watched silently, my red veil acting as a barrier, as he stepped closer and our gazes locked.

My heart raced as I reminded myself why I was there.

I knew that, to secure the future of my people, a political marriage was essential.

If the unthinkable happened, and Artur ascended the throne, the people would suffer.

We stood in silence for a moment, the weight of our future together palpable in the air.

Then, slowly and with the utmost care, Doran reached out his hand.

He gave a slight smirk, followed by a raised eyebrow.

Taking a deep breath, I placed my hand on top of his and nodded solemnly.

Queen Aleyna of the Winter Court.

A title I promised to bear with dignity and resolve.

We stepped into the water, and the sun glistened off the wet sand beneath us.

As the sea water lapped around me, my

red wedding dress, with its intricate lacing and jewels, felt heavy against my skin.

A cold sweat trickled down my back as my legs trembled and my heart thudded, yet I didn't move.

The priestess waited in the water, her eyes narrowing as her wet robes clung to her body. "Who comes before me?"

"I come," I said firmly. "I, Aleyna Han, Imperial Princess of Ilanya, come to this sacred place with-" Doran was unlikely to be his real name, but I paused before uttering his title. "-with my betrothed, The Winter King."

The Winter King. The Butcher of Calan. Monster.

My husband.

The priestess nodded, her gaze flickering between us. "Do you both come before me, to make this sacred vow of marriage?"

This was it. The moment of truth.

"Yes." I pushed away the sorrow that welled within me. With only Isra as my witness, I stepped forward and joined my fate to his. "We have come to share our lives, and to be joined in an everlasting bond."

Doran's hand tightened around mine, his calloused fingertips brushing against my skin.

My mother should have been here to witness this moment. Her only daughter, trading her safety for the safety and security of her people.

Her wedding comb felt heavy on my scalp. My eyes drifted to Doran's face, and I found strength in his gaze.

How would married life be with him? Did he have a heart?

"And you, Winter King, or whatever your true name may be," the priestess said. "Do you accept this woman as your wife and pledge to honor her in sickness and in health?"

The corner of his mouth twitched as if he was suppressing a smile. "I do."

I echoed his words, my voice ringing clear over the waves. "We do."

The priestess stepped back and gracefully lifted her hand, her fingers adorned with rings. "Step forward into the sea."

Hand in hand, we stepped forward, taking three enormous steps.

She carefully tied seaweed around our wrists, the wetness of it sending a chill through our skin.

Warmth passed through me when his fingers intertwined with mine.

I looked into his eyes, feeling the intensity of the moment before glancing away.

His thick, black eyelashes brushed against his cheeks as he gazed at me.

A small smile tugged at the corner of my lips as I remembered how he looked at me when we first met. Hunger and curiosity.

That same look kept me in my place.

The priestess's low, melodic voice echoed through the air as she recited ancient vows and blessed our union.

And when it was all done, she stepped back.

It was time for the gift exchange.

The situation hit me like a ton of bricks and my heart sunk in my chest.

Doran hadn't been informed about this custom - the exchanging of gifts to symbolize the binding of our vows.

Taking a deep breath, I slowly glanced up at him and saw the recognition in his eyes.

He raised an eyebrow as my throat tightened.

Did he think I was trying to deceive him? Or worse, take advantage of him?

Scrambling to find an explanation, I kept

my eyes lowered as I felt the spray of the waves against my skin.

The priestess stepped forward and severed the slippery seaweed that bound our hands.

As it unraveled, she said, "Gifts may come and go, but your vows linger, a reminder of your commitment to one another. May your union never falter, even during times of hardship."

Gifts may come and go. But a Fae deal, once it is made, cannot be broken.

The priestess turned to me.

A gentle glow shone on her face as the sun turned her white robe a delicate pink.

"Aleyna, the spirits have bestowed upon you the gift of writing your own story. Make the most of this opportunity, you won't get another. What blessings do you wish to give your husband?"

I turned to Isra.

She handed me a sword made of white gold, its weight heavy in my hands.

Husband of Aleyna Han, imperial princess and crown princess of Ilanya. Winter Queen.

By tradition, his name should be etched into it, but as he hadn't given me a name, I carefully inscribed my own.

I had always been an untraditional princess.

The blade glinted in the light, freshly sharpened, and the hilt was encrusted with sapphires.

"This sword is a symbol of our union." I handed Doran the ivory hilt, and he ran his fingers along the intricate carvings.

The sword gleamed in the pale light, and I knew it would serve us both well.

"This sword I give to you, my husband," I said. "Let this blade guard our loyalty, and may no force be strong enough to divide us."

He ran his fingers over the engravings of my name, tracing them delicately before taking hold of the hilt.

He gripped the blade, his fingers curled around it like a vice as he lifted it in a graceful arc, letting the light catch and reflect off its shining surface.

The ritualistic gesture seemed to signify something more. But what I couldn't tell.

He bowed his head in my direction, the light of the sun reflecting off his glossy hair.

A flood of comfort filled me.

He acknowledged my gift and our union.

This was a symbol of our shared commitment, no matter what the future held.

"My present for you is something that cannot be held in your hands." Doran's voice was low, but it reverberated within me. "My gift to you is a vow of loyalty and shelter, promising to stand with you through anything we may face. I swear by all that is sacred that I shall never forsake you or our union."

I was left speechless, my lips parted in surprise. I hadn't expected this—a Fae oath to me, from a king with a ruthless reputation.

His sharpness exceeded my expectations—not only did he grasp the concept of gift-giving, but he also made a promise to me that was more generous than what we had discussed.

His unwavering stare and promise of a Fae oath created a sense of awe in me, as if I had stumbled upon something far greater than what I had initially expected.

My heart swelled with emotions that were hard to describe—relief, peace, and something more powerful, a deep trust in my choice to accept the deal.

This kind of loyalty was an unexpected boon.

The Fae were prudent and never parted with anything without a price.

But here I was, standing in front of a Fae king who offered me his loyalty and protection without any conditions.

I knew then that this deal was going to be unlike anything I'd ever experienced before—and I was strangely grateful for it.

But what would this gift cost me?

Everything had a price in this world, but the Fae were particularly unforgiving in what they expected in return.

The priestess smiled as she stepped forward. "Your marriage has now been imbued with a timelessness that will never be broken. Cursed are those who seek to undo this sacred bond."

Isra and I turned to each other and shared a knowing smile.

Although we both knew this was an arranged marriage, something shifted.

Power.

As I stepped out of the waves, my dress and veil clung to me.

Doran walked towards me and extended his hand, helping me back onto dry land.

The sand clung to our feet as we moved forward, and a wave of emotion hit me—we were married now.

A wall of snow appeared, the cold flakes glistening in the sun.

My eyes widened as I looked at Doran.

"A mortal wedding isn't enough to bind a Fae. Allow me to perform the traditional Winter wedding ceremony."

I nodded, and a shiver ran through my body as an icy chill descended.

He pulled a white dagger from his pocket, the sharp point reflecting my face back at me.

A delicate rune was inscribed onto the hilt of the sword, and a single drop of blood sparkled in the light.

He cut his hand, and blue blood oozed out.

Was the drop on the knife mortal blood?

He reached for my hand, and cut my hand as well.

As our blood mixed with the blade of the dagger, the sharp sting of the blade quickly subsided.

Red and blue entwined and formed a majestic, deep purple.

He smeared the blade with our mingled blood, and a symbol formed. A rune of eternity that marked our bond forever.

"This is a symbol of our union," he said, his voice ringing out over the snow-covered beach. "Our blood is bound." He held the dagger up, lifting his eyes up to the sky. "Let the earth and sky serve as witnesses to our union."

The blade of the dagger pulsed with a vibrant purple light as light shimmered around us.

The icy sensation of frost spread up my arm as Doran lowered his hand and the blade.

A strange sensation grew in my gut, accompanied by a faint ringing in my ears.

Power emanated from the blade, and I knew that this union was now sealed with something far greater than mere words.

Doran held out his hand in the fading light, and a heavy golden chain materialized in it.

He softly draped the chain around my neck and the dagger clattered against it, a reminder of our union.

He kissed the top of my head. "Never take this off," he breathed. "We are bound together, united as one. This necklace shows the world that we are bound."

Peering up at Doran through my thin veil, I licked my lips. "We must make this union official."

No wedding was complete without a bedding ceremony.

Chapter 4

Marriage Bonds

The silence was unbearable.

In the dimly lit room, only my ragged gasps and his even breaths filled the silence.

Sweat trickled down my forehead, and my throat was so dry I could hardly swallow.

Remain calm. The price of peace is marriage.

My feet cracked on the wooden floor as I carefully walked towards the dresser, my long veil trailing behind me.

Doran followed closely behind me.

He had a reassuring aura, but his presence was still somewhat intimidating.

I felt the heat of his gaze on me as he intently watched my every move.

He took a step forward, the sound of his shoes on the floor echoing off the walls.

His fingers brushed against my cheek, and I felt the urge to blush.

His fingertips were gentle as he slowly pulled the veil away from my face.

I felt exposed, as if my emotions were laid bare.

I detested it.

He was my husband, and I was his wife now. But I was more than that. More than simply a wife.

He gently tugged my wedding comb out of my hair, and it clinked softly as he placed it on the dresser.

His hand lingered on my neck, and I steadied my breathing.

The air was thick with anticipation.

But he turned away and unbuckled the clasps of his shirt, the metal clinking softly.

As he removed the garment, his toned body was revealed, the outline of his muscles glinting in the light.

His blue tattoos glowed in the soft, dim

lighting.

No.

They shimmered with power.

My stomach churned.

It was time.

My fingers quivered as I peeled back the layers of my dress to reveal the ivory buttons of my wedding gown.

Doran's breath hitched, and my face flushed in response.

I clumsily fumbled with the buttons on the dress, trying to undo them.

I made a sound to get his attention, and he spun around. "Would you mind helping me?"

He stepped closer, guiding my hands away from the buttons.

His fingers deftly undid the dress, one by one.

I studied the intricate patterns of his tattoos through the reflection in the mirror. "What do these mean to you?"

The swirls were intricate, and I couldn't help but be mesmerized by their beauty.

"They are symbols of strength and protection," he answered, his voice gravelly with emotion. "The runes tell a story. I'm a warrior, and I solemnly swear to fight for my people with every ounce of my strength."

He stepped back, his hands hidden behind his back.

I carefully peeled off my red dress and felt the cool air on my skin.

The beading on the fabric glowed in the dwindling light, creating a cascade of glittering colors.

My heart thudded as Doran stepped forward, his warm breath fanning my neck as he moved closer, his lips just brushing my ear. "Don't worry, little wife. No bedding ceremony will take place tonight."

What did he mean?

His lips were soft and gentle as they brushed against my cheek.

I reached up and ran my finger along his jawline, feeling the softness of his skin. "You want a child? Am I not to give you one?"

Did he regret his decision and wanted to renegotiate our deal?

Was my mortal status too shameful for him?

His eyes crinkled. "We will conceive no child tonight. I don't believe in forced bedding ceremonies. When the moment is right, we will become one."

I shuddered. "An alliance."

He fixed his gaze on me. "Yes, what's truer than two people bound by a singular purpose that they have no intention of breaking?"

A child for a throne.

A marriage to seal the deal.

His words washed over me like a soothing balm, and my shoulders relaxed.

No bedding ceremony.

His fingertips lightly brushed against mine as he walked towards the canopy bed.

My eyes followed him as he lay down, the sheets billowing around his body.

"Come and lie next to me tonight," he said, his voice soft and inviting.

I walked towards the bed and carefully laid down next to him, his warmth radiating onto my skin.

He pulled me closer to him, and I bit my lip.

His breath was hot on my neck as he whispered in my ear, "It's time for us to fight for our future. Together."

Curiosity filled me as I stared up at my husband, the man who promised to fight for his people and protect me.

"Am I not desirable?" I asked, my voice barely audible.

He leaned in and kissed my forehead, his lips cool against my skin. "Your beauty is incomparable." He looked up at the ceiling. "I want to see you on your knees, begging me for it. I don't take a woman against her will, even if she is my wife."

My eyes narrowed.

Was he testing me?

"What would you do if I said I wanted you?"

Doran was a beautiful man, but the very idea was ludicrous.

Lust was destructive. It was self-indulgent and self-centered. When the stakes were this high, lust only led to ruin.

He smiled, and a twinkle appeared in his eyes. "Then I would call you a liar. I can feel your heart fluttering, and I can see your eyes wide with fear. You don't know what you're asking for." He ran his fingers through my hair, sending gentle tingles down my spine. "But I do."

I swallowed hard and forced myself to look away.

Doran was right- I didn't know what I was

asking for.

It was eerie how he could read me so well- like he had some kind of canny insight into my innermost thoughts.

"You can feel my heart fluttering?" I asked with trepidation.

He nodded. "Yes, I can. And I know what you're feeling. You're scared and unsure of yourself. They have pushed you into a corner, under pressure to decide. But I can also feel your curiosity. You want to explore, to see if our union can work."

What?

That should be impossible. There was no way he sensed my emotions.

His look of amusement told me otherwise.

"When two people in the Winter Court marry, it is more than just a ceremony; it is a commitment that will last forever. We are connected. Your strongest emotions and desires become my own."

A wave of fear flooded me, my breath catching in my throat.

He could feel my fear as if it was his own. He could sense the turmoil of emotions in my heart- the anxiety and trepidation that seemed to increase by the second.

My most private thoughts were exposed.

All I wanted to do right now was to run away. Hide in the palace, praying he wouldn't come looking for me.

But I stayed put, my gaze locked on the man in front of me- the man who read me better than anyone ever could.

I swallowed hard. "You can feel that?"

He nodded, his eyes brimming with understanding. "It's okay," he whispered, stroking my hair. "I know you're scared, but the bond goes two ways. I can feel your fear, but you can also feel my strength. Focus."

And suddenly, I could.

As if his words opened a door in my mind, I felt the strength of his conviction radiating onto me. He was determined and unyielding in his beliefs.

His words filled me with a strange comfort, and I closed my eyes. "Can you manipulate it?"

He shook his head. "It's a bond of unity, not a bond of subjugation. I cannot control you, and neither can you control me. You have my word."

The Fae were masters of manipulation, but rarely made promises.

It was part of a marriage bond, but it wasn't clear to me what it meant to the Fae.

"Can I stop you from accessing my innermost emotions?"

He closed his eyes. "I can block the bond. It will filter out most emotions, but the most intense emotions will still be shared."

"Yes, please." I took a deep breath and nodded, feeling his strength coursing through me before it stopped. "What now? What is our next move?"

He lay on his side and looked at me, his gray eyes searching my face. "The only way forward is together. As one. You shall introduce me to your family. And I will introduce you to my household."

I turned to face him. "I will have to warn them about you."

A grin appeared on his face as he chuckled.

"But it will have to wait. My stepmother's family is in Ilanya, and it would be unwise to arrive unannounced."

He laughed, a deep rumble that filled the room. "I am no stranger to courtly politics. We will make our own announcement, and it will be one they cannot ignore."

And the one advantage I had, the surprise

element, would be gone.

"They will leave in two days. After that one last dinner, I will invite you to my father's court."

His mouth was set in a firm line and his eyes hardened, conveying a stern seriousness that was unnerving. "I can accompany you if you'd like. The Selwyns are not to be underestimated."

My mind raced as I considered the implications of his offer. It was a risky move and one that I undoubtedly didn't want to take.

Doran was a formidable ally, but his presence risked stirring up further complications.

I kept my face carefully neutral, hiding my inner turmoil with a careful mask of politeness.

I knew he could sense emotions, and I was determined not to give him any sign of manipulation.

"It would be great to have your backing, but unfortunately I must go it alone. It would be too dangerous. You're my husband and the leader of a powerful family—if you were by my side, they would take it as a sign of hostility. I would prefer it if you stayed away."

He nodded, his face revealing nothing. "Your wish is my command. I will await your return, my queen."

My queen.

The words made me feel powerful and safe all at once.

His reaction surprised me the most.

He was willing to take the risk of trusting me, knowing full well that I could turn against him at any moment.

A glint of something flashed in his eyes, and I knew he saw the flicker of emotion that crossed my face.

He might have blocked the bond, but he was still an observant person.

He needed that to stay ahead of his enemies.

He smiled, a gentle curve of his lips that reminded me of a wolf's smile. "If I sense you are in danger, I will be there in an instant. No matter the consequences."

Chapter 5

The Golden Lion

As I approached the entrance, two red banners adorned with a golden lion fluttered in the wind—the banner of the Selwyns.

Two blue banners, with a golden sun, the emblem of the Han family, stood proudly next to them. Smaller and more subtle.

That was deliberate.

I shot a look of disdain at the golden lions before I softened my expression.

Everyone in the palace watched each other with suspicion, like they were all snakes in the same pit.

The servants paused and looked up as I

strode through the ornate archway.

The marble walls gleamed and the grand staircase led to an open courtyard where aristocrats, merchants, and diplomats mingled.

My stepmother's golden hair shone with the rubies and pearls adorning her crown.

She smiled at my father, who stood behind her, looking content.

The curls of her dress danced in the light of hundreds of candles that adorned the walls.

She was the center of attention, always the belle of the ball.

Observing her from afar, I felt a pang of envy. Though I admired my stepmother's poise and cunning, I could never quite replicate the confidence she carried.

Every time I saw her, I felt a complicated swirl of emotions—disdain for her controlling nature, trepidation over her power, and appreciation for the knowledge she'd instilled in me.

Our relationship had its own unique set of challenges.

The servants bowed their heads to me as I smiled.

The weight of my crown settled on my head and I forced myself to stand tall like the princess I was.

I did not know what the night would bring, but I kept my worries hidden.

I did all I could do, and I prayed it would be enough.

I glanced at Emre, the butler I had known since childhood. "Emre, would it be possible to send the musicians for a bit of entertainment?"

Emre smiled at me and nodded. "Of course, princess Aleyna. I'll see to it right away."

I shifted my gaze to the other servants, their shadows flickering in the candlelight.

The brightness in their eyes gave me a feeling of hope that this night could be a success.

"I am truly grateful for all your hard work. All of you have done a terrific job."

They bowed their heads as I looked at the crowd below.

Violinists, harpists, and flutists played a gentle melody as I walked down the stairway.

I slowly scanned the room, feeling the atmosphere of the space.

My stepmother and father were still in the center, the sounds of their polite conversation blending with the murmur of voices from the others around them.

Where was Artur?

I looked around, but he was nowhere to be seen.

What was my brother up to?

My steps echoed through the stairwell as I descended. Despite the tightening feeling in my stomach, I kept walking.

No matter what happened tonight, I had to keep my composure—just like my stepmother.

But what if she knew?

If she knew, she would never forgive me.

Her rage would be so fierce it would put my father's temper to shame.

I could try to tug at his heartstrings and have him disregard the situation. The Winter King's reputation would please him.

But the possibilities of what she would do next were inconceivable.

I looked up to the ceiling above, closing my eyes and silently whispering a prayer.

After what seemed like an eternity, I reached the bottom of the staircase.

My stepmother extended her hand to me. "Aleyna, come. You have greeted no one yet."

My father nodded his approval as I took

her hand.

No flaw in etiquette or expression would be overlooked.

The charade of the perfect family needed to be maintained.

I curtseyed before my stepmother and father—dutifully and obediently, but with a hint of a smile.

"Don't be silly, Aleyna." Queen Genna's eyes twinkled as she kissed me on both cheeks. "Family is family."

"Mother," I said calmly. "Your presence honors me."

My father beamed at me with a warm, loving smile.

His curly, salt-and-pepper hair was pulled back in a tight bun and his mustache twirled over his thin lips.

"My daughter." He placed his hand on his heart. "You are a sight to behold."

The queen nodded, her golden earrings jingling softly.

I was relieved that I appeased them both.

For the moment, my family seemed content. Now all I needed to do was to keep this up.

"You are indeed a sight to behold, Aleyna. A sight for the sore eyes of our court."

The insult hadn't escaped me. Ugly as a sight for sore eyes, indeed.

I lowered my head slightly and smiled gracefully.

Her words pricked my skin, but I refused to give her the satisfaction of a reaction.

I was used to her subtle remarks and veiled insults.

"Your mother is indeed a force to be reckoned with." The king's voice was filled with admiration and awe as he gazed upon the queen. "She just arrived from her father's court and organized this dinner with remarkable speed."

I gritted my teeth as I watched my stepmother enjoy the praise.

That woman was not my mother.

Neither had she lifted a finger to help the servants prepare.

I kept my thoughts unspoken, my mouth closed.

My stepmother's fingers dug into my flesh as she smiled. "You should be proud of her, dear husband. Aleyna has been a great help. She's a diligent and dutiful daughter." Her eyes flicked up to mine and her lips curved into a thin, unnatural smile. "Your future looks bright, and I'm sure you'll stay on this path."

Or else.

She didn't need to say it; I knew.

"Her husband will also be proud of her," the queen said, her tone implying a warning.

My future was in her hands.

But her tutelage taught me one thing—to be crafty and cunning.

Her words echoed in my head: never be outdone, remain one step ahead.

So I did.

I glanced over my shoulder at her. "Your grace and benevolence are appreciated more than words can express. Everything I am today is because of the lessons you taught me."

More than she could ever imagine.

The queen's face softened, and a warm chuckle escaped her. "I'm truly touched by your kindness."

My father raised his glass, and the guests echoed his action by raising their own. "To our princess," he said. "May her wisdom and loyalty endure for all time."

With a loud creak, the doors burst open

and my brother sauntered in proudly.

He glanced around with a self-satisfied grin, his eyes twinkling with a hint of naughtiness.

Silks and linens were thrown about his shoulders and feet, in stark contrast to the other guests.

Their caftans with fur linings and detailed embroidery represented Ilanya.

Unlike the attire of my brother and stepmother.

On his collarbone, I spotted a red mark.

Well, well, well. Someone was up to no good.

I kept my emotions in check and raised my glass, the clinking of the crystal echoing around me.

The queen cast a look at my brother, her eyes narrowing with disapproval. "If it isn't the prodigal son."

A sinking sensation filled my stomach as dread settled in.

I knew what was coming next—she would make this my responsibility.

Whenever my brother caused trouble, she would always make me answer for it.

"I attended one more gathering before I arrived here, mother."

The smell of alcohol and smoke lingered in the air, and I was relieved that at least he was honest enough not to deny it.

A self-satisfied smirk crossed his face as he remarked, "It's a good thing my sweet sister takes after you."

The queen's eyes grew darker, and my body tensed, fighting back the urge to roll my eyes. "You will be the one to handle this, Aleyna."

I nodded, already knowing what to do.

Artur was my responsibility. I would take care of it.

Just like I always did.

"Boys will be boys." Father chuckled and waved his hand, dismissing the issue. "I remember when I was his age."

My brother smirked at me, a silent challenge in his eyes.

The queen raised an eyebrow, unamused. "Ilanya requires a man instead of a boy," she said, her voice thick with a warning.

I grabbed my brother's arm and weaved him through the crowd and out of the room.

Guests' laughter filled the room as they

watched us.

I couldn't control my brother, but I could protect him, even if it was against his will.

"Goody two shoes," my brother muttered under his breath.

The acrid smell of alcohol made me cringe, and I rolled my eyes in exasperation.

"Not everything revolves around you, Artur."

He laughed, but I saw the fire in his eyes. He was ready to erupt at any moment.

I tightened my grip on his arm and led him out the door, simmering with anger.

I had no choice but to be the reliable one, and it weighed heavily on my shoulders.

We walked in silence and I let his drunkenness pass before glancing at him with disapproval. "You were lucky this time. Next time, I might not save you."

He shrugged carelessly as he stumbled behind me. "Mother loves me," he slurred. "She'll understand. She will forgive me."

Unlike you were the unspoken words.

I audibly sighed and tightened my hold on his arm, guiding him away from the grand, bronze statue that shadowed us.

"Love has nothing to do with this," I said. "You can't keep playing with fire like this and expect no consequences. You need to take responsibility for your actions. That's the only way you will ever truly become a man."

He stopped and looked at me, his eyes bloodshot and glassy. "I know," he hissed. "You always were the perfect daughter. Perfect, but useless."

I let out a bitter laugh and shook my head. "That is me, the perfect daughter with no authority."

A sudden lull of exhaustion rocked my body.

I wanted to be finished with this, to be set free from all of it.

The responsibilities. The expectations. The manipulation.

All I desired was the freedom to make my own choices without a heavy hand weighing me down.

"One day you will understand," I said, my voice soft. "One day, you understand it is not about pleasing everyone, but pleasing yourself first. Become the man that you want to be."

He nodded, but I could tell he wasn't listening. He was too drunk and exhausted for this conversation.

He scoffed and tugged his arm from my grip. "You think you know it all? A king doesn't need to be a gentleman."

I rolled my eyes. "No," I said firmly. "But a prince does."

He glanced away, mumbling something inaudible.

I knew he would never admit it, but deep down, he knew I was right.

His lips curved up into an amused smirk. "Fine. I'll try to be better, okay? For mother and you."

"No Artur," I said, taking his arm again. "For yourself. You are a prince, and you must learn to take responsibility for your actions."

"King," he said with a half-smile.

I shook my head, exasperated. "Not a king, but an imposter of one until you learn to act responsibly and take ownership of your actions."

Servants bowed their heads as they passed us.

"What would you do as king? Lead by example," I said gently. "That's what a proper king does."

Artur scoffed. "Viziers and counselors will

tell me what's right and wrong."

I smiled. "Yes, they can advise you, but you must be the one to choose the right path. You will be judged by your actions and decisions, not those of others."

Artur's face flushed with anger, and he clenched his fists. "You think you can lecture me on responsibility? What do you know about it?"

His eyes were full of intense hatred that made my heart sink, and I heard a low growl escape his lips.

More than you could ever know, I thought.

Partying and drinking all night was easy. Taking responsibility for your actions and making wise decisions, now that was hard.

His breath was heavy with the smell of liquor as he took a step forward.

He pushed me with such force that I nearly lost my balance, stumbling back.

"I am a prince," he spat out, his voice full of venom. "You can't tell me what to do! You may be a queen one day. But not today."

I took a deep breath, trying to remain calm. "Father decides who will be the next ruler and who will not," I said calmly. "You can either earn his trust or you can lose it."

Artur scoffed, as I steered him towards his

quarters.

The golden doors glinted in the moonlight, a reminder of the power that awaited him if only he could learn to control his temper.

The guards opened the door for us, and I smelled incense as I pushed him inside.

He stumbled forward, tripping as he crossed the threshold.

I sighed, the sound reverberating through the room, as I saw his bowed head, his figure slumped in defeat.

"Clean up, Artur, our guests are waiting."

Chapter 6

Unexpected surprises

"Your brother has been behaving himself, I take it?"

As I placed a savory, stuffed grape leaf between my teeth, my father smiled at me from across the table.

I nodded. "He just needs some time to think."

My father gave my hand a reassuring pat. "My daughter, you have so much wisdom to share."

As I felt a warmth spreading throughout my chest, I couldn't help but smile. "Thank you, father. Your words mean more to me than you know."

The queen grabbed my arm, her nails digging into my skin. "You are a blessing, Aleyna. We need more like you."

The scent of her butterscotch perfume filled my lungs.

I offered a courteous smile, yet I felt a wave of uneasiness.

Her words were laced with a hidden agenda, her true intentions veiled in sweetness.

"We are not the only ones who have noticed it. Ambassador Bölek visited your father today."

I arched my eyebrows in surprise. "Why?"

The ambassadors only visited father when they had official business to discuss.

A playful sparkle entered the queen's eyes as her lips curved into a sly grin. "He was here to inquire about a marriage proposal for you." Her eyes gleamed. "King Alois has noticed your kindness and strength, and he believes you'd make an ideal wife for his son Cyril."

Cyril, the third son.

A solid match.

This union would open up a world of new opportunities for our trade relations with Arcadia.

Not to mention Cyril was kind, intelligent, and handsome.

It would've been a match I'd gladly accept if I hadn't already pledged myself to another.

I glanced at my father, whose lack of words was almost deafening in the room.

His gaze was fixed on me as if he were waiting for my response.

I cleared my throat. "What did you say, father?"

His mouth curved into a smile, his lips pressed tightly together. "I said we would consider the offer."

That meant no. He didn't want me to marry the prince.

I nodded, my shoulders slumped in disappointment.

It wasn't the first time they denied me a chance to marry a prince.

Artur laughed, his voice full of bitterness. "Who would want to marry her? It isn't like she's some sort of beauty."

My father laughed goodheartedly and shook his head. "You know better than that, Artur. Aleyna's compassionate heart is more valuable than any physical beauty she may possess. You might not see the appeal in your sister, but others have noticed."

The queen cleared her throat, her expression stern. "Artur," she said firmly. "You will apologize to your sister. Now."

Outright insults were strictly forbidden.

What would people think?

Artur glanced at me, his expression tight. "I'm sorry," he muttered through gritted teeth.

"Our Aleyna doesn't deserve low-ranking suitors." The queen flashed a toothy grin, but her eyes remained emotionless. "She deserves a king."

My father would not permit any king to crown himself king of Ilanya. He'd make Artur his heir instead.

A clever plan, but one that I couldn't accept.

I knew what she was trying to do—position me as a pawn in her game of power.

"I'm fortunate enough to have such a kindhearted family."

The king smiled, his eyes crinkling with delight. "You shine brighter than the stars, my daughter. We will put our utmost effort into finding you an appropriate match."

I closed my eyes and felt comforted by his gentle touch as he absentmindedly stroked my hair.

The queen's gaze softened as she leaned in closer to me. "We will make sure that you find a king who is worthy of such a remarkable daughter. Yet the frown on your face shows you're not too keen on the idea."

I swallowed down my frustration. "No, I'm grateful for your kindness."

The queen smiled indulgently and squeezed my arm. "In your position, you should only care about your children. Our situation doesn't leave room for love. Heed my advice and choose a course of action that will ensure their future."

She then straightened her posture and glanced at my father before turning her attention back to me.

"It's rare that people find something as special as what your father and I share. A marriage filled with mutual respect and deep affection. If the outcome is uncertain, you must make the decision that will benefit them the most."

I clenched my teeth tightly, and the sensation reverberated through my jaw.

Love?

Only one of them was in love, and it wasn't the queen.

I glanced at the queen, my eyes narrowing. "A wise sentiment, your majesty. I will weigh my options. Watching your marriage has been a source of inspiration to me."

Love was a foolish pursuit that brought nothing but heartache.

I refused to be a pawn on anyone's chessboard.

The queen sipped her tea, the sound of the china cup clinking against the saucer, her eyes twinkling as she glanced at me. "We will find a king with a just and honorable nature. It might seem like I despise you, but in reality, I'm just striving to make sure you're set up for success."

I smiled, my lips pressed together. "Thank you, mother."

The sound of my father's laugh brought a smile to my face, its deep reverberations surrounding me.

"Pay attention to what she has to say, my daughter. She's a clever woman."

"Being a ruling queen is not easy. Don't be impulsive."

A dull ache filled my heart.

The right decision was obvious, and it didn't include love or happiness.

"I understand."

My father smiled. "Don't be worried. I promise to choose the best possible spouse for you."

The queen nodded in agreement, her crown glinting in the light as she glanced at me. "I will help."

"Aleyna is already married to a king," a voice said from behind me.

Everyone in the room paused and shifted their gaze towards the window, the curtains rustling in the breeze.

Doran leaned languorously against the frame, his lips curled into a smirk.

Pale diamonds were nestled in his hair, and his gray eyes glinted with a cold amusement.

He looked like a devil, descending from the shadows to claim me as his own.

The guards stepped forward, their hands on their swords as they advanced towards him.

My father jumped out of his seat, but the queen held up her hand. "Winter King."

Her voice shook as she nervously glanced at Doran.

"No." I stepped between them and Doran. "I invited him."

"Winter King." Artur placed his hands on my shoulders, his voice stern. "You need to leave immediately. You are not welcome here."

Doran's smirk widened, his eyes blazing with triumph. "It seems I'm already welcomed. I have taken your sister as my own, to be my wife."

I glanced at my father, and his expression was a combination of shock and fury.

The queen's expression was unreadable, but I saw the glint of admiration in her eyes.

Doran nodded and stepped towards me.

He grabbed my hand and planted a soft kiss on it, his eyes sparkling with mischievousness. "I apologize for being late."

With a trembling hand, I stepped forward and offered my hand to Doran, my eyes meeting his. "You arrived at the perfect moment. Your presence warms my heart."

The room was silent as Doran and I stood there, our hands clasped together.

The queen's mouth dropped open in shock, but she quickly composed herself. "It seems I was wrong about you, Princess Aleyna. Your political astuteness is much more impressive than I expected."

I ignored her and focused on my father.

His face became gentle as a small smile graced his lips.

"Father," I said, gesturing to the Winter King, who stood tall and proud. "I'd like to introduce you to my consort. Husband, my father, the king of Ilanya, Deniz."

"I've heard of your accomplishments. You are a man of impressive feats."

Terrible feats. Terrible deeds. Terrible secrets.

My heart ached for what I had done, but I smiled.

Doran only inclined his head. "I've also heard tales about you."

The queen smiled. "It seems like you two have an interesting tale to tell."

My father nodded in agreement, his eyes twinkling.

Doran's gaze fell on me before he turned to my father, the silence between us deafening. "I was so eager to meet my wife's family that I couldn't wait until tomorrow."

A gleam appeared in my father's eyes. "When did this union happen, dear?"

Doran took a step forward. "We wed in the

ocean's embrace, surrounded by the sun, moon, and stars."

The queen coughed, her voice was barely audible. "How romantic."

My father smiled, a hint of emotion in his voice. "It certainly is. I am glad for you both. I wish to raise a toast to the newlyweds."

My father raised his cup of boza and everyone followed suit.

The room was deadly silent as we all watched my father.

He looked around the room before his eyes rested on me. "To our princess and the Winter King, may their marriage bring them many blessings, and may they find true happiness with each other."

The room filled with a lackluster, muted clapping.

Artur tossed a grape up and grinned as he caught it between his teeth. "To my sister, who will leave us for many adventures in the Winter Court. May she find what she is after, and may she be safe from harm."

My father smiled before throwing his arms around me, holding me close. "Love is the greatest adventure of all. I wish you both joy in it."

The queen nodded her head; her face unreadable as she watched us. "Does this mean you will leave us for the Winter Court as its queen?"

Doran sneered. "We shall leave tomorrow."

I turned my head to look at him.

That wasn't what we agreed.

He looked at me and cocked his head, as if daring me to challenge him.

My heart raced, and I took a deep breath before turning to the queen. "I will be returning to Ilanya, but I will make sure that I visit the Winter Court often. Allies should always keep in touch."

The queen nodded and smiled, her lips tight.

My father laughed, a twinkle in his eyes. "It appears our daughter is a match for the Winter King, in more ways than one."

∞∞∞

I shoved Doran against the wall, the blade

of the dagger glinting in the light as I held it across his throat.

His eyes widened with shock before they softened into a gentle expression.

"Do not underestimate me, Winter King," I said through clenched teeth as I pressed the knife into his neck.

Doran's expression changed to one of amusement, his lips curling into a smile. "I would never dream of it, my queen."

"What are you trying to do?"

A smile tugged at the corners of his lips. "You don't have to fear me," he whispered, his skin hot against mine as he moved the dagger closer to his throat.

A line of blue blood emerged.

"You are an oath-breaker," I said in a soft voice, my eyes never leaving his. "You can't be trusted."

"I may have broken the spirit of some promises, but I will never break the one I made to you." He grabbed my chin, forcing me to look at him. "I will never break my vow to you, Aleyna. A deal is a deal."

My knuckles whitened as I clenched the dagger, my gaze averted.

Doran chuckled and slowly removed my

hand from his throat. "You are a force to be reckoned with."

"How do I know you won't break it?"

The deal.

Doran smiled, his eyes twinkling. "We shall return, little wife, and I shall keep my word."

I stared into his eyes, searching for any hint of untruth. But all I saw was sincerity.

I slowly removed my hand and stepped away, sheathing my dagger. "How will this make me queen?"

His body coiled as he stepped closer. "Ah, little one, they have already crowned you the queen of Ilanya. You just don't know it yet. This will make sure people will want you as their queen and that you are kept safe."

He brushed a strand of hair from my face, his touch gentle and reassuring. "I will not let them harm you. I can keep you safe from any threat, but only if you are standing by my side."

My heart was pounding as I turned away.

Could I really believe in his word and put my trust in him?

Doran grabbed my hand and pulled me towards him, his breath warm against my ear. "Let's make a deal, shall we? We will go to the

Winter Court and I will protect you from any danger. And in return -"

"Are you threatening me?" I interrupted him, my voice shaking.

Doran's laughter filled the room as he threw his head back. "No, I am offering you a chance to become the queen. A chance for greatness."

My heart raced as I stared back at him, the possibilities running through my mind.

"The others want you dead. I looked into their hearts and saw the truth," he said, his eyes full of conviction. "But I can protect you from them and keep you safe."

My skin prickled at his words.

Was I really in danger?

I swallowed hard, my throat suddenly dry.

He nodded slowly and then leaned his lips to my ear. "You knew. That's why you approached me, little wife. Don't worry, I protect what is mine."

My hands trembled slightly as I crossed them in front of me. "No deal, Doran. Unless you guarantee my safety and the throne of Ilanya."

I felt his breath on my neck as he chuckled softly. "What if I do both? Will you accept my offer, then?"

For a moment, I almost accepted his offer. But then my mind cleared, and I stepped away.

"No more deals, Doran. I will manage on my own."

He bowed his head in respect. "As you wish, little wife. Our deal is off."

"You didn't offer me anything the original deal didn't."

He grabbed my arm and pulled me back, his gaze intense. "Clever girl. But you are proving to be a bright one. You found out the true purpose of the wedding dagger."

"Stabbing my husband when he displeases me? The Fae have unconventional ideas on marriage."

"What is marriage without a little excitement?" He chuckled, and the sound reverberated off the walls. "That was one of its purposes, yes," he said. "It's a sign that you will fight for your own survival as well as the survival of your family."

I nodded, still not sure what to make of it all.

"It is a dangerous world, Aleyna. Be careful who you trust and who you make deals with. And remember, if all else fails, you can always come to me."

Chapter 7

Welcome to Frosthome

The blaze of the fire reflected in my eyes as I watched it spread along the walls, consuming everything in its path.

My stepmother's cold eyes burned into me. "You are a little girl with delusions of grandeur."

Red banners and flags were proudly waving in the wind, while blue banners hung limply along the walls.

My father's men shouted insults as they yanked me towards the carriage.

I couldn't think, couldn't breathe.

All I felt was rough hands grabbing at me, throwing me inside.

The door slammed shut with a deafening

thud, and I cowered in the corner, bracing for the inevitable.

This was not how things would end.

I refuse to die like this.

Before I could brace myself, a looming figure blocked my path.

I peered down and the hilt of the dagger protruded from beneath my dress, the blade glinting in the light.

I grabbed it and looked up.

My stepmother pointed a long, accusing finger at me as she closed in.

She shifted her form, turning into a snowy white wolf with eyes that gleamed in the light.

Doran's wolf.

This was not real, it couldn't be.

The wolf lunged at me and I thrust the dagger forward, stabbing it.

I opened my eyes, and I heard unfamiliar voices whispering.

The room was filled with the smell of burning, and a thick smoke hung in the air.

Three figures towered above me.

Instinctively, I rolled and fell from the bed, scrambling to my feet.

This wasn't a dream, it was real.

Someone was out to get me.

My eyes began to tear up from the smoke, and my lungs burned as I coughed and struggled for breath.

Reaching out, I felt along the wall and found a window.

When I pulled the window open, I peered downstairs and saw the narrow banner that prevented my escape.

Shit.

One of them stepped forward, the scarf around his face obscuring his features.

He brandished his dagger and lunged at me, the metal glinting in the light.

I quickly ducked and spun away, narrowly avoiding him.

My heart raced, and my mind began to work.

I reached for the only thing I had—a candlestick standing nearby. I grabbed it, and with a firm grip, thrust it forward.

It clashed against his arm, and he staggered back, holding his arm in pain.

I hurriedly darted forward and wedged my body under my bed as soon as I got the chance.

Through the thick smoke, the assassin's shadow was visible, and I could hear his low breathing.

My heart pounded as I clutched the dagger beneath my nightgown, surrounded by the sound of the assailants' feet shuffling.

I waited.

A strong arm grabbed my arm and pulled me out from under the bed.

I tightly clutched my dagger in my hand and lunged forward, aiming to slice the assassin's arm.

He stumbled back; the dagger missing its mark.

I wasn't going down without a fight.

I took a deep breath and slowly raised my feet, using every ounce of strength to push the assassin back.

Another arm grabbed my braid and tugged my head back. The burning sensation on my scalp was unbearable, but I refused to give in.

I would not die today.

A sudden wind blew through the room.

The door opened.

A thin layer of frost appeared on the walls and floor, spreading outwards from the doorway.

An ethereal figure stepped through the threshold, his body was draped in a deep black cloak and his face hidden by a silver mask.

Doran.

He slowly scanned the room with his eyes, eventually settling on the bed.

The yank on my braid vanished and the hold on my arm relaxed.

The frost in the room spread, and a layer of ice now covered the assassin's feet, preventing them from moving.

Doran stepped closer and grabbed the arm of the assassin in a tight grip.

The assassin screamed as the ice spread up his body until it completely encased him.

My husband, my unlikely savior.

I loosened my white-knuckled grip on the dagger and I released a shaky breath.

I survived—but more importantly; I won.

The other two assassins begged as Doran encased them in ice.

As I crawled from underneath my bed, I let out a long sigh of relief.

His hand reached out, and I clasped it, the calluses on his palm rough against my skin as I stood up.

I was taken aback when I saw my hand shaking uncontrollably.

Doran placed his fur cloak around me as shivers ran down my back.

I could've died.

He held my gaze for a moment, his eyes searching my face, before he turned away and waved his hand. The attackers shattered into a million pieces.

It was easy for him to do that. It made me realize how powerful he was. The Fae were not mortal. Mortal ways could not stop them.

Doran faced me again, his face unreadable. "Your enemies move fast, but your courage surpasses that of many."

He held my chin up with one hand as my heart raced. "You are safe now. Calm yourself, wife."

He stepped back, and I slumped against the wall, my eyelids heavy. "Without you, I'd be dead."

My voice quavered.

He nodded, the silver mask catching the light of a dying candle.

He offered me his arm, and I took it, resting my head on his shoulder as he walked me to my living room.

It looked as if a wild animal had ripped it apart.

The curtains were torn from the windows, and the furniture lay in pieces along the floor. I ran my fingers along the bare walls and felt my heart break at the sight of my artworks lying in pieces on the floor.

Everything was in disarray—except for the large ottoman in the center of the room, which remained unscathed.

Its soft velvet cushions were still intact, and its dark wood frame held strong.

Why would they do that?

Small bottles and paper were scattered around the perimeter of the ottoman.

I bent down to examine them and discovered that it was a suicide note left by the assassins.

It looked like my handwriting, but I knew it was not.

That was why.

I shivered as I realized how close I came to losing my life. I would have died by now if Doran hadn't been here.

This was planned. Someone wanted me

gone.

My legs trembled as I made my way to the closest chair and fell into it.

My husband stood a mere foot away from me, his eyes fixed on mine.

He slowly pulled away his mask, revealing his stoic and unwavering face to me.

He leaned close, his breath warm against my face. "Let us not forget this moment," he said in a low voice.

He stepped back, and I nodded, my heart still hammering.

Bells rang in the distance. The chirping of birds outside filled the air.

Life was still going on. Despite everything, that just happened.

Someone tried to kill me.

Someone send assassins to murder me.

Dead.

Someone wanted me dead.

Deep down, I knew who did it. But I could never prove it. I wasn't sure I wanted to.

Doran observed me. His face was unreadable, and his shoulders were tense. "The enemy is hidden, but the battle is far from over," he said. "Speculation will do no good. The only thing that matters is that you are safe."

A single tear escaped my eye, the chill of the night air lingering.

I was safe - for now. I needed to figure out how to survive in a world that wanted me dead.

He grabbed my hand and looked me in the eye. "You are strong. I will be with you through it all."

The comfort of his touch and the compassion in his voice bolstered my confidence.

He squeezed my hand, and I looked up at him, his gray eyes still burning bright in the darkness.

We stood there, the atmosphere so still it felt like forever, but the clock only ticked away a few moments.

He cleared his throat and stepped back, his face turning serious. "Let's not waste any more time. Be prepared. Visitors arrive."

His pointed ears twitched, and the door creaked open.

Guards flooded in with a heavy thud, their swords drawn and ready.

Their blue and silver coats glowed in the moonlight, and for once, the sight didn't fill me with safety.

The assassins couldn't have entered the palace without their help.

Doran stepped in front of me, blocking my view and protecting me from their glances.

My father entered the room. A sword hung from his belt, and his armor was only half-fastened. His steps were heavy with anger as he came closer to me.

He put his hands on my shoulders, his gaze intense as he stared into my eyes. "I will make sure this never happens again."

The hitch in his voice betrayed his sorrow.

I nodded, too overwhelmed to say anything.

My father gathered me in his arms and held me close. He was trembling, his breath coming out in quick gasps as he tried to suppress his tears.

His hug was tight yet gentle, and a surge of heat spread through me.

I closed my eyes, took a deep breath, and savored the moment, allowing myself to feel safe in his arms again. I heard his heart beating steadily, a reminder that I was still alive and that he loved me.

After a few moments, he pulled away, his expression still heavy with emotion, but now also filled with determination.

His hands moved lightly over my face. "What happened?"

I glanced at my husband.

His face was a wall, giving nothing away. Despite the distractions around him, he remained focused on the guards.

I wanted to tell my father everything, the truth, but I simply said, "Someone wanted me gone."

Gone. Such a simple word.

My father nodded, his face solemn.

He hugged me close, and I smelled the faint scent of his cologne. Lemon, musk and oranges.

"This will never happen again," he said firmly. "I failed you once. But never again."

"It appears you have enemies lurking in your own city. You should take care of them," Doran said in a crisp voice.

My father looked at Doran, his face turned red. "Yes," he hissed. "Who would do this? I'll destroy them."

I grasped my father's arm, and he stopped. "Whoever hired the assassins must have had a lot of resources at their disposal."

I observed the hardness of his jaw as his expression tightened in response to the information.

Doran's expression shifted as he slowly raised an eyebrow.

But I subtly shook my head.

My father could never fathom that someone in our family would turn on me. He loved us too much.

And I knew the Winter King had the same suspicions. Only a family member could've done this. It was the obvious choice.

My father nodded, his features solemn. "We will find them and bring them to justice."

His love would ruin us.

Doran stepped forward. "We must leave now."

His voice was low and firm.

My father nodded, a hint of surprise in his eyes as he looked at me.

I looked down and saw the stains of tears and blood on my silk nightgown, a reminder of what just happened.

The blood also stained my fingers, and I felt it on my face.

I was still alive, and that mattered most of

all.

Alive to see another day.

Doran grabbed my arm and pulled me away, his fingers gentle yet firm. He urged me forward, his voice soft but insistent.

My father followed us, his arm still around my shoulder as if he was afraid I would disappear if he let go.

"No matter what," he whispered in my ear, "I will always be here to protect you."

I swallowed. "Thank you, my king."

His love nearly cost me my life.

Chapter 8

Wolves and mushroom circles

"Are you not impressed?" Doran asked, and a frigid chill ran through me as I saw his smile.

A dangerous edge lurked beneath his words.

When he said we'd travel through a fairy circle, I was expecting something magical and full of wonder.

Not an ordinary mushroom circle in the forest.

"I suppose," I muttered, eyeing him warily.

He laughed, and the sound echoed in the courtyard.

He pulled me into his arms, and for a

moment, I felt secure.

The next thing I noticed was the crunch of frozen dew beneath my feet.

My eyes widened in awe as I took in the breathtaking scene before me.

Large silver trees glimmered in the pale moonlight, casting long shadows across a glistening, snow-covered landscape. The snowy mountains loomed in the distance, hiding secrets beneath their icy peaks.

A carriage drawn by two white horses appeared out of the shadows, carried on a gust of wintry wind. A glittering cloud of frost formed around it, and Doran stepped forward.

He gave me a gloved hand and helped me into the carriage, before settling next to me on the velvet cushioned seat.

The carriage moved, and my heart raced.

The Winter Court. A place of secrets and lies. A place of beauty and danger.

The stories of the court flitted through my mind, tales of deadly games and unexpected alliances.

Mortals never strayed too close... but here I was, headed right into the heart of it.

I pressed my face against the window, feeling the glass cool against my skin as I took in the unreal sight.

Above us, streaks of vibrant color filled the night sky. Soft auroras danced in the air, casting a luminous glow over the snowy landscape below.

I examined my fingers. The rusty hue of dried blood remained, but soon the marks would fade.

"They've never done this before."

My stepmother and my brother didn't like me, but they weren't the type of people who arranged assassinations.

At least I didn't think so.

My stepmother was crafty, but she was well aware of the dangers of a move so audacious.

The carriage moved up the mountain, and I realized that my father's love provided me with one last chance to save myself.

No.

My husband's protection.

He was the one who provided me with the means to escape.

When I peered out the window, the snow-capped peaks glistened before slowly vanishing.

"But deep down, you knew."

Doran's voice brought me back to reality.

I nodded, acknowledging the truth in his words.

I didn't want to admit it, but I knew there was a real risk that this would happen.

"Family can be beautiful, but can also be an open wound. Tricks, deceptions, and betrayal can lurk in the shadows. You must be careful."

Family could be a blessing, but it could also be a curse.

I looked outside of the window. "They are my family and I love them. The queen has treated me fairly... in her own way. I won't forget that she gave me a chance."

Not a mother, but a mentor. Her teachings hovered in my mind, a legacy of her life.

I looked out at the night sky and the star-filled horizon made me feel insignificant.

She could've sent me away. She could've forgotten about me.

But she hadn't.

"Family matters can be complex, and you don't need to justify them to anyone."

A faint smile curved my lips, but it was tinged with sadness.

The only way to get what you wanted was

through power and influence. And marriage was the ultimate currency.

I grew up surrounded by people who constantly tried to control me, and that fear never truly left me. With every step I took, I felt the weight of their expectations on me.

Love was a luxury, and I learned to protect myself from it. And family was no different.

I didn't expect to find such acceptance in a stranger. In his own way, he was kinder to me than my family.

My family wanted me dead.

He gave me a chance to be free, and I was determined not to squander it. It was a heady feeling, and I wanted to savor it. It also frightened me, I realized.

I was playing a game I didn't understand, and I didn't know what the outcome would be. I hoped I made the right choice.

I looked out the window again, knowing that I was free—for now.

The icy landscape stretched for miles in front of me before a large lake appeared in the distance. Perched upon the lake was a magnificent castle, illuminated in the pale moonlight.

I spotted marble towers, ramparts, and

battlements.

It was as if the stars came down to these strange lands.

A white city, a new home.

It was there that I would finally make my stand.

Silently, I vowed to never let them control me again. I was done with being a pawn in their game.

From now on, I was my own woman—fierce and unafraid.

"Welcome to Frosthome."

"Not the Winter Court?" I asked, a weak smile tugging at my lips.

"The Winter court is how others see it. But to us, it's Frosthome—our home."

Our carriage winded its way through the city streets, passing by colorful stalls and shops draped in layers of fur and blankets.

Blue marble statues of bears and dragons watched us silently as we passed by.

People bowed their heads in respect as we made our way to the castle gates. Not all of them looked humanoid.

Some had wings, others scaly skin, and some had features I couldn't even comprehend.

The gates opened, and a group of guards welcomed us.

I looked up at the banner which hung atop the entrance: a pale blue flag with a white rose in the middle. Frost covered its petals.

We finally arrived.

My feet sank into the snow as I stepped out of the carriage. I breathed in the cold air as I looked around.

As we entered the castle walls, heat flooded my body. Large chambers draped in silver silk lined the walls, and a grand staircase greeted us, leading to the upper floors.

My eyes were alight with wonder as I took in the beautiful sight.

The marble on the walls glowed in the light.

But as I looked closer, I saw something else—something deeper. The castle was cold, almost empty.

The lack of furniture and decorations made the place seem like a museum. It was a stark contrast to my home, where the palace was always bustling with activity.

Here, there was nothing but coldness. I expected warmth, but I found an almost palpable void.

What was winter without love?

Without warm embraces?

Without laughter?

Doran observed me, his gray eyes twinkled.

He placed a hand on my shoulder. "This is your kingdom now," he whispered, his voice carrying a hint of amusement. "You can shape it into whatever your heart desires."

"I do not understand. This is your home, not mine. Why should I change it?"

"When a new king or queen ascends, they must make the court their own. To transform it into a place that speaks to their identity and wishes."

I folded my arms as we walked. "Why didn't you?"

His cloak rustled as he raised one shoulder in a small shrug. "I was never one for decorating." Despite the lackluster reply, the strain in his voice betrayed his true feelings. "This reflects me—a place of cold, where nothing has changed for centuries."

Cold like his heart, I thought to myself.

But despite his words, I refused to accept what he said.

A warm home could be a refuge for a bitter man if he was willing to accept it.

"But it doesn't have to be that way," I said, determination in my voice. "You can still make this place yours—in your own way."

Doran smiled, but it didn't reach his eyes. "Well then, if you truly wish for it. Decorate it. It might even endear you to your people as their new queen."

Queen?

The word echoed in my mind as I looked around.

I came here to make a stand. Now he offered me the chance to make my mark.

My eyes narrowed. "Queen? We agreed I would be the ruling queen of Ilanya."

Was he trying to take control again?

"Yes, the ruling queen of Ilanya and the queen of Frosthome," Doran replied calmly. "You married the king of Frosthome. The title, the power, it is yours to wield."

I clenched my fists. I knew what I wanted —independence and autonomy. "And if I refuse?"

He held up his hands. "Don't forsake potential allies. This could be a powerful foundation for your rule in Ilanya."

Doran was right. I couldn't give up an opportunity like this.

I was a princess. Now I would be a queen.

A huge white wolf crossed our path, startling me and breaking my thoughts.

The wolf seemed to sense my change in mood and stopped to gaze at me, before walking to me and nudging me with his nose.

As he licked my hand, I felt the warmth of his soft fur against my skin.

When I leaned down, I heard the gentle rumble of the wolf's purr and marveled at its softness and strength.

His head bumped against my hand, and I smiled.

"He's never done that before. He rarely likes anyone."

I looked up to see Doran's expression of surprise.

I smiled, as I felt something I never experienced before—power.

Here was a creature that accepted me without question.

"I'm easy to love if you give me a chance."

"Fickle as the winter's winds may be, if you embrace them, they will warm your heart."

He was right.

I came here to find my footing as a ruler. To gain allies and make a mark on this world. The way forward was clear—I would make Frosthome my own.

Decorating these icy walls was the first step in achieving my goal. I would make it my home. Until I could hear my laughter echoing through the halls of my home again.

Chapter 9

The Iron Sword

The silver light from the windows shone across the room as I stepped into the dining hall.

Spirits were soaring among the courtiers, and their hearty chuckles could be heard echoing through the air.

For a moment, it almost felt like home.

As I stepped in, the room fell into an eerie silence, and I could feel the stares of everyone in the room upon me.

My heart raced as I looked around the room. I expected a nicer reception.

But how could I blame them?

I was an intruder, an outsider in their midst.

I walked past them with my head held high, my footsteps echoing off the walls of the room as I attempted to appear more confident than I felt.

The Fae were a sight to behold.

Yesterday I glimpsed them, but the sheer diversity of creatures here was breathtaking.

A few I recognized from the childhood books the queen read to Artur.

The brownies with wrinkled skin and lithe frames, their eyes twinkling with mischief, seemed to be everywhere.

Redcaps, their hats dripping with blood, lurked in the shadows while will-o'-the-wisps, glowing orbs of light, flitted about the room.

The High Court Fae, like my husband, were a sight to behold. They had ethereally beautiful faces and their clothes were made of gossamer and silk, shimmering in the lamplight. They were the embodiment of grace and elegance, seemingly untouched by time.

As I stepped up to the dais, their eyes were upon me, judging and assessing my every move.

But despite my anxiety, I stood tall and proud.

I was mortal, with all the flaws and vulnerabilities that entailed, but I was determined to make them accept me.

How did one deal with these creatures?

Not creatures, but Fae.

People.

Strange people, but people all the same.

The main table was empty except for two thrones, and one of them was mine. Decorated with silver thread and adorned with pale blue gems, it made me pause.

Queen of Frosthome.

The last thing I wanted was to isolate myself from the people. First impressions were crucial and I was determined to make a good one.

The tables seemed to be divided into different factions. Each group of Fae looked distinct from one another. Not based on species, but on alliances and allegiances.

The colors of their clothing, the way they interacted and spoke with each other, everything pointed to a secret and complex world of politics.

I needed to navigate these waters carefully and choose my words wisely.

I didn't want to accidentally insult people. The Fae had long memories for slights.

At one table, ladies dressed in pale blue were seated. Silver crowns adorned their heads and their voices sang in a high-pitched chorus.

They were closest to the main table, and I noticed one of them watching me.

Her eyes were as dark as night. Her face seemed unnatural still, like a mask made of blue porcelain. On her chest a crest was embroidered, depicting a raven with its wings spread wide.

The others wore similar symbols, and I realized they were the ladies-in-waiting.

Or Frosthome's version of it.

A neutral force that carefully monitored the proceedings. Never interfering or taking sides.

The perfect table for me.

I straightened my back and walked towards them, my footsteps echoing in the silent hall.

My approach had the desired effect.

The tension in the room seemed to ease as I approached their table. They exchanged glances and nodded, a sign of approval.

A test of my diplomatic skills, but one I passed.

I was about to sit down when one of them spoke up. "Winter Queen, you are a sight to behold. We were almost ready to surrender our dream of a new queen."

A sight to behold?

I smiled politely.

What kind of queen did they expect me to be?

A kind one, I hoped. A wise one. But most of all, a strong one.

The Fae of Frosthome were a different people, and I needed to prove that I was up to the challenge.

I had my work cut out for me.

The brownie at the end of the table nodded in agreement. "Welcome, your majesty. You honor us with your presence."

The ladies bowed their heads.

"Thank you for your kind words. I'm both honored and humbled to be here." I seated myself in the middle. "The king is a handsome man. Surely he would have married soon."

The joke had the desired effect. Smiles lit up their faces as they exchanged glances, as if they knew something I didn't.

Maybe I could find some answers to my husband's mystery? A man like that must have a story.

The one that watched me earlier leaned in.

"My lady, a man can never be sure of himself. Although his manners are impeccable, he lacks the endearing charm of most people."

The group smiled and chuckled, the sound of their laughter warming the room.

I was surprised at her frankness, but also intrigued.

Was this why he had never married?

Was he so different from the others that no one found him attractive enough?

The very idea amused me. A man with that face, but no one wanted him?

I kept my expression neutral. Inside, I was bursting with curiosity. "We are all different, yet we can all be valuable and respected. I'm sure my husband is no exception."

It was a good sign they ridiculed their king openly. It meant that fear didn't keep them from being honest.

The ladies smiled and nodded in agreement as they continued their conversation.

The lull in the conversation gave me a chance to look around.

Glancing at the spread on the table, the pickings were slim. Bloodied hearts, strange glowing fruits, and meatless dishes.

All strange fare for a breakfast banquet.

I felt the stares of the courtiers upon me as I picked up a fruit, giving it a wary look before taking a bite.

Red liquid ran down my chin as I wiped it with the back of my hand.

It tasted sweet, but with a hint of bitterness. I tasted nothing like it before, and I didn't know if I liked it.

Food was the least of my concerns.

I needed to understand their culture, get along with them, and earn their trust.

The ladies at the table exchanged amused looks.

The brownie spoke up again, her voice full of pity. "After your journey, I'm sure you must be absolutely ravenous. We have created a selection of dishes from our homeland for you to savor."

She motioned to the others, and they laid a plate of exquisite delicacies before me.

Loaves of bread, cheeses, fruits, and even a few savory dishes. Rows of colorful dishes, each more tantalizing than the last.

My hand reached out before I even realized it, as a fruit rushed in front of me.

The Fae of Frosthome chuckled at my

surprise. "Winter Queen, you must be careful. These are no ordinary fruits and vegetables. They contain powerful magic and can be quite dangerous."

"They bite," one lady joked, making everyone laugh.

I smiled in thanks and sampled the food.

Unlike other plates, my food didn't run away when I touched it.

Nor did my food try to bite me.

My mouth tingled with spices and the sweet tartness of fruits. But below it, all was a subtle richness that reminded me of home.

Salty, deep, and comforting.

The ladies watched me as I savored each dish, their eyes dancing with amusement.

They seemed pleased with my reactions and nodded in approval as I complimented the cooks.

Their hospitality was touching. They wanted to make me feel welcome even though I was a stranger in their court.

My fork clattered against the plate as a brownie brought me a steaming cup of tea, its sweet aroma wafting through the air.

I smiled again and sipped from the cup.

"The king never opened his heart to the ladies, my queen. But we hear tell of your love story."

Was this a warning? A test?

I placed the cup on the table. "Our story is not a tale of love, but of an alliance. Our two courts have come together and our marriage is a symbol of that union."

The ladies exchanged looks. It seemed like they were not quite ready to accept this explanation.

"But here you are, and here we are." One courtier turned to me as blood dripped down her plate. The hood on her cloak shifted, revealing a set of piercing eyes. "A mortal queen amongst the Fae. You honor us with your presence."

I bowed my head in respect. "I deeply appreciated your words. It's a great privilege to be here."

Expectations were high. I needed to get used to this life quickly if I wanted to succeed.

"I hope to create a peaceful and harmonious atmosphere in Frosthome."

"Is that what you intend to do, my queen?" A woman asked from one of the other tables.

At first, she looked like a figure of stone. When I looked closer, I saw the glitter in her eyes.

The cracks in her face mirrored my own.

The surrounding ladies smiled.

"Yes, with the help of all of you. Not to change the way you live, but to bring us all closer together and build a stronger kingdom."

As I talked, I noticed several people in the room exchanging glances, letting me know that they were all paying attention.

I sipped on my cup. "I was thinking about sprucing up the palace," I began. "I want to bring a bit of warmth and color into this place."

The Fae adored beauty in all of its forms, so they exchanged enthusiastic nods and smiles across the room.

I lifted my chin. "So, what do you think?"

A night flyer flew up to me, her black wings shimmering in the candlelight. "We think it is a grand idea." Shark-like eyes locked on mine, her expression serious. "The castle could use some freshness and color. We would be most pleased to help you in any way we can."

"It's been too long since we've seen the castle adorned with beauty," one courtier with rich, russet brown skin and silver hair that reached the ground said. "Why, it would be a shame to not see what you can bring to this place."

"With the help of you and the others, we can make something truly remarkable."

I was sure it would be a sight to behold. The fashion of Frosthome would serve as inspiration.

Soft winter hues of blues, grays, and whites. Rich velvets and silks. Intricate embroidery on their gowns and cloaks, sparkling in the firelight.

The castle would become a place of beauty and magic once again.

The bare bones were gorgeous, but it needed more.

"Do you have anything in mind?" one of them asked. A man, his beard and hair a glorious shade of auburn.

Would I keep true to my word or fail to bring the promise of not changing Frosthome?

"I'd like to look at the old pieces of furniture and tapestries that were collected by my husband's ancestors. Maybe I could combine the old with something new, crafted by some of our best artisans. I think it will give this place a unique look."

They tittered in approval, but a level of skepticism still lingered in the air.

"Yes, that would be very nice," one of them

said. "We will take you to the vault to see the pieces yourself. You will find something special."

"But first breakfast and introductions," another courtier said. "We must all get to know one another better."

I lowered my head in respect. "My name is Aleyna, and I am your new queen."

Wide eyes stared at me before respect replaced the skepticism in them.

That was an odd reaction to a name.

Was it because it sounded familiar?

I highly doubted that.

There were many royal kingdoms, and I wasn't extraordinary enough to know by name.

But I didn't have time to ponder on it, because the courtiers began introducing themselves.

"I'm the Iron Sword." The leader of the table nodded. "I'm pleased to meet you, my queen."

The other courtiers introduced themselves and I smiled, as titles instead of names were used.

Was there a taboo about using names, I wondered?

Should I not use mine either?

"Unlike the king, we rarely visit the mortal realms, so mortal customs about names are unfamiliar to us," the Iron Sword explained. "I haven't had the chance to pick one for myself yet. That's why I go by the Iron Sword."

Names must have a different meaning here in the Fae realm. They were more attached to their titles and possessions than anything else.

They were not mortal, after all.

Naming conventions even differed among mortals, never mind the Fae.

"I hope that with time, I can learn more about your culture and traditions."

The Iron Sword smiled. "We are honored to have you here with us and look forward to teaching you all about our ways."

"And why are you called the Iron Sword?" I asked. "If I'm not being too bold."

"It is my honor to be called by this blade." The Iron Sword drew her sword and held it up for me to see.

An iron blade, with intricate designs along the length of it.

"As a courtier and loyal servant of the king, I've been entrusted with this weapon of deathly power. It is my sword, and I must protect the king and his court with all of its might. No other sword is as sharp and resilient as mine. I am known for my skill in the art of fencing."

"Impressive. It is an honor to have someone as accomplished here in our court."

The iron sword, though plain, fit in perfectly with the atmosphere of Frosthome. Winter seemed to push its way through the castle, and this blade of iron was like a shield, protecting us from whatever dangers might come our way.

"I will be your guard and lady-in-waiting, my queen," Iron Sword said. "I am ready to serve you in any way I can."

Did I need protection? I was the queen of Frosthome, after all.

Or was the title of Iron Sword more than just a name?

Whatever it was, I accepted the offer with grace.

"Thank you for your service. I am sure your help will be invaluable. I'm sure I'll have a lot of questions for you, as my understanding of Frosthome is very limited."

"It would be my pleasure to help in any way I can." She nodded. "Frosthome has much to offer. Together, we shall explore everything this place has to give."

"The Summer King is due to come to us within the week - can you believe it?" a courtier by the name of Chrysanthemum said. Her purple and pink dress made her stand out, and her rosy cheeks seemed to almost sparkle.

Was she from another court? The liveliness in her voice made me think she must be from one of the other Fae realms.

I raised an eyebrow. "From what I understand, the relationship between the two courts is... strained."

Why would he visit now? Did my arrival have something to do with it?

"That is true. But your marriage has helped to bridge the gap," Chrysanthemum explained. "The Summer King wishes to offer his congratulations in person."

The Iron Sword turned her head. "Even a man of his limited character knows that courtesy must be maintained."

Less of a bridge and more of a tightrope.

But I supposed it was better than nothing.

"Well then." I straightened my shoulders. "Let us welcome him with hospitality, then. What can you tell me about him? What should I expect when meeting him?"

The courtiers looked at each other and

smiled.

"You will see," Iron Sword said, her voice full of mirth. "He is a strong, proud man. But flattery and charm can easily sway him."

I nodded.

I could do that. Anything to help the kingdom move forward.

"We shall find out what he has in store for us soon enough," Iron Sword said. "Until then, let us enjoy our days here with each other."

"That means we have a lot of preparations to make before he arrives." Determined to make this a success, plans for the formal reception were already forming in my head. "The castle is going to look beautiful."

The Summer King was coming, and I was more than ready to make a good impression.

Chapter 10

Summer King

"That lout of a king better be on his best behavior when he arrives," Iron Sword said, her voice stern. "He shows no respect to anyone who isn't of noble Summer birth."

I nodded.

This fierce Fae woman meant business, and I was grateful for her help during our preparations. This was my first official act as queen of Frosthome, and I wanted to make a good impression.

"Don't worry." I turned to her. Her silver hair reached the ground and the iron sword on her back glimmered in the light. "We will make sure that he knows Frosthome isn't to be underestimated. We tolerate no weakness."

Night flyers flew around me, their iridescent wings glittering in the night like a thousand stars.

The wispy curtains blew in the wind, and I looked out over the court.

The castle was transformed into a winter wonderland of silver and blue, adding warmth and depth to this castle.

Thick rugs and plush, luxurious chairs were placed all around the court, inviting guests to sit and chat in comfort.

Soft moonlight shone down from the crystal windows, shining like thousands of tiny stars.

In the distance, I heard the deep notes of horns and drums, announcing the Summer King's arrival.

I took a deep breath as I straightened my back.

It was time to be the queen of Frosthome.

Iron Sword gave me a sly smile. "I am certain that he will be. Let's hope he gives us something worthwhile instead of just idle chatter."

Furniture was made from dark woods, trimmed in silver, and adorned with intricate carvings of animals and frosted leaves.

Snow-covered trees lined the walls, while crystals and snowflakes hung from the ceiling like a wintery chandelier.

I glanced around. "Yes, that would be something."

I carefully crafted everything to evoke a feeling of strength, power, and beauty. It was a palace fit for a visit of a Summer King.

"Let's give him an unforgettable welcome and dazzle him with our might and strength."

Iron Sword nodded in agreement, her face resolute.

The blue fabric of my dress flapped in the breeze, and the yellow trimmings glowed in the silvery moonlight.

As I walked towards the throne room, my husband eyed the changes with a bored look on his face.

His dark hair fell in a cascade of waves down his back, bringing out the sharp angles of his face and the mischievousness in his eyes.

His midnight velvet cloak was trimmed with silver, shimmering like stars as he moved.

His eyes met mine, and his lips curled in a smirk.

He nodded and gestured to the throne

beside him. "You look." His voice was low and smoky. "Like a queen of the Winter Court, ready to take on any challenge."

I grabbed a goblet of grenadine. "Isn't that what I am?"

His possessive smile widened. "A delightful queen indeed. Now let's make sure that the Summer King knows it too. My little wife isn't one to be trifled with." His eyes narrowed and his lips pressed into a serious line. "He's a charming fellow, but don't let him fool you. He's a dangerous one."

My lips twitched in an almost smile.

Flashes of jealousy raced through me, but I pushed them away.

I eyed him, laughter dancing in my eyes.

The determination in his eyes made it clear that he would do anything to keep me safe.

"Oh, don't tell me you're worried about me?"

His eyes narrowed. "You don't have to worry about the Summer King. You're well-protected. If you need me, I'm here."

Feeling bold, I stepped closer to my husband and bumped my shoulder against his. "Or is it something else? Are you worried I will fall for his charms?"

Checkmate.

His eyes hardened, and he leaned in close. "Most women can't resist him. He's a cunning fox, able to weave powerful tales. But I know you better than that."

He glanced away, his gaze distant.

"You are true. Our alliance is unbreakable." He looked back at me, his eyes hard. "Make sure he knows it as well."

"Jealousy doesn't suit you," I said, my voice teasing.

His lips quirked in a faint smile. "Then it's a good thing I don't have to be jealous."

His desire to possess me made me smirk. I knew he wasn't really concerned about the Summer King's advances, but his protectiveness was endearing.

Out of the corner of my eye, I noticed the Winter courtiers watching us with rapt attention.

Hushed whispers echoed through the palace as they discussed our interactions.

The Iron Sword lifted a goblet when my gaze stopped on her. I winked at her before focusing on Doran again.

Doran and I waited patiently until we

DEAL WITH THE FAE KING

heard the rhythmic sound of hooves clopping against stone.

The heavy smell of snow and ice filled the palace as the Summer King arrived.

Irritation rippled through me, but I forced a smile onto my face.

I looked at my husband and realized it wasn't my emotions I was feeling, but his.

The Summer King must truly agitate him. This was the second time he breached the barrier of our marriage bond today.

Murmurs and whispers filled the hall as the Summer King stepped forward.

He undid his robe and handed it to one servant.

His hair spilled out in golden waves, each lock caressing his high cheekbones and framing his eyes.

His broad shoulders were draped in a sleeveless robe of purest white, adorned with gold embroidery and gems that sparkled and glimmered in the soft light of the whisping torches.

I knew better than to be taken in by his appearance.

Despite his beauty, the room was filled with an eerie stillness of unease and uncertainty.

I stepped forward and nodded gracefully, my silver headdress glinting in the light.

A bright smile appeared on his face as he observed us.

Something about him seemed off. Too polished, too slippery. It was the slick smile of a man who was used to getting what he wanted.

His handsomeness wasn't enough to make up for his untrustworthiness.

But I was the queen, and an entire court of people watched my every move.

So I smiled as needed to welcome him to Frosthome with all the decorum that was expected of me. Even though I knew in the depths of my soul that this man could never be trusted.

We observed as the Summer King made his way through the court, bowing his head to the nobility and casting his gaze around the room.

When his eyes rested on me, a chill ran down my spine.

Finally, he reached the throne and smiled seductively at me. "Good evening, Winter Queen," he said in a deep, rumbling voice.

His touch was delicate as he took my hand and kissed it softly.

His golden hair cascaded down his face, obscuring his features.

Gold sparks flew from his lips as electricity ran down my arm.

Fae tricks were not something I was used to, but I kept my composure.

I dragged my hand and nodded. "Welcome, Summer King," I said coolly.

Besides me, Doran stiffened.

He gripped my arm, and his anger radiated off him in waves.

The Summer King stepped away, a faint smirk on his face.

He made his presence known, whether or not I accepted it.

I glanced at Doran, my eyes wide with warning.

He nodded, but the jealousy in his eyes still lingered.

I reached out and ran my fingertips along his arm, squeezing it softly.

I focused on the Summer King, thankful that he remained in his place.

I pretended to smile, although inwardly I was seething with rage. He would not manipulate my court, no matter how much he might wish to.

Smarmy bastard.

I met his gaze evenly. "You can call me Aleyna."

His eyes widened in delight, as if he hadn't expected me to give him such an intimate title.

He nodded and said, "Aleyna, it is then."

He didn't offer a name in return.

The slight was intentional, and I raised an eyebrow in response.

Doran moved closer to me. He laid a hand on my shoulder. His protective presence surrounded me.

The court watched as we sized up each other's strengths and weaknesses.

The silver bracelets on my arm tinkled as I crossed my arms. "What brings you to our court this evening?"

The Summer King smiled, and his eyes shone with mischief. "Surely you know." He paused, looking around the room. "I never expected the Winter King to be the first of us all to marry. Especially not to such a delightful creature," he said with a sly smile. "Aleyna, you have my admiration."

My husband stepped forward, his voice

icy. "The Winter King is more than capable of protecting what's his, Summer King. I suggest you take your admiration elsewhere."

The Summer King paused, his eyes glittering like diamonds. "Come now. I mean no harm. Beauty in a place like this isn't taken for granted."

Smarmy and overconfident as he was, I couldn't help but admire his flamboyance. That took guts.

I kept my expression neutral. "Perhaps you should take your own advice and find something else to admire tonight."

Taking a seat, I gestured for the Summer King to join us.

"My husband married me for my strength, determination, and will. We want nothing more than mutual respect and understanding - something that can only be achieved through honest dialogue. If you wish to gain favor in our court, I suggest you abide by these terms."

He tsked. "You are wise beyond your years, Aleyna."

The Summer King gave a barely perceptible nod, his gaze never leaving mine.

"You certainly changed this place in a week," he said, his voice husky with admiration. He paused and then added, "I am curious to see what else you changed."

My husband's jaw clenched when the Summer King crooned my name.

Was he truly jealous? Or was it something else?

There were many things at stake. But the very idea of a rival king interested in me made my heart beat faster. I couldn't deny it.

How would Doran react?

I smiled graciously. "Change is inevitable, Summer King. I am sure you understand that better than anyone else."

The Summer King's gaze flitted between Doran and me as he took a seat next to me. "Seasons pass and seasons grow."

Doran lounged against his throne, his head tilted back and eyes closed.

His dark hair brushed against my shoulder, and I could smell the faintest hint of winter in his presence.

"Are you here just to feed your ego or do you have something useful to offer?"

The Summer King smiled, but there was steel in his voice. "I will never deny my ambition. But my curiosity should never be confused with foolishness. I am here to observe and to help however I can."

He paused and gestured around the room.

"I am sure you have heard tales of my court. I can tell you that whatever you have heard is true."

I nodded, understanding the subtle warning in his words.

He came to watch and report back.

I expected as much, but it was still unnerving.

The Summer Court was a powerful force, and I had to tread carefully in his presence.

Their presence in the mortal realms brought a new danger. The people of Ilanya deserved better.

But the context of the conversation shifted once more with Doran's next words. "If you are here to help, then I suggest you start by respecting my wife's wishes."

The Summer King sighed and looked away, clearly understanding the silent warning from my husband.

The Summer King may have been a dazzling sight to behold, but he was nothing compared to the beauty of my husband. Winter's chill seemed to dance around him, his captivating presence far outshining the Summer King's flamboyance.

What did the Summer King think he could offer me I didn't already have?

His attention and admiration were certainly flattering, but there was no way I would ever consider it over my husband's loyalty and protection.

His alliance with the Selwyns proved his untrustworthiness.

Insincere flattery didn't impress me.

∞∞∞

"Dear Aleyna." The Summer King sipped on his glass of mead. "What dark secrets does the Winter King have over you to make you marry him?"

This accusation was greeted with a chorus of gasps.

Doran's gaze sharpened as the courtiers rose, his posture becoming more rigid.

A chill ran up my spine and I raised my chin, eyes narrowing. "He has not."

Around me, the Winter courtiers bristled,

clearly ready to defend their king at any cost.

He looked delighted. "Tell me you didn't. Why would you ever do that?"

I lifted an eyebrow, my ears perking up in interest.

He thought I blackmailed the Winter King?

His eyes widened in astonishment as I erupted into uncontrollable laughter. "He didn't have to. I married my husband because I wanted to - not out of fear or obligation. Speak plainly. What is your game here?"

The Summer King's lips twitched in surprise. "What did he want from you?"

My husband leaned forward, his voice low and menacing. "My wife is not a bargaining chip, Summer King. She is the queen of Winter and shall be treated as such."

The Summer King bowed his head in deference, a gleam in his eye.

He pushed, but he knew better than to push too hard.

Wife.

I liked the way it sounded coming from his lips.

I paused.

Why did I think that?

My heart raced as I realized the truth.

He chose me.

No one else, just me. A powerful ruler that chose me for his queen.

The very idea appealed to me. No one ever picked me, but he did.

Not even my family.

"My husband answered your question. Wife. That is my title and it will be respected. And that is what he wanted. Me."

And my firstborn.

I would not give him any insight into my life. Speculations be damned.

The Summer King sighed and leaned back in his chair. "How boring. What would make you betray your own husband, Aleyna?"

Chapter 11

Challenges to Power

My husband stood up from his throne, the jewels on his crown sparkling in the light. His jaw was clenched, and his eyes were blazing with fury.

He never looked so angry before - not even when assassins tried to murder me.

I could barely breathe, my heart pounding in fear as he pointed a finger at the Summer King.

"You are not fit to ask such a question," he hissed.

The Summer King raised his hands, a gesture of surrender.

The glint in his eye was still there, but something else eclipsed it. Fear? Respect? I couldn't say for sure.

Doran took a step forward as frost covered the tables.

I needed to step in to de-escalate the situation. The Summer King's boldness and arrogance get the better of him.

"Why would I ever do that?"

His gold hair glinted in the candlelight as he turned to look at me. "Winter snows are cruel," he said simply.

Doublespeak.

He was reminding me of the power his kingdom held.

Humans and Fae were more alike than we cared to admit; even in our differences, loyalty was a concept we both seemed to understand.

The Summer King straightened himself and stepped back, his gaze still fixed on my husband.

The tension in the room was thick enough to cut with a knife.

I lowered my gaze, and a tight smile appeared on my face. "Are they? Winter snows are cruel, but summer isn't any more forgiving."

Doran's chest rumbled with a low chuckle as he sat down. His hand found mine, and I slowly squeezed it.

A power move, but one that showed loyalty and respect.

I leaned forward as the Summer King sat down. "The trick with summer is that it likes to fool others—it can be a warm front that hides something deeper and darker."

A gentle sensation spread across my hand as Doran's knuckles lightly caressed mine. "Well said, my wife."

The Summer King's eyes narrowed as he looked between us.

My husband's eyes shimmered with a spark of power as he raised his hand and frost formed in the air.

The Summer King drew back instinctively, a look of anger crossing his face as an icy wind swirled around him.

His expression shifted, and his hair darkened to a deep, chocolate brown, with a thin scar tracing the side of his eyebrow.

The golden facade was gone.

"My wife can see the true nature of the Summer Court. I suggest you do not play games here."

I felt the tension in the room as I glanced between the two of them.

I would pay the price if the two came to blows.

No matter how powerful I was, this was a battle between two Fae kings. Their magic was too strong for me, and I needed to tread carefully.

The Summer King smiled, though it did not reach his eyes. His eyes blazed with a fire that could not be quenched, and his lips were pressed into a thin line that revealed his intensity.

"I never take things seriously in your court."

The surrounding air crackled with the power of his rage.

He turned to me, his gaze still as intense as ever. "The Fae are more powerful than mortals, Aleyna. Your fear is understandable. Brutes like us can be quite intimidating, after all."

My heart was still pounding in my chest, but I held back my fear.

"A facade that hides something deeper and darker," I muttered. "The summer has always been deceptive and treacherous. But the winter can be just as calculating and merciless."

Doran's lips curved into a cruel smile. "The Winter Court has its own devious ways, Aleyna."

My husband's hand tightened around mine and I knew he was trying to keep me from speaking out.

"That may be true. But with the Winter King at my side, at least I know I'm safe."

Doran gazed at me intently. The unguarded hunger in his eyes burned bright, and it felt like a fire was lit inside me.

I heard my own breath echoing in my ears as I turned away. The intensity of his gaze was too much.

The Summer King chuckled in amusement. "Very well." He clapped his hands together. "A fair warning from a powerful woman. I will take heed."

The irony was not lost on me. It was usually the other way around—the Summer King warning others of his power. But here I was, a mere mortal, standing up to two powerful Fae kings.

My husband smiled and squeezed my hand again in appreciation.

"Tell me more about your court," I said, power surging through me.

The Summer King's eyes widened in surprise before he smiled. "What would you like to know?"

"Everything."

The Summer King raised an eyebrow as he

stared at Doran. "Greedy little thing."

His eyes were half-closed as he kissed my fingertips, sending a tingle up my arm. "Mine."

∞∞∞

Brushing a lock of hair from my face, I stared at my reflection in the mirror. Dark eyes, lips set in a determined line, and beauty spots gave away my mortality.

No glamor or illusion could ever hide the truth.

Mortal. Flawed. Insignificant.

Dinner shone a light on the differences between us.

I was a mere mortal, while they were powerful Fae kings.

My husband was a Fae. A powerful, ancient being. And his power was undeniable.

But I saw the look in his eyes when he looked at me, and I knew that what made him powerful was not just his magic—it was his desire for legacy.

But I also understood that he could still be untrustworthy, and that feeling clung to me like a chill.

Tales of tricks and treachery were common among the Fae, and our deal never promised me safety in the future.

I was taking a risk by standing at my husband's side, and I knew it.

My husband pushed the door open and stepped into the room, the light from the hallway spilling in behind him. An ominous energy followed him.

His features relaxed when he laid eyes on me. But only for a moment.

He sat behind me, taking up the brush and running it through my hair. Soft strokes and gentle caresses.

His hands were a reminder that no matter how powerful he was, the power he showed me was a mere fraction of what he truly was capable of.

I looked at him in the mirror, noting his tense expression. "What's wrong?" I asked softly, as his gray eyes met mine. "Why were you so tense today? Did you think I would betray you? Betray our alliance?"

He paused before he continued brushing

my hair. "I study a person before I'm willing to make a deal with them," he said. "I need to know who they are. What did I find out about you, Aleyna?"

My lips curved in a smile as my eyes glinted with amusement. "That I'm a queen who doesn't realize she is one?"

The brush stopped, and my husband looked at me through the mirror.

A slow smile formed on his lips, and then he leaned in close to whisper. "Oh, you are a queen, but you are much more than that. You understand the consequences of your decisions, but you never let fear guide them."

I lifted an eyebrow, my smile broadening. "Am I a warrior, then?"

His breath tickled my ear as he replied. "No. You are a tactician."

He said nothing else, but the warmth in his voice told me everything I needed to know.

I turned around to meet his gaze, understanding that a powerful alliance was the only thing we could rely on.

I lifted my chin, my eyes steady on his. "As long as I have you at my side, at least I know I'm safe." I turned to the mirror again. "But that's not all that you think of me."

He resumed brushing again, taking my hair in a gentle grip. "No, that's not all." His voice was low and serious. "I can see how you maneuver through the court, how you balance between two Fae kings. But your need to please others will be your downfall. You don't acknowledge your own conviction and strength. Indulging in a little selfishness can be a rewarding experience."

I smiled.

He knew me better than I thought.

He was right. I put others before myself too often, but I will try to be more mindful in the future.

"Maybe I will," I said as he nodded in agreement. "You make me sound like I'm a fool."

My husband shook his head. "No, not a fool. But someone who can see the bigger picture and understand its complexities." He leaned in close, a smirk on his lips. "You are wise beyond your years, Aleyna. Wise enough to know that sometimes you just have to take the risk."

Taking risks was an essential part of being a queen, no matter how much it scared me. I was ready to take this risk, and I felt it would be worth it in the end.

He chuckled. "There's more to life than attempting to meet the expectations of your father and your country. Let yourself yearn for what you want, and don't be afraid to reach out and grab it. You deserve to be queen, not just out of fear of what your brother would do, but because of your own aptitude and power to rule."

A lump formed in my throat, and I had to force myself to swallow.

His words pierced my skin like shards of ice.

I nervously glanced away and whispered, "I married you."

He paused, his gaze lingering on my face, before he smiled. "And that is why I know you have what it takes to be a great queen—one who follows her heart and her head. Your attempts to make everyone around you happy will come back to haunt you. Taking care of yourself should be your number one priority."

I nodded slowly, my mind spinning with conflicting emotions.

But in the end, I trusted his words and knew that it was time for me to take a risk and put my own desires first.

I needed to follow my path. To be selfish and to follow my own convictions. There was nothing wrong with that.

Releasing a deep breath, I looked up and met my husband's gaze.

He smiled, his eyes crinkling in the corners, and then I felt his hand in my hair, brushing in a steady rhythm.

I closed my eyes, allowing myself to drift away from my worries and insecurities. "That might be true," I whispered. "But every time the Summer King said my name, you tensed up. I felt your anger, and I don't understand why."

I opened my eyes and caught his gaze in the mirror, the intensity of it making me still.

Smoky gray eyes watched me warily, as if he knew I was about to say something that would change the entire course of our conversation.

He released a heavy sigh and stepped away from me. "I think you already know the answer, Aleyna."

"Why?" I asked softly, my lips curving into a teasing smile. "Does it bother you he called me Aleyna? It's a name. A regular name. It has no special power."

He released a deep breath, his gaze searching my face. "It's your true name, and you give it away like it's meaningless."

Anger flared in his eyes as I searched for the right words. "I don't give it away," I said softly. "A name has no meaning. It's only the person who it belongs to that gives it power."

He nodded and stepped closer, the faint sound of his breath brushing against my neck as he pulled me in. His hands shook as they clenched and released, the sound of his knuckles creaking in the silence.

"To the Fae, names have power. When someone knows your name, they can control you."

Control?

"But I'm mortal—I'm not bound by the same rules as you."

"All these peasants and that unworthy scum of the Summer Court know your true name," he said, his voice rough with emotion. "They know my wife's name. My queen's name. It's a precious thing, not something to be taken for granted and treated as if it's insignificant."

I smiled, and the warmth of his embrace surrounded me as I ran my fingers through his hair.

The possessive way he clung to me when jealous was strangely endearing.

Underneath my husband's physical strength and dominance lay a vulnerability that few ever got to see.

He feared losing me, and by using my name so freely, his actual feelings showed.

Perhaps, in this game of power dynamics, we were more evenly matched.

A name might not have any power, but if it came from the heart, it could be an anchor.

An anchor that would keep me safe.

"You have my name," I whispered. "No one can take it away from you. I'm your wife." A teasing smile curved my lips. "And you're the king."

He smiled, pressing a soft kiss to my hair. "That I am."

As our gazes met in the mirror, I knew he understood what I was saying. That I wasn't going anywhere.

A deal was a deal.

He squeezed my waist before stepping away.

"So tell me, husband, why have I not seen you this week?"

He chuckled. "Isn't it obvious?"

I shook my head, amused. "We are newlyweds. I can't read your mind."

"My presence would undermine your position as queen. To be seen in public with me would mean the court focuses on me instead of you. How can you win their hearts when their ears are all attuned to me?"

"Your generosity is impressive," I said, my voice low. "But you don't need to do this for me."

He smiled again, a knowing glint in his eyes. "It's selfishness, not generosity. A wife reflects the power of her husband, and I need you to be strong. To show everyone that we are a unified front."

Our alliance depended on it.

He paused his brushstrokes, looking into the mirror and meeting my gaze. "And I think it's working. Your words today have shown everyone how strong you are."

Why did he find this important?

"And how will you show them how strong you are?"

"By sleeping in your chambers tonight," he said, his voice low and serious. "They will see that I have claimed you as mine. That our marriage is genuine."

He took my hands in his, looking into my eyes with a seriousness that I never saw before.

"And are you making me scream today, husband?" I asked, my voice barely a whisper.

He chuckled, the intensity in his eyes fading as he smiled down at me. "I don't see you begging yet. Wickedness is a two-way street."

He leaned in and kissed my forehead.

His lips brushed against my skin so lightly that I barely felt it.

My core clenched. "Let's see who comes out on top."

"A challenge." His lips brushed mine lightly before he stepped away. "I accept it."

Chapter 12

A truth for a truth?

The ground trembled beneath the polar bear's thunderous roar as it charged across the ice.

I inhaled sharply, anticipating the force of the impact.

But before the bear could get close to me, a wave of icy enchantment rolled over it and it stopped in its tracks.

My husband smiled, his gray eyes piercing even through the cold. "Dangerous creatures," he said, his voice as smooth and seductive as his icy powers.

He carefully traced the outline of my face with his fingertips. "But you will need to ride along with your brave husband if you wish to be safe."

I reached up, and my fingertips glided across the smoothness of his cheek as I stroked his face. "Stupidity has its advantages, I suppose."

The courtiers watched with delight as his cackling laughter reverberated throughout the courtyard.

"You should take more risks, Aleyna. Life is too short to be so controlled and cautious."

I rolled my eyes, but couldn't help the smile that played on my lips as I watched the bear slowly thaw and slink away. "Our marriage may be unconventional, but it's certainly never boring."

If reading a bear's intentions wasn't enough of a challenge, I had to take on the icy depths of my husband's gaze.

He was unreadable as he watched me, and I felt that if I didn't answer his silent questions correctly, he would never let me live it down.

I took a deep breath and squared my shoulders, trying to appear more confident than I felt. "What are you thinking?"

He smiled, a slow curl of his lips that sent a thrill through me. "Whether you'll be bold with me."

My heart skipped a beat.

Bold in the bedroom?

A flush reached my cheeks, and all I wanted to do was run away. But I forced myself to stay still and meet his gaze head-on.

"I can handle it."

I hope.

He stepped closer and his gaze drew me in like a moth to a flame. "Are you sure, Aleyna? I don't want to take you too far outside of your comfort zone."

My mouth was so dry that I licked my lips, trying to find the courage to speak. "I'm not afraid of anything you might throw my way."

He leaned in, his breath fanning across my face and setting my skin alight. "We'll see, won't we?"

I nodded, not trusting myself to speak.

He was competitive, but so was I.

The bear approached us. The enormous creature raised its head and regarded us with a solemn stare.

My husband extended his hand and whispered something under his breath.

The bear stopped in front of us, sniffing the air, before turning to look at me. It seemed to size me up.

"You are all bones and no blubber," it said with a huff before turning and walking away. "I have standards, you know."

Talking polar bears? Cruel and witty polar bears?

Welcome to my world.

I bit my lip and glanced at my husband, who still watched me with a knowing smile on his face. "It seems I'm not the only one with standards around here."

I passed a test I didn't even know I was taking, but he gave me the key.

My expression was serious as I stepped closer and looked up at him. "A polar bear isn't a suitable companion for either of us."

My husband brought his face close to mine, and I could feel the slight tickle of his breath on my lips.

"No, it isn't." He paused, letting the anticipation build between us. "But I believe I found you a more suitable companion."

Before I processed his words, Doran took my hand and guided me toward a giant moose.

"This is Farnos."

The majestic beast bowed its head in my direction, and I swear I heard it snicker.

"It seems Farnos and I are going to get along just fine."

My husband pulled me close. "I thought you might appreciate the company."

The moose snorted and stepped away, clearly ready to get going.

"Come on, little wife."

I grinned as the moose snorted, and I shook my head. "You're impossible."

"And yet," Doran whispered in my ear. "You keep coming back for more."

The moose watched us with trepidation before huffing again and trotting away.

I looked up at the towering animal and raised an eyebrow. "It looks... comfortable."

Doran clicked his tongue, shaking his head. "It's not about comfort. It's about taking risks and having faith in yourself."

The conversation we had a week ago crossed my mind. Was this his way of pushing me outside of my comfort zone?

"Alright then." I stepped closer to the moose, still wary of its size, and placed a hand on its neck. It didn't move, and I smiled in satisfaction as I turned to my husband. "See? Nothing has eaten me yet."

He placed his hands on the small of my back as he steered me toward the moose. "No, nothing has eaten you yet." His eyes lingered on mine, and my heart fluttered as he leaned in closer. "But if you're not careful, someone might."

I shivered as his breath brushed against my neck, and I forced myself to take a step back. "Perhaps it's better if I stay on the safe side and keep my distance."

He smirked and leaned in closer, his lips brushing against my ear. "It's up to you, but I think you can handle it."

His words made me feel a warmth that spread from my head to my toes, making me shudder.

I could handle the moose, but my husband? That I wasn't too sure of.

What monster had I unleashed by challenging him?

The moose shuffled, its tail swishing back and forth.

I tentatively reached out and patted its neck, feeling the warmth radiating from it.

The moose dropped to its knees. "Would you mind?" I asked it, wondering if it feared us.

The moose shook its head, and I carefully

climbed up onto its back, nestling my hands into the thick fur of its neck.

Doran clambered up beside me, my heart swelling at the sound of his arm wrapping around my waist.

His eyes were intense, and he leaned in close, holding my gaze. "Ready?"

I nodded, gripping the moose's fur tightly. "Let's go. But why are we riding together?"

The moose snorted before leaping forward and taking off into the night.

I gasped as the wind hit my face, and I clung to Doran as the moose ran faster and faster, each stride taking us further away from the safety of the castle.

My skin tingled with a delicious warmth as my breath came out in little puffs of air.

Despite sharing a bed, we'd never been this close.

Doran tightened his grip on me. "Because of this."

The other Fae raced through the forest on their polar bears, as the steady beat of the hooves of Farnos echoed through the snow.

As we galloped away, it was as if I was flying.

I turned to Doran. "You just want an excuse to hold me."

The cold air stung my cheeks, and my hair blew wildly in the wind, but I laughed and pressed closer to Doran, feeling a thrill course through me as we raced away into the night.

"Your curves are much more comfortable to hold than a riding post," he joked, his breath warm against my ear. "Squeezing you tight helps me keep my balance."

His muscles tensed around me as we rode.

I pressed my lips together, feeling my cheeks flush as I looked up into his eyes. "Well, I certainly don't mind," I said, my voice barely audible above the sound of the moose.

But he heard me, and his eyes darkened with an emotion I couldn't quite understand.

He pulled me closer, and our gazes locked. "Tease."

His lips curled into a smirk.

The moose suddenly stopped, and I turned to see a pack of wolves stalking us from the shadows.

Doran tightened his grip on me, but he made no move to get off the moose. He just held me closer. "This is my domain."

The wolves stopped in their tracks. The moose snorted as it turned around and continued on its way.

I glanced back at Doran, my heart still pounding from the encounter.

He smiled down at me, his eyes twinkling with mischief. "Don't be afraid. As long as I'm with you no one can hurt you."

"And if they try?"

Doran chuckled amused.

I could feel the thick, coarse fur of the moose beneath my hands as I leaned back into Doran, and I felt his arms tighten around me in response.

"How about we trade a story for a story?" I asked, my voice barely above a whisper. "A truth for a truth?"

"Until?" he asked, his voice just as soft.

I looked up at him and smiled. "We won't be able to tell stories anymore."

Doran hummed in agreement, his lips a feathery touch against my ear. "What's your story then?"

"That's not how this works. You need to ask me a question. Anything you want to know."

He was quiet for a moment, his chin

resting on my shoulder as he mulled over his question. "What is the most daring thing you've ever done?"

I laughed and shook my head. "Getting on the back of this moose."

His muscles tensed and he squeezed me tighter. "Not summoning me?"

"Summoning you was easy. Looking death in the eye and riding off into an uncertain future... that's a whole other level of courage." I pulled away and looked up at him, a small smile on my face. "Not to mention the polar bear."

Summoning him was an act of desperation.

"Your courage is inspiring, little wife."

"Courage is not the absence of fear," I whispered. "It's the choice to face it."

Doran's smile widened, and he nodded. "I think you choose wisely, my lady."

"How about you? What's the most daring thing you've ever done?"

His muscles tensed, and he leaned in close. "Marrying you. There's no greater risk than that."

"Be serious," I said, swatting his arm playfully.

He sighed and looked up at the night sky. "I

am. You're the most daring thing I've ever done—a mortal princess choosing a Fae king to be her husband."

I leaned back against him, feeling the strength of his arms around me. "Well then, my king, I suppose we can call it even."

The moose continued through the snow-covered forest. Silver trees with white snowcaps glittered under the moonlight as we rode.

"Your first heartbreak?"

I froze, my breath catching in my throat. I hadn't expected this question, and for a moment I was too scared to answer.

"Losing my mother."

Doran tightened his arms around me. "Losing a parent is difficult. I lost both of mine. When my father died, it felt like the world had gone dark."

I looked back at him, my eyes searching his. "How did you lose them?"

His gaze softened. "They murdered my mother, and my father went mad with grief. He ended up taking his own life."

They?

I leaned back against him, and the feel of his chest rising and falling with each breath brought tears to my eyes. "I'm so sorry."

He nodded stoically, his gaze sweeping across the dense trees of the forest. "We all experience sorrow, yet it's our resilience to overcome them that shows our true character."

"When my mother died, my whole life changed," I said after a few moments. "I didn't know who I was or what I wanted to do with my life anymore. My father was so lost without her, he barely noticed I was still alive."

His fingers traced lazy circles on my arm. "But you eventually found yourself again."

"I needed to step up. I wanted to make everyone happy so that they wouldn't feel the sadness and pain I felt. If I could make everything better for other people, then maybe it would make me feel better, too?"

I looked away, embarrassed.

I'd never talked about this with anyone before, and it felt strange to be so open in front of him.

Who was this man that I could tell him something so personal?

Doran stayed quiet, his arms still around me. "You were so young, yet you showed such courage."

After a while, I spoke again. "Who was your first love?"

He paused and looked ahead, his face softening as he smiled. "It's not a who, and more a what. After my parents... That's when I discovered painting. It became my solace and my passion."

Surprised, I turned to look at him. "I never knew you were artistic."

"It's something I keep close to my heart. A private joy that others don't always understand."

"What do you like painting most?"

He paused again as the moose trotted on. "The way a sunrise casts its light onto the buildings, the way a person's face can tell a thousand stories. Every moment has something special to it." The gemstones in his hair glittered as he turned to me. "That's what I like to capture most in my work—that feeling of being alive."

"It sounds like you have an incredible gift."

He leaned forward to brush his lips against my cheek. "Perhaps it's not so much a gift as something that helps me make sense of the world. My turn," he whispered. "Who was your first love?"

Chapter 13

Bonfires

"I didn't know we were taking turns."

His chest shook with deep, rumbling laughter. "Come on, you can tell me. Your dazzling smile must have stolen the hearts of many. A ravishing woman such as yourself."

His teasing brought a warmth to my cheeks, and I couldn't help but smile.

"My romantic entanglements were never long-lived."

"Did they not appreciate your wit and beauty?" he asked, his eyes gleaming in the night.

I looked away. What had I just gotten myself into?

His face broke into a coy smile as an amused hum filled the air. "Were they not worthy of your attention?"

The ones that weren't pushed out of court were unreliable. How could I trust someone my stepmother approved of? There was a hidden agenda, and I couldn't be sure of anyone.

"I'm hesitant to open up to anyone."

He nodded sagely. "The fear of not knowing if you can trust someone with your heart can be a heavy burden."

"My first love was Isra," I said shyly. "Not romantically, of course," I added quickly. "She was my best friend and confidante."

He lightly touched my face, sweeping away a strand of hair with his fingertips. "I'm glad you have someone you can count on in times of need."

Did he have that?

His eyes turned bright. "People get to know each other before getting married. We hardly know each other. But I think it's a start, don't you?"

His words felt like a balm, soothing away my worries and fears. He was right—sometimes all we need is a chance to get to know each other before making any big decisions.

I held his gaze. "Yes. It's a start. Knowing each other is important for a strong marriage."

His lips quirked into a half-smile. "Maybe," he said, his voice low and husky. "But it's insignificant to know someone's favorite foods, the things that keep them awake, or the way they prefer to spend their day." He gazed in front of him. "None of that is important. It's more important to understand someone's intentions and motivations."

"Uncovering someone's favorite dishes and activities can provide an insight into their character." I met his gaze. "The little things they do demonstrate the kind of person they are."

Doran shrugged. "That level of intimacy takes an entire lifetime to achieve. In our positions, it's hard to know if someone is being genuine. The risks are too great."

I looked down.

I wanted a marriage based on tenderness, not one of convenience. Despite by fears, I craved the feeling of connection that comes with loving and being loved.

Doran gently tilted my chin up, his gaze intense. "I know it's not what you asked for. But I promise to be honest with you and to do whatever I can to make this marriage work. Our child, should we have one, will never lack a parent's love and attention."

His words hung in the air between us like a promise.

The tenderness in his eyes told me he meant what he said, and that made me feel a little better.

"Thank you," I mumbled. "I appreciate it."

The moose eventually stopped in front of a cave, and Doran slowly slid off its back.

He clasped my hand as I stepped down, the warmth of his touch igniting me with a pleasant heat.

He led me into the cave. "Come, let us join a proper winter feast. We can dance and be merry."

Maybe this marriage wasn't such a bad thing after all? Maybe it was the start of something beautiful.

Not love, but something just as precious.

Companionship.

Looking up, gemstones twinkled from the walls, creating a rainbow of color on the dark stone. Waterfalls trickled from the sides and an enormous bonfire roared in the center, illuminating everything. People danced around it, the sound of their laughter and singing providing a rhythm to their movements.

Tree branches with twinkling flowers hung from the ceiling and fireflies hummed around us.

This wasn't a feast like I ever experienced before.

Doran looked down at me. His eyes twinkled. "Care to join them?" he asked, gesturing towards the people.

I slipped my hand into his. "Let's dance."

His hands were gentle on my waist as he pulled me close, his lips lightly grazing mine.

Color flooded my cheeks as I looked up at him, my heart pounding in my chest.

"Let go of your fears, Aleyna," he whispered into my ear. "For tonight there is just us, no one else."

I let the rhythm of the music sweep me away, a contented smile on my lips.

Harps and flutes echoed from the cave walls, stirring old memories. Of dancing in the courtyards and singing in the halls. Drinking boza and playing games with father.

Doran held me close, his hands gripping my waist tightly as we moved in circles, the dizzying sensation of spinning overpowering us as we went faster and faster until we were both breathless. Our movements were met with enthusiastic cheers and claps from the surrounding people.

Snowflakes descended from the sky, and I gasped in delight.

Night flyers flew around us, their colorful wings reflecting the light from the floating gems.

Another grabbed my hand, and I smiled shyly at Doran before spinning away. The redcap led me away, and I laughed as we whirled around, our feet barely touching the ground.

∞∞∞

In the corner, servants laid out flower crowns and ribbons. All different colors glittering in the firelight.

I turned back to the Iron Sword, who was observing me. Her bright blue skin was decorated with pearls.

"What do they mean?" I asked as she passed me a crown of moonflowers.

She smiled, her dark eyes twinkling in the firelight. "They are symbols of the night, and a reminder to remain true to yourself. Always."

I placed the crown on my head, taking a moment to let her words sink in.

She smirked. "Giving your crown away is a sign that you want to take things to the next level with someone."

I placed my hands on my hips as I smiled at her. "I never knew you felt that way."

Her skin turned a light blue. "Never let the Winter King hear you say that. He would..."

I raised an eyebrow. "He would do what?"

She bit her lip. "He would be... displeased."

I laughed and shook my head. "Noted."

I looked back to the dancefloor, where Doran was spinning with another woman. The firelight illuminated her auburn hair, and she gave him a sly, knowing grin.

My heart raced, and my eyes darted away.

A true beauty.

My throat tightened.

Doran glanced in my direction, and our eyes met. A mischievous twinkle glimmered in his eyes as he held out his hand to me. An offer that was too tempting to ignore.

The Iron Sword touched my arm gently. "Go on, give him your crown."

"Surely, I can't," I shook my head. "It would be improper."

Our relationship wasn't like that. We shared laughs and meaningful conversations, but nothing more than that.

She raised her eyebrows knowingly, a hint of a smile tugging at the corner of her mouth. "He's your husband. You can do whatever you want. The women at court are well aware of that fact. Give it to him and show the court that you appreciate him."

I looked back at Doran, my heart thumping wildly in my chest.

He smiled, silently urging me to join him.

Taking a deep breath, I held the flower crown in my hands and stepped out onto the dancefloor, the vibrant colors of the lights reflecting off the floor.

He bowed down; the breeze ruffling his hair.

I placed the crown on his head. "As the queen of the Winter Court, I think it's only proper that I bestow my husband with a crown."

Doran grabbed my hand, and I felt the exhilaration as he spun me around, the fabric of my silk dress brushing against my skin as it twirled with us.

"Don't worry, little wife," he murmured into my hair. "Who can love a monster?"

With flushed cheeks, I realized he felt my moment of insecurity and wanted to reassure me.

I pulled away and looked into his eyes. "I see no monsters here." Before I rested my hand on his biceps, I twirled around him. "Monsters don't surprise their wives like this or save their wives when they don't need to."

"Monsters are greedy and selfish," he said, a wry smile playing on his face.

"No, not monsters. Kings. Why shouldn't you?"

The corners of his eyes crinkled as he pulled me closer. "Has the Iron Sword told you what the crowns mean?"

"They're symbols of the night — and a reminder to remain true to myself. And a symbol of affection."

"She has understated it." He spun me around again, the flower crown glimmering in the firelight.

Redcaps leaped around us, their laughter ringing out in the night.

"They mean you wish to spend the night with me," he said, his voice low.

I looked away as my back rested against his chest. "Doing what?"

He grinned, his arms wrapping around my waist. "Things that only can be done in the dark," he whispered.

He twirled me around and I raised an eyebrow. "If you are doing them only in the dark, no one will know."

Doran's face softened, and he looked deeply into my eyes. "Oh, they'll know," he murmured. "They always do."

"And what will they know?" I asked, my heart thumping in my chest.

Doran put his hand on my chin and raised it until our eyes met. A dangerous smile curved his lips. "Whatever unspeakable pleasure we can find in the night."

Heat rushed through my body, and a familiar thrill ran down my spine.

A knowing look appeared in Doran's eyes.

"Then," I said, my voice shaky, "Let's stay in the dark."

"You are not begging yet."

I held his gaze. "You've not convinced me yet."

He lifted me off my feet as he spun me

around. "I'm just getting started?"

I wrapped my legs around his waist. "Maybe you need to convince me a little more?"

He lowered me onto the floor, his lips close to mine. "I can do that," he said, his voice a low whisper.

My eyelashes fluttered against my cheeks. "Or... You'll beg me."

He chuckled softly, lifting me up again and spinning me around in the air. "Or we could just stay in the dark and never know."

As he set me down, I felt my lip trembling beneath my teeth, a smoldering smile etched across his face. "Let's bask in the comfort of the dark."

"And do what?" Doran asked, his pupils dilating as his gaze met mine.

I looked into his eyes, and I knew he already knew my answer. "Everything."

A chill ran through me as Doran's thumb grazed my jawline. "I can think of a few things we could do," he said, his voice husky. "Anything?"

I nodded, eagerly. "Anything." I swallowed hard, my heart racing. I could just imagine it. Him. It would be my undoing. "But I'm not convinced yet."

His lips curled into a smile. "You'll be

convinced soon enough, little wife."

He grabbed my hand and pulled me close.

Doran brushed his lips against the back of my hand, sending a wave of electricity through my body.

His touch was electrifying as he kissed along my knuckles, his tongue teasing each finger before finally pressing his lips to my palm.

His warm breath sent shivers down my spine, and I could feel a deep desire stirring in my core.

Harsh breaths escaped his lips as he whispered in my ear, "We can stay out of the light and explore all the pleasures hidden in darkness."

My breath hitched as his soft lips brushed against my ear.

I opened my eyes, a deep longing stirring inside me.

A teasing smile spread across Doran's face, but he stepped back, his hand lingering on mine. "The night is young, and my people are waiting for their king. But before we go," he said, his voice teasing, "Will you beg me to stay?"

I met his gaze and grinned, lifting my chin in defiance. "No, queens don't beg."

"Kings don't either," he replied, his eyes

twinkling. He leaned forward and kissed me gently on the forehead. "Their prey begs."

"And I'm definitely not your prey," I retorted, deciding to break the tension with a bit of playful banter.

He laughed and stepped back. "Little wife, you are an exceptional, rare creature."

Chapter 14

Grievances

"You want me to do what?"

I had to be mistaken - it was impossible to believe. There was no way he wanted to grant me that much power.

"To listen to the petitioners," Doran said, his voice serious. "For only one day. You will handle the judgments, pass the laws and decide what is best for our people. I give you my blessing to do as you see fit."

Did he trust me to do this? To put the fate of his people in my hands?

I was at a loss for words.

"I... I won't let you down," I said after a moment. "I promise to be fair and just in my judgments. The people of Frosthome shall have the best possible leader today."

Doran smiled and nodded his head, a gesture of approval that warmed my heart.

"I know they will. You have full control," he said, his voice low and steady. "Trust your judgment and do what you believe is right."

My mouth went dry.

He handed me the power to shape the future of Frosthome, and I could feel the magnitude of the task ahead.

The people deserve nothing less than my best.

Taking a deep breath, I nodded my head in agreement. "I understand your trust in me. And I won't let you down. But what if you disagree with my judgment?"

Doran chuckled. "Then I will trust your wisdom to be greater than mine. You are the queen of the Winter Court. The title, the power, it is yours to wield," he enunciated each word carefully, as if he was speaking a spell. "I give you my full blessing."

I bowed my head in reverence. "Thank you for this opportunity."

Doran nodded his head, the corners of his mouth lifting into a subtle smile. "You are welcome."

It was a strange feeling to be taken so

seriously. To be thought of as an equal. To be trusted with so much power.

I raised an eyebrow. "And what will you be doing?"

He clapped his hands together. The opal stone on his ring shimmered in the light. "I will be near, but not too close. The Autumn King asked for my help in a delicate matter."

Curiosity burned inside me.

What was Doran involved in? But I dared not ask.

His eyes softened, and he placed his hand on his face. It made him look more vulnerable. More like a normal person rather than the king.

"I'll be here when you return. I look forward to hearing all about your day."

He grabbed something from behind him. He turned back to me, revealing a deep blue cloak with silver embroidery and fur trim.

"My cloak," he said, holding it out to me. "This symbolizes the authority I will grant you today. The people of Frosthome will recognize it immediately and obey your orders."

I reached out and took the cloak, feeling its heavy material between my fingers. I thought of how much power this cloak represented, and a sudden surge of courage ran through me.

"It's beautiful," I said in awe.

He stepped forward and wrapped the cloak around my shoulders; the fur tickling my skin.

"It looks stunning on you," he said, his voice barely above a whisper. "Take this to heart. You are now the one deciding. What you decide will be the ultimate outcome. Don't let it slip away."

I gave a small nod of my head, and a thrill of excitement filled the air around me. "Thank you."

I nodded and grasped the cloak tight.

His eyes narrowed in thought. "What do you want in return?"

I looked outside the window. Dawn just arrived, and the horizon was painted in shades of pink and orange.

"I want you to paint me." I bit my lip, not wanting to say too much.

Doran's mouth widened in surprise, then slowly slid into a smile. "A painting of you?"

He stepped closer. His hair caught the light of the moon and, for a moment, he looked like a painting. A beautiful painting of a warrior king that could have been plucked from a fairy tale.

"That's all? It's little to ask for such a

monumental task."

Handing me power, trust, and now a painting of myself? Doran was spoiling me.

I smiled coyly. "A beautiful representation of your queen," I said simply. "I want to be immortalized forever in a painting made by your hands."

Smolder crept into his gaze, and he nodded slowly. "As you wish, little wife."

Little wife.

The phrase sent shivers down my spine.

"Until next time," I said, taking one last look at Doran before turning around and walking out the door. "Husband."

∞∞∞

The Iron Sword cut in front of me to stand guard as I stepped into the throne room. The audience chamber was filled with people, all of them staring at me with diluted expressions.

Taking a seat on the dais, I nodded to them in greeting. The whispers of surprise rippled through the room, a few people even gasping at my presence. The blue cloak I was wearing served as a reminder of my newfound power.

I smiled to myself, feeling the effects of Doran's words still ringing through me.

Doran's wolf appeared at the edge of the room, its bright blue eyes watching me intently.

Its presence seemed to unnerve everyone in the room, but I felt only comfort. I knew that wherever I went, the wolf would be there to protect me from any danger.

It was comforting to know Doran granted me this small piece of himself - a token of his faith in me.

The wolf bowed its head in reverence, before stepping back into the shadows to watch over me.

Yes. Today was mine to wield.

"Today I will hear your grievances," I said, my voice loud and clear. "I will listen to your stories and decide in the best interest of our people."

The audience was silent, their eyes glued to me as if a miracle had been bestowed upon them.

Did Doran's cloak really make them think of me as their ruler?

"Now speak."

The people talked, their grievances spilling out of them as if someone lifted a heavy burden from their shoulders.

It felt strange to be in the throne room, as not a bystander, but a decision-maker.

The closest I'd ever come to rule was sitting on my father's lap while he listened to his courtiers.

His throne was made of gold, while mine was forged from silver.

The words of the people floated around me like a river. But I listened, and when the time came, I made my decisions.

The Iron Sword clanked as she moved about the room in response to my orders.

A young couple stepped forward, asking for help with a dispute between families. I listened closely and made my ruling. A farmer asked for a loan to help his struggling business, and I approved it.

The air in the room was tense but hopeful as I spoke. But underneath all of that, I could feel something else — a growing tension.

I swept my gaze across the room, noticing how some of them were whispering.

One of them seemed to be a merchant. The detailed designs of his clothes told me he was someone important. The man's stare was intense, as if he were trying to evaluate me.

I held his gaze for a few moments before turning away. I needed to remain calm and collected, but the man seemed determined to test me.

When it was finally time for him to speak, the merchant stepped forward, his eyes blazing with fury. He bowed deeply to me. "Winter Queen, I come to you with news of a great injustice-"

But a man shouting from the back of the room cut him off. "Lies!" he said, his voice filled with rage. "The Winter Fae are trying to take what isn't theirs!"

The strings of hair silver and gold glimmering in the candlelight set him apart from all others. Gold hair and bold patterns stitched onto his cloak — a Summer court Fae.

Only he could pull off a feat like this, claiming the attention of everyone in the room.

The Iron Sword immediately stepped in front of me, ready to attack at my command.

"Ah! I apologize for his outburst, Winter Queen," the Summer Fae merchant said quickly. "We were just discussing some trade disputes between our courts. Nothing more."

The room erupted into chaos. People

started shouting, their voices filled with anger and distrust.

I took a deep breath and stood up. "Enough!" I said, my voice echoing through the chamber.

Silence fell, and all eyes were on me.

Taking a step forward, I surveyed the room. "We will settle this dispute fairly and justly. As your queen, I promise that."

The murmurs slowly died down, and the Iron Sword stepped aside.

I sat down on my throne. "What is the meaning of this? What is the truth?"

Doran's wolf stepped forward and sat down next to me. I placed my hand on its white fur.

The Summer Fae stepped forward. "Winter Queen." His voice trembled as he looked me straight in the eye. "The Winter Fae are trying to take what isn't theirs. They're using lies and deceit to do so."

He was trying to use my mortality to endear himself to me? Winter had a dark reputation among mortals.

The Summer Fae took another step forward, his expression still filled with anger. But before he could speak, the Winter Fae merchant stepped forward and bowed deeply in respect.

"Winter Queen, I accept your judgment," he said solemnly. "I'm Tall Oak, a merchant from the Winter Fae Court. I will accept your ruling, whatever it may be."

"Present your case then."

The Winter Fae presented his evidence recounting the events that happened. A tradesman had been swindled by a Summer Fae merchant in an unfair transaction, leading to the current dispute.

The Summer Fae rose to his feet, shaking with rage. He argued his case passionately, detailing the unfair treatment of Winter Fae merchants.

I listened closely to both sides and considered the evidence before me. After much deliberation, I finally reached my decision.

"Both parties have grievances," I said, my voice ringing out in the silent room. "But justice must be served. The Summer Fae will pay restitution to the Winter Fae merchant, and I settled the matter."

"But Winter Queen," the Summer Fae said, his tone pleading. "I -"

"It is decided," I said firmly but kindly.

"The Summer King will hear of this."

The wolf growled low in its throat, and the Summer Fae quickly backed down.

Behind him, Doran stepped out of the shadows. The rest of the room didn't seem to notice he was there. His eyes blazed with undiluted rage, but his face remained stoic.

I glanced at the Summer Fae, giving him a small nod. "Let him come. My decision stands. I will settle this dispute in accordance with justice and fairness. That is all."

The room was still, the air heavy with tension. But other than the sound of my breathing, there was only silence.

Another petitioner stepped forward, but I waved them away. "We will reconvene tomorrow."

The court bowed and dispersed, and the tension in the room slowly faded away.

Doran stepped forward, his gaze burning with a fierce intensity. He seemed to study me as if trying to determine the strength of my conviction.

After a moment, he approached me, his steps slow and deliberate.

"Wife." He inclined his head in respect, "How has ruling been? Are you satisfied by the justice you have dispensed here?"

"It's been a challenging but rewarding experience." I stroked the fur of his wolf as Doran eyed us with great interest. "How long have you been here?"

"Long enough to know you handled yourself masterfully." He paused for a moment, as if considering something deeply before continuing. "But it's a mortal's justice, not a Fae's."

I glanced at him, and his gray eyes seemed to sparkle in the light. Not a single flicker of feeling crossed my face. "It doesn't matter if it's mortal or Fae justice, as long as it is fair and just. That's all I care about."

Doran nodded in agreement, his gaze still burning into me.

"Have I disappointed you?" I asked quietly, my eyes meeting his.

He sighed, and a small smile tugged at his lips. "No, Aleyna. You have exceeded every expectation."

The tightness in my chest eased.

"Thank you."

He nodded and stepped back, his gaze still locked with mine. "You have done well, little wife."

I stood up. "But not how you would have done it."

His eyes blazed, and he leaned close, his lips brushing against my ear. "No," he murmured. "I would have been much more.... ruthless. The Summer court scum would have been begging for mercy."

He stepped back, his gaze still intense.

My silver rings clinked as I clenched my hands.

"But," he continued with a smirk, "I'm sure you'll figure it out soon enough."

My cheeks flushed as I met his gaze. I was aware of his every move, and I couldn't help but wonder what else he could teach me.

"I look forward to learning."

He flashed me a wicked grin, as if silently challenging me. "As do I. But let us celebrate our successes."

I lifted an eyebrow as he handed me a glass of mead. "Indeed."

He chuckled and clinked his glass against mine, his gaze still smoldering with an intensity that left me breathless.

"To justice," he said, a hint of mischief in his voice.

"To justice," I echoed as I observed the blood-red liquid.

"And to a job well done," he added, his voice low and seductive.

I smiled and touched my glass against his once again.

"Our success? Did your meeting with the Autumn King go well?"

"Oh, yes." He grinned dangerously, taking a sip of his mead. "He agreed to our terms."

"Then this is indeed a success."

He arched an eyebrow. "Will you not ask me what the terms were?"

I took a sip of my mead, my eyes twinkling with amusement. "No, I think I can guess what they were. I'm sure you got the best possible outcome in the end."

He eyed the wolf, and it rushed out of the room.

"There was no need to do that."

"He was interfering in a private conversation. He should know his place."

I frowned. "But he is still a part of our kingdom, Doran. We must treat him with respect."

"Regardless of rank, the king and queen

will always show respect. But he must also show respect in return, or there can be no balance of power."

I mulled over his words. "Ruling is more than just making decisions, isn't it? It's also about enabling people to make them."

"Ruling a kingdom is a craft," he said, his voice filled with pride. "And it takes skill to master it."

I nodded, my lips curving into a smile. "A craft that requires justice and fairness to be settled in accordance with rules and regulations."

"But it's not art without the proper cunning and grace. So tell me, my queen, did you like it?"

I laughed and recounted the events of the court.

He listened intently, adding his own insights here and there as I spoke. Context into the feuds and alliances, the power plays, and diplomacy.

When I finished, he smiled and took my hand in his. "That's how you rule a kingdom. With wit and grace. You are a natural, Aleyna."

I blushed at the compliment and squeezed his hand gently. "Thank you, Doran, for your counsel and advice. I wouldn't have been able to do it without you."

"You don't need me, Aleyna. I'm just a humble servant to your brilliance."

I chuckled. "Liar."

He lifted my hand to his lips, brushing them against my knuckles ever so gently. "Let me just say that it has been an honor serving you, my queen," he said solemnly.

My heart fluttered at his words, and I smiled warmly at him. "Charming words, but I think you should let your actions speak louder than words."

He raised an eyebrow, a hint of mischief in his eyes. "What did you have in mind?"

I leaned closer, a playful smirk on my lips. "When can I expect my portrait?" I asked, my tone light. "You promised that if I was successful, you would paint me. And I believe I am becoming quite the master of courtly politics."

His eyes sparkled with amusement. "You are. And I stand by my promise. You shall have your portrait soon enough. You are most persuasive, my queen."

I grinned and took another sip of mead. "Good. I will look forward to it then."

He smiled and ran his thumb across my knuckles, sending a shiver down my spine. My heart pounded in my chest and I couldn't help but wonder what else he could teach me.

"I will capture that look of power, grace, and wit."

"I'm sure you will."

He grinned and released my hand, a satisfied smirk on his lips. "How about we go for a walk?"

"That sounds delightful," I said, a soft smile on my lips. "But are you sure you are up to it? I don't want to tire you out too much."

"Oh, I'll be just fine." He walked towards me deliberately before he stopped before me. "Besides, I'm sure you have plenty more stories to tell me while we walk."

"Extravagant flattery." His lips lingered above mine and my stomach fluttered. "But, yes, if you insist."

Chapter 15

Ancient magic

Outside, the sun was setting, painting the kingdom in shades of gold and pink. As we entered the gardens, the tall spires of the castle loomed above us, casting long, deep shadows on the ground.

Snowy pines lined the pathways, swaying gently in the chill winter breeze.

All around us were delicate blooms of different colors, some shining with a brilliant luminescence, while others moved around.

Sparkling snow covered the ground, with soft blankets of frost sparkling on the lush grass.

In the center, the tall fountain sparkled and glittered as the water cascaded from it. A thick layer of ice encased it, giving the illusion of a crystal palace.

I shook my head in wonder. "Truthfully, I'm relieved that the day is over."

"It takes a toll," he agreed, squeezing my arm gently. "Ruling is no straightforward task."

A light chuckle escaped my lips as my mouth tugged into a smile. "Speaking from experience?"

A snowflake drifted down from the sky, and he caught it in his hand. "As my father always said... A clever ruler uses trickery as a tool, but never loses sight of justice and righteousness."

I raised one side of my mouth in amusement.

The snowflake melted in his palm, and he opened his hand, watching as the droplets hit the ground. "If one can learn to balance both, then they are truly a master of courtly politics."

I leaned against him, a giddy laugh erupting from my lips. "That is a Fae way of saying, 'Don't be a jerk.'"

"A bit more eloquent than that, but yes."

My heart lightened. His presence made my worries seem so much smaller.

As I spun around, I could feel the snowflakes tickling my face and the wind blowing through my hair. "I suppose I should heed your words of wisdom, then."

He smiled and watched me, his eyes filled with admiration. "I think you already have."

My heart raced as I stopped spinning, my eyes locked with his.

Why did he have such a firm belief in me, despite my own doubts? The faith that was placed in me, when I had done nothing to deserve it, was overwhelming.

He took me to the fountain, and I was mesmerized by the gentle trickle of water echoing in the air.

I trembled slightly, and he embraced me, my skin tingling as his arms wrapped around me.

He regarded the fountain thoughtfully. "It is a fitting tribute to our success."

I cocked my head to the side. "How so?"

"In the winter, we must be resilient to survive. But if we can endure the cold and come out on top, then the sweet reward will be worth it."

I lifted an eyebrow. "And a fountain of ice and snow tells you that?"

He gave me a knowing smile. "Yes. It is a reminder that even in the worst of times, there is beauty to be found. A king must take the risk if the reward is worth it."

I smiled, transfixed by his words. "My father always says a wise ruler is like a skilled weaver who can make a beautiful tapestry out of even the most tangled threads."

"A mortal way of saying that ruling is like parenthood," he said, his lips curving into a smile. "You must be firm and decisive when needed, but never forget the love that lies at the heart of it all."

I smiled and nodded, my gaze distant as I contemplated his words. "A wise ruler is like a parent," I said slowly, the words resonating in my heart. "They must guide and protect, but also nurture and encourage growth."

He chuckled softly and drew me in closer, his powerful arms wrapping comfortably around my waist. "It is a difficult balance."

He raised his hand and the fountain burst into life, the icy waters cascading down in a mesmerizing display of color. Blue. Purple. Silver. Green.

His expression changed, but I couldn't quite place what it was. Regret? Longing? "Beauty and resilience."

His eyes met mine, and a hunger stirred within me.

His gaze never wavered from mine. "The

perfect combination for a queen and her king."

My breath hitched in my throat, and I nodded slowly, my heart hammering against my chest. Yes, it was the perfect combination.

The wind blew my hair around, and I shivered as the chill hit me. "Why do you want a child?" I stepped away.

His muscles rippled under his blue robe as he moved. It was hard to tear my eyes away from him.

He placed his hand on his heart. "To be the best father I can, of course. To show them all the love and kindness they deserve. The Fae are not known for their fertility, so when a child is born, it is a great blessing. I want to be part of that."

I crossed my arms behind my back, my fingers interlaced. "To have a family to share your joys and sorrows with. That is a blessing."

He nodded solemnly, his gaze never wavering from mine. "To have something to love and protect that is all yours." He paused, inhaling the fresh air deeply before continuing. "And to pass on the legacy of our people for generations to come."

I bit my lip in thought. "That is a noble ambition," I said softly, my voice barely more than a whisper.

His hand was warm as it gently cupped

my cheek tenderly. "I'm the last of my line," he said, his voice heavy with regret. "Or at least I was before I married you. I want to continue my legacy, and the only way forward is to have children."

His touch was electric, sending a shiver down my spine and making my heart beat wildly. His warmth was so comforting that all my doubts melted away.

"Legacy is not just determined by blood. It is also determined by character and deeds."

He smiled at me. "Not that type of legacy. I want to create something lasting, something that will outlive me and leave a mark on the world."

He stepped away and walked to the fountain, his hand playing with a strand of my hair as he gazed upon it.

"A king needs an heir, someone who will carry on his work - both in spirit and in truth."

I released his hand and stepped away, my ears perking up at the sound of birds in the trees.

A firstborn for a throne.

The words echoed in my mind, and I shivered again as the chilly night air enveloped me.

That was our deal. And I would do my part.

Whatever it took.

"It's time to go," I mumbled. "We mustn't linger."

He reached out to me, his fingers curling in a silent invitation for me to join him. "I wish to show you something."

I followed him, my heart pounding in anticipation.

We reached the edge of a cliff, and he pointed at the night sky. "Look up," he said softly. "And you shall see."

My eyes widened in awe as I saw what he meant. Dancing across the sky was a brilliant display of night flyers, shimmering like diamonds in the night.

I gasped in amazement, my mouth agape.

He reached for my hand and intertwined our fingers together, both of us standing mesmerized by the beauty of it all.

"Beautiful," I breathed, my voice barely a whisper. "What are they doing?"

"It's ancient magic." The night flyers dipped and soared in graceful arcs, their movements almost like a dance. "A reminder of how far we have come, and that even in the darkest of times, there is beauty to be found and a way forward."

I shook my head. "Is that what they would say if I asked them?"

He smiled. "No, but it is a lesson that can be learned from sight."

I watched in awe as the night flyers gracefully moved around, the moonlight glinting off their wings.

"Breathtaking."

He leaned forward, his eyes boring into mine. The black flecks in his eyes seemed to shimmer in the light. "Indeed, it is. And I am glad you are here with me to experience it."

"A parent's love is like that," I murmured, finally understanding the meaning of his words.

He nodded. "It is tenacious, and relentless in its pursuit of what is best for us. We must remember to be firm and decisive when needed, but never forget the love that binds us all together."

I nodded, feeling the truth of his words deeply. The wings of the night flyers flashed against the sky, and I knew he was right.

He glanced at me. "So why were you so tense in the gardens earlier?"

I smiled sheepishly. "It's just... a lot of responsibility."

He brushed a strand of hair away from my face. "Children are a blessing, but they can wait. Take your time and make sure you are ready before you take this step."

I looked at him. "That's not what I mean. Our deal is binding; if I don't fulfill my end of it, I'll be an oath breaker. A wretched thing in a land where honor is everything."

His eyes still lingered on me, as if he was trying to see into my soul. I met his gaze unflinchingly, my expression serene.

"I understand. But remember that you are not alone. I'm here to help you and do whatever I can to make this easier. We will make sure the sky is full of hope for our future generations. I sensed your apprehension, and I want you to know that I will always be here for you."

I looked up at the night flyers, then back at him. "It's not that I don't want children... Children are a blessing. It's just..."

"But you fear the idea of a child of your own," he finished, his voice gentle. "A child with me."

I turned away. "No, I don't fear it. I'm just... cautious," I said, my voice wavering slightly. "I don't want to bring a life into this world unless I'm absolutely sure it won't be taken away."

His eyes flashed. "You think I'd harm our

child? Or you?"

"No, of course not! I only fear what the future holds. How would I ever be able to keep a child safe under such scrutiny? We never even discussed what we would do if our child was born. How will we raise it in a world that expects so much?"

He cupped my face in his hands and looked deep into my eyes. "This won't be easy, but it will be worth it. I promise you that no matter what the future holds, we will face it together. And our child will always have my undying love and protection."

I felt a warmth radiating from his gaze. Tears welled in my eyes, and I looked down. "I don't want our child to be another casualty of political games. I want it to have a chance at life."

Unlike myself.

He smiled, and the warmth of his kiss lingered on my forehead. "Our child will have more than just a chance at life. It will thrive."

I looked up at him. "How can we guarantee that?"

He glanced at the night flyers, their wings still shimmering in the moonlight. "We can't, but we can do our best to ensure that we give our child every opportunity to succeed. Let us swear this day to always stand together in the fight for our child, and to guard it with our lives."

"A Fae's oath is binding, but a mortal's oath is not," I said, trying to make sense of his words.

He nodded slowly. "The oath of a mother and a father? That is something that will never be broken."

I smiled, feeling a sense of peace wash over me.

His reassuring words filled me with confidence and provided me with a sense of security for our child's future.

"Agreed," I said as we looked out into the night sky together.

This time, I knew what he meant when he said "forever." And I was ready for it.

"What do you expect fatherhood to look like?"

He looked out into the night sky, the full moon illuminating the horizon. "I will be a father who loves and respects his child," he said slowly. "I will be there for them no matter what, providing guidance and strength when they need it the most. I want to teach my children the importance of honor and respect, as well as the value of hard work. Above all else, I want to show them the joy of living life to its fullest."

I smiled and squeezed his hand. "That

sounds perfect."

I could visualize our child in my head. My curly hair and his gray eyes, running through the fields of our home.

It was a beautiful dream.

I looked up at the stars. "But what does it mean to the Fae? To be a parent of a Fae child?"

He smiled and looked down at me, his expression infinitely tender. "A parent is a parent, no matter what kind of child they have. They must provide stability, guidance, and unconditional love. That is the only thing that matters in the end. But that's not what you are asking, is it?" His expression was carefully blank. "You are asking, what does it mean to parent a Fae child?"

I nodded, my throat tight.

"Your fear is understandable, but I can promise you this," he said. "Our child will grow up in an environment of acceptance and understanding. We will nurture them and help them develop. We will show them the beauty of our cultures, teach them our beliefs and customs so that they will always remember where they came from."

It was a beautiful sentiment. One I wanted to see come true.

He smiled, his expression filling with

pride. "They will grow up knowing that their parents are both Fae and mortal. Our child will understand that their story is not one of division, but one of unity."

I crossed my arms around myself as I looked at the stars. "You must think I'm a fool for worrying."

He shook his head and brushed away the tears that spilled onto my cheeks. "No, my Aleyna. You are brave and strong for believing in something bigger than yourself, even when it seems impossible. That makes you incredible."

His gaze softened, and he cupped my face in his hands.

"We will make this happen. I promise you that."

I smiled, feeling a lightness inside of me as I leaned into him. His breath was a reassuring warmth against my skin, and I knew I could always rely on his strength no matter what.

He pulled me closer. "Do you fear my Fae blood?"

My smile faltered. "No, I do not fear it. I welcome it."

"Do you fear me? What kind of parent I will be?" His voice was barely above a whisper.

I rested my forehead against his chest. The

fur trimmings tickled my cheeks. "No, I know you will be a devoted father, just as I will be a devoted mother. I fear no longer."

He smiled and brushed a strand of hair away from my face. His lips were so close, and it tempted me to kiss him. His tongue darted out, wetting his lips, and my heart fluttered.

I looked downwards. He was the most attractive man. It was the truth, after all. His presence was so captivating that I felt like I was under an enchanted spell when I saw him.

His long, black hair was pulled back, showcasing his high cheekbones and defined jaw. His full lips turned up into a smirk, and his gray eyes sparkled with intensity.

He chuckled to himself as I wrung my hands, trying to hide my nervousness.

"Our child will be the luckiest Fae," he whispered against my lips. "The luckiest Fae of all."

"The luckiest child." I breathed as his lips met mine and we sealed our promise with a kiss.

His lips were soft and warm as they met mine. The faint scent of sandalwood and mint clung to his skin, teasing my senses.

His hands brushed against my cheeks lightly, and I let out a soft moan in response.

His tongue entwined with mine, gentle and teasing.

I ran my hands up his back, feeling the strength of his muscles ripple beneath my fingertips.

His lips moved to my neck, leaving a trail of fire in their wake.

I gasped as he sucked gently on my earlobe before tracing a line down to the hollow of my throat.

His hands moved lower, caressing my hips and pulling me closer. I felt the heat emanating from his body, and it sent a shudder coursing through me.

His mouth moved back to mine and his kiss intensified, the taste of his lips lingering on mine.

My knees weakened as he explored my mouth with his tongue.

His hands moved up to cup my face, and the feeling of his arms around me sent a wave of bliss through my body.

"Our child will know what it feels like to be loved by both parents."

I smiled and closed my eyes, leaning into his embrace. "Yes."

He kissed me again, and for a few moments, we were lost in each other, allowing the world to pass us by.

He pulled away slowly, his eyes still dark with desire. "Yes," he said, his voice full of certainty. "Our child will be the luckiest Fae of all."

But it would be a child born of a trade deal, of a political alliance. Not a child born of love. Two parents with different beliefs and customs, but one shared goal: to create a better future for their child.

Lust was hot and fiery, but it lacked the depth and devotion of love.

I nodded as I looked downward.

Would that be enough?

Chapter 16

Portraits

"I guess now I can add 'painted by my husband' to my list of accomplishments." A hint of teasing crept into my voice as I looked around the room one last time.

I saw Doran's hand in all the portraits of his ancestors that lined the walls, the colors and brush strokes of each one seeming to come alive in the dim light.

The meticulous detail in each brushstroke, the muted shades of color, the careful selection of hues that complemented one another—it all spoke of a man with an artist's eye for beauty.

I turned towards him. "How have you hidden this from me? How did I not notice this before now?"

He smiled at me in that knowing way, the one that said he had been aware of my admiration for a while now—and enjoyed it. "It's all about the presentation", he said with a twinkle in his eye, as his arm wrapped around my waist. "And you, my little wife, are a masterpiece."

I blushed and smiled, feeling the warmth spread through my body as I stepped into his embrace. Softly I spoke, "Well," my gaze meeting his. "You must be proud to call this work of art your own."

His breath tickled my skin as he laughed softly before pressing his lips against mine, sending a pleasant chill down my spine.

"Yes," he murmured against my skin, his breath fanning across my cheek.

I leaned into him, savoring the moment and the feeling of our connection.

His lips moved from mine, and I felt a shiver of pleasure as he kissed my ear.

"You can always count on me to make sure your efforts are rewarded with the recognition they deserve."

The corners of my mouth tugged up in a smile as I stepped back, the warmth of his body still lingering around me. "I'm looking forward to beholding the beautiful creation you will make."

"So, how do you want me to paint you?"

His deep, melodic rumbling filled the air, and his eyes shone with a hint of naughtiness.

I bit my lip, feeling the heat rise in my cheeks as I stepped back. "What about something that takes your breath away?" I met his gaze with a challenge of my own.

"That's not much of a challenge," he purred, his lips curling into a smirk.

I looked at the portraits of his ancestors again. Before my gaze fell on his other portraits. The ones that captured the beauty of life, the details and the emotions.

"Show me my soul through your art," I said finally. "Allow me to witness the world through your eyes."

Doran looked at me for a long moment, his gaze intense and thoughtful. And then he nodded, a smile tugging at the corner of his lips. "As you wish, my lady," he said, and I could feel the electricity between us. "A change of scenery is needed, and I have the perfect place in mind."

"Oh?" I lifted my eyebrows in surprise. "Where are we going?"

"Ahh." He took my hand in his and guided me out of the room. "That would be telling, little wife."

I laughed and followed him out, already looking forward to seeing what he had in store.

Whatever it was, I knew it would be nothing short of amazing.

After all, the man was an artist.

He conjured two coats for us, and we were soon on our way. A carriage with two horses in tow waited outside, and with a click of his tongue, they were off.

The air was cool, the night sky clear, and I couldn't help but marvel at my husband's ideas.

Where would he take me? To what place would Doran's brush bring us?

"Any hints?" I asked as I settled into the carriage.

He grinned, his eyes twinkling with amusement. "You'll see soon enough."

He winked at me before tapping on the roof of the carriage. It moved, and anticipation rose inside me.

I leaned in, my hand lightly caressing his thigh as I moved closer. "Come on now," I said with a playful pout. "What's the mystery? The suspense is killing me, don't drag it out any longer."

He smiled, his eyes twinkling mischievously as he looked down at me. He lightly ran his fingers across my cheek and then moved downward, tracing the curve of my jaw with his fingertips.

"Patience, Aleyna," he murmured. "The truth will be revealed in time, so just wait and see. Patience brings its own rewards."

I trembled, my body responding to his touch as I moved closer, my lips pressing against the crook of his neck.

My breath was warm against his cheek as I whispered, "But I don't want to wait," before pressing my lips to his in a passionate kiss and drawing back with a teasing smile. "I need something to give me a hint, anything at all."

His lips curved into a smirk, and he leaned in to whisper in my ear. "Trust me, it will be a memory that will stay with you long after the surprise is revealed."

I gasped at his words, feeling goosebumps break out over my skin. "Promise me it will be worth the wait," I said, my voice barely louder than a whisper.

He smiled and nodded, his hands warm and comforting as they moved to cup my face. "I promise you this." His gaze locked onto mine, his pupils so wide and dark that it felt like I was being enveloped in flames. "No matter what happens, I'll make sure you never forget it."

I raised an eyebrow. "We'll see about that."

He smiled and his fingertips were light and warm as he brushed a strand of hair away from my face before leaning in to button the top of my coat.

His lips curved into a playful smirk as he caressed my skin before pulling away.

Tease.

For a man who wanted a baby, he sure was good at teasing.

As we settled into our seats, the horses' hooves clattered loudly against the cobblestones beneath us, leading us to wherever Doran decided to take us.

The horses clopped steadily as we drove deeper into the forest; the anticipation growing until they eventually came to a halt, and we hopped off.

The night was dark, the stars twinkling brightly above us, and a thrill of excitement rushed through me as Doran took my hand in his.

His eyes sparkled with eagerness as we made our way through the woods to the abandoned cottage, the sound of twigs snapping beneath our feet.

He grinned at me as he opened the door, and I gasped at what I saw inside.

The room was illuminated with a soft, golden glow from hundreds of flickering candles, their scent of incense lingering in the air. A feast adorned with petals of winter roses was displayed in the center of the table.

A large canvas was propped up on an easel in the corner, and I could feel my eyes growing wider with each extra surprise.

Doran smiled at me as he poured us two glasses of grenadine, his fingers lightly brushing against mine.

I felt his eyes on me, heavy and intense.

He took a sip from his glass, and then gently guided mine up to my lips, whispering, "Drink, darling. Allow yourself to be swept away by the night."

I smiled as the syrupy sweetness of grenadine filled my mouth with every sip.

I hummed thoughtfully. "I'm still waiting for the painting that you promised me."

"And I shall deliver, but a lady must be patient. This is a place of creativity and beauty, and I thought it would be the perfect setting for me to capture you in all your glory." He stepped closer, and my eyes were drawn to his, the intensity of his gaze causing my breath to catch. "Let the night carry you away, Aleyna. I promise it will be a journey you will never forget."

His words made my throat clench with anticipation. I did not know what was in store for me, but I had a surprise of my own.

I leaned in and kissed his cheek, whispering, "Let's see who will be more surprised when the night is over."

He chuckled before taking my hand and leading me to the canvas. "Ready?"

"Almost."

I slowly undid the buttons of my coat, the smell of my perfume wafting out. I raised my dress to reveal the pale blue corset, which had a delicate lace trim.

A sharp hiss passed his lips as he ran his eyes over me, his expression full of shock.

"Surprise," I said with a sly smile.

His eyes were wide with a desperate, ravenous hunger. But then I noticed something else.

Something that made my heart race and my stomach flutter.

I licked my lips and stepped away, my eyes sparkling. He was going to have a hard time concentrating on painting me.

"Oh sweetheart, you truly do not know what you do to me," he murmured as he stepped closer and ran a finger along my collarbone.

Goosebumps appeared on my skin.

"As I paint your image tonight, I will ensure that no one else lays eyes on it. It will be ours and ours alone."

I laid down on the couch and let him take control, my body tingling with anticipation as his brush glided across the canvas. Every stroke was thoughtful, every line intentional, and I felt the intensity of his gaze on me.

"You may speak. What's going through your mind?"

"A truth for a truth?"

He smiled and nodded, the bristles of his brush creating a soft scratching sound against the canvas.

"I feel like I'm in a dream. Frosthome is nothing like I'd ever imagined."

He cocked his head to the side, regarding me with a newfound interest. "Frosthome has always been a place of inspiration for me, and I feel grateful to share it with you." He smiled and looked down at the painting. "Most people don't see the beauty of winter, but you do."

"How can they not? Winter is magical." I cocked my head. "Without winter, how can we appreciate the warmth of spring?"

"The winter can be harsh, but it's a necessary part of the cycle. It makes us appreciate the good times when they come around."

"Without the challenge of winter, we will never appreciate the beauty of spring." The pearl necklace I wore sparkled in the light as I leaned back. "There's beauty in all things, even in the darkness."

Doran's ear twitched, his brush still moving across the canvas. "And that's why I'm here, to capture the beauty of you."

He waved his hand, and a plate of sweets with a sweet aroma appeared.

A variety of fruits and cakes lay on the plate, including figs, apples, and honey cakes, their juices dripping down the sides. The plate moved silently towards me, its surface reflecting the light of the room.

I took the plate and heard the crunch of the honey cake as I bit into it. "Magical indeed."

His eyes seemed to glimmer in the light as he watched me eat, and a low hum filled the air. "Indeed."

Honey dripped down my fingers, and I licked them.

The desire and intensity in his gaze sent a shiver down my spine. "Why are you not painting me?" I asked, my voice a soft, throaty whisper.

Chapter 17

Figs and honey

"How can a starving man paint when the most exquisite feast is right in front of him?"

I felt my cheeks burn, and I glanced downwards, flustered by his boldness. I held my head high and challenged his gaze with a smirk. "Then come feast."

"The poor artist needs no more inspiration than your beauty. How could I ever deny myself the pleasure of celebrating it? His eyes were like magnets, drawing me in as he stepped closer. "Except art is in the beholder's eye and I am most eager to paint your vision."

"Even more than feasting?" I teased, my heart pounding in my chest.

"I made a promise that I would surprise

you," he said with a sly smile. "And I always keep my promises."

I stood up and stepped closer to him, the plate rattling slightly in my grasp, and saw the look of anticipation on his face. "Then let me feed you."

I plucked a fig from the plate and brushed it against his lips, my eyes lingering on his. His tongue lapped eagerly at my fingers, and I could almost taste the sweetness myself.

Juice dripped down his chin, and I leaned in and licked it off. His skin was smooth against my tongue, and the flavor of him sent a wave of excitement through me.

His muscles rippled underneath his shirt. "Starvation never felt so sweet."

I stepped away and lay down on the couch. "Join me and I will illustrate to you the sweetest of pleasures."

He smiled and sat down beside me. His hand was soft as he slowly reached out to brush my hair away from my face, the sound of his breathing the only noise in the room.

His eyes were dark and intense, and I could feel his warm breath on my face as he leaned in. "Allow me to paint your vision."

His lips were gentle and tender against mine when I closed my eyes. He tasted like honey and warmth; like a promise of something magical.

I opened my eyes in surprise, my breath catching when he pulled away.

The room was filled with light; the walls adorned with a beautiful mural of snowflakes and ice. My gaze shifted to Doran in disbelief as I took in the sight before me.

He grinned, his eyes crinkling with amusement. "You asked for a kingdom, and I provided it."

I smiled back. "But that's not the kingdom I wanted."

He chuckled and kissed me again, his hands gently cradling my face. "What is it you desire, little wife?"

His eyes were burning with intensity as I licked my lips. "My painting. Just like you promised."

He nodded and kissed me one last time before standing up. He grabbed the paints and brush and painted, the smell of oil paint and turpentine filling the room.

I lifted my eyebrow. "Tell me, what do you see when you look at me?"

He looked down at the canvas, his brush never stopping its movement.

"I see beauty, strength, and passion," he murmured. "I see a woman that can conquer the world if she wants to."

"I see a man that can make the impossible possible," I replied. "Someone who believes he's a monster but is really a hero."

He paused, and our eyes met. "I'm a monster. I'm Fae, and many fear us."

"The way you treat your subjects shows your true character. You protect them, and you care for them more than any king I've ever met."

"To be Fae is to be powerful, and that power can be used for the greater good," he said, looking back down at the canvas. "Frosthome is my domain. I will protect it until my last breath." He paused, his brush still in motion. "I will slaughter anyone who dares to threaten it. I will be their shield, and I will not falter."

"That's not a monster, that's a king."

"A monster and a king. That is who I am." His sharp eyes fixed on me. "It is who I will be forever. My titles do not define me. I define them. The Butcher of Calan, Darkness of Fae, king of Frosthome. I am all of them and none of them. You are my wife, and my kindness will be yours as long as I live. But I will never forget who I am and what I am capable of. Death is my strength, and it defines me."

I frowned and looked down. "You are not malevolent, you are loyal. Your strength should be celebrated and respected, not feared."

He remained still for a moment, his expression unreadable, and the room was filled with an eerie quiet.

He erupted into a hearty laugh. It was a deep, rich sound that filled the room and made me straighten up.

"You've not seen my darkness, but you know it's in me. When you see it, I only hope you won't be afraid."

His words lingered in the air. I looked up, and his eyes were intense as they met mine.

The Butcher of Calan, Darkness of Fae, king of Frosthome. Maybe he was all these things and more.

Tales of his past, both good and bad, would follow him wherever he went.

But I was certain of one thing. He made me feel special and valued, unlike any other man I had known before. That was something I would never forget.

"A truth for a truth?" he said, his eyes never leaving mine.

I let out a breath I didn't know I was holding. "Yes, a truth for a truth."

"Tell me about your childhood."

I placed a fig between my teeth and felt the crunch of its skin. "My mother was the proud daughter of successful merchant traders. She was a kind but firm woman who taught me the value of hard work. She always told me to reach for the stars, regardless of what anyone else said."

I paused. I didn't want to mention the darkness that lingered in our home.

"My father was a good man," I said finally, "But he's also a king and a leader, and I think that shaped my view of the world." I swallowed hard. "At home, he was a kind father who did his best to raise me the right way. He believed in me and I'm grateful for that."

He frowned. "And your stepmother?"

The Selwyn stepmother.

I hesitated, not sure how to answer him. "My stepmother was kind to me."

He scoffed.

I raised an eyebrow. "What?"

He shook his head and laughed softly. "Aleyna, don't deceive yourself. Your stepmother showed no compassion or kindness towards you."

I sighed and looked away.

He was right; she wasn't.

"You are right," I said finally, "Not in the traditional sense, but despite her faults, she's a strong, independent woman and she taught me what it meant to be a leader. I'm thankful for all the life lessons she has shared with me."

She taught me to be independent and to believe in my own abilities.

"Do you love her?"

The disbelief in his voice was clear.

Our relationship was a tangled web of emotions. I didn't expect others to understand. I didn't even fully understand it.

Before answering, I thought for a moment. "No," I whispered, as my voice threatened to break. "She made me feel like a stranger in my house, and I don't think I can ever forgive her for that. She was the only mother figure I had." I looked back at Doran, my eyes meeting his. "That's my truth. Now it's your turn."

"My parents were great rulers," he said, his voice chilling. "But as parents, they weren't always there for me. I was mostly alone. Trying to make sense of the world around me." He paused and looked up at me. "But I learned a lot about myself in those moments of solitude."

A lump formed in my throat. "I'm sorry."

"Without those moments of quiet, I wouldn't be the man I am today." He observed me with a bemused look. "For worse and for better, those moments shaped me."

With the strength borne from his broken childhood, he became a powerful man. I couldn't help but admire him for his resilience and courage.

Our eyes met, and a current of understanding passed between us.

"Thank you for sharing that with me," I said. "It means a lot."

"My childhood may not have been conventional," he said. "But I wouldn't trade it for anything."

"You are a remarkable man, Doran." I flashed him a bright, cheery smile, hoping to lift the atmosphere. "You're in the middle of painting a woman with half her clothing off, and you still want to share stories with me."

He shot me a knowing smile. "How could I not be eager to share my stories with the most captivating woman in all the Fae Courts?"

His kind words brought a blush to my cheeks, and I gave him a coy look. "Flattery will get you everywhere, my king."

"I hope so."

∞∞∞

We sat, talking for hours about our childhoods, our hopes and dreams, and the future that lay before us. It was a beautiful moment. One I'd never forget.

As we talked, the sun slowly descended and day turned to night. But neither of us wanted the night to end.

"Do you want to see your portrait?"

I smiled and nodded. "Yes,"

He rose to his feet and held out his hand.

I took it, my heart fluttering as our fingers intertwined.

He guided me to the other side of the room, and I was awed by the vivid colors of the painting.

It was me - but not me. I wanted to be like the woman in the painting, her inner confidence and beauty radiating from the canvas.

Curly hair and deep brown eyes, my lips

full and soft. Dressed in a gown, my confidence and grace shone through.

The image captivated me. A better version of me.

My eyes widened as I looked at the painting, my heart aching with emotion. "It's beautiful. Is this what you see when you look at me?"

His hand squeezed mine. "I felt overwhelmed trying to capture the essence of your being with my brush."

I looked up and smiled, feeling strangely at peace. "Thank you for capturing this moment," I said softly. "But why not the corset?"

He grinned, a hint of mischief in his eyes. "That's an image for me alone," he said, pulling me close.

His breath was warm on my skin, and I shivered in anticipation. "It's our secret," he whispered, his lips brushing against mine.

My heart raced as I looked into his eyes, feeling like I was about to take a leap into the unknown.

How would it feel to submit to him? To fully submit to him?

I wanted to find out.

Control was a tricky thing. It could

intimidate and paralyze, but it could also be liberating.

I feared Doran's power and influence, but I also knew that it didn't have to mean the end of us exploring a physical relationship.

Fear shouldn't stop me from taking a risk and exploring something new.

I ran my fingers along his jawline, feeling the sharp edges of his cheekbones as I moved.

He closed his eyes and leaned into my touch, a soft sigh escaping his lips. "I can feel your heart." His breath fanned my face. "I can please you, if you let me, Aleyna."

How would it feel to submit to him?

My heart thudded in my chest, and I met his gaze. "Yes," I breathed. "I want to try."

He smiled and leaned in, pressing his lips against my collarbone.

I shivered in pleasure at the sensation of sharp teeth grazing my skin.

"But I'm not looking for a moment of weakness," he murmured, my skin tingling as his lips moved against mine. "If you'd just let me, I'd give you the world and all its beauty. The kingdom. Everything. It's yours for the asking."

I closed my eyes. I wanted to trust him and explore this newfound connection between us.

But something inside me was hesitant. I had to be certain that I was safe and in control.

"I can feel your fear." He breathed in my ear, his fingers lightly tracing patterns on my bare skin. "I can give you the freedom to explore without fear, Aleyna. You don't have to be afraid."

His pupils were dark and inviting when I looked up into his eyes.

He stepped away. His body heat lingered, but his gaze remained fixed on mine. "The willing submission of one being to another is something that can't be bought or sold. It has to be earned," he said, his voice low and husky. "And I will not take it lightly. Without full trust and understanding, I won't take it from you."

I swallowed hard. "You want me to submit?"

To control?

"Queens don't submit, they demand."

He disappeared into the shadows, his words echoing in my mind. I touched my lips, still tingling from his kiss.

Demand. The word reverberated through my head.

I wanted to demand, needed to demand.

Demand everything I knew he could give

me.

Without emotion getting in the way.

Without fear.

Take control. Demand my pleasure. Demand my desire.

Chapter 18

Greed is a dangerous thing

This was it. I couldn't go back.

Doran opened the door, and I felt my heart racing as I looked into his dark, passionate eyes.

I stepped in and the heavy wooden door thudded shut behind me.

It was the first time I entered his chambers.

I meticulously examined the details of the room as I looked around. The room was almost empty, with only a few essentials and minimal decorations, a stark contrast to my own luxurious chamber.

As I stepped further into the room, the only thing that adorned the wall was a painting of a woman with dark eyes that seemed to be following my every step.

It was me.

The red veil and the intricate jewelry were unmistakably my own.

It was me on my wedding day.

Doran's eyes sparkled as he watched me take it all in. "Why are you here?"

I opened my mouth, but a whisper of nervousness stopped me.

Spirits, what was I doing?

Doran leaned against the door. His eyes crinkled as he gave a slow, languid smile.

The challenge in his eyes was undeniable.

Arrogant bastard.

I squared my shoulders and met his gaze, determined to make my demand. "You know why I'm here, husband."

He stepped forward, his hand reaching out to cup my face. I closed my eyes and leaned into his touch. It was almost hot against my cheek, and I suppressed a shiver.

He pressed a languid kiss behind my ear, and I shivered. "Ask, Aleyna." His voice was low but commanding.

A strangled moan escaped my lips.

I just needed him to touch me.

Everywhere.

I opened my eyes and looked into his, feeling the heat of his gaze like a touch.

The tense silence stretched between us as I weighed my options again. Carefully, like I hadn't already done so many times before.

I could leave, never knowing what pleasure he could give me. Or I could take a risk and demand exactly what I wanted from him.

His fingers tightened slightly, and he leaned in, his lips skimming my forehead. The warmth of his breath spread through my body, and I inhaled sharply as I clenched my fists.

My insides clenched tightly. That was how he affected me. I needed him. No, I craved him.

His eyes hungrily devoured my face, and I looked down.

"The lands of frost and snow are dangerous," he whispered, his voice a soft murmur. "It's not for the fainthearted. But together, we can brave the icy winds and find heat in each other's embrace."

Slowly, I raised my eyes to meet his.

His gaze was intense, and he waited for me to answer.

A million thoughts ran through my head, but in the end, it all came down to one thing.

I wanted him.

I sighed. Now was the moment to be courageous. Doran was a man. A man like any other.

Liar.

I stepped forward, placing my hands on his chest. "I'm here to make a deal."

He leaned back, and a slow, satisfied smile spread across his face. "Let's hear it."

My fingers fidgeted with the fabric of his shirt as he waited for me to speak. "I want to make a deal, but what can you offer me? What do you want in return?"

He pressed forward, his gaze never wavering from mine. "My dear Aleyna." His thumb idly stroked my cheek. "What I offer is far greater than what you can imagine. Everything you desire is mine to give."

He leaned down, his lips brushing my ear so gently I almost thought I was imagining it. His breath was warm and inviting as his thumb traced down my bottom lip.

My tongue danced against it, as if daring him to continue.

Without breaking eye contact, I sucked his thumb into my mouth. I bit down, sliding my tongue as his gaze grew heated. Releasing it with a plop, I pressed a gentle kiss against his palm.

I knew I was powerless in his arms, but so was he in mine.

"Power, pleasure, freedom. These things and more," he whispered.

My breathing grew shallow as his hand slowly roamed over my body, side to hip to back. "And what do you want in return?" I asked, my voice barely audible.

His lips curved into a smirk. "Your complete surrender."

I shivered at the thought, my heart pounding.

He pulled back, not so much physically as much as with intent, his eyes still locked with mine. "I want your pleasure. All of it." He placed kisses on my forehead, my cheeks, my nose, and then finally my lips.

My body trembled with anticipation as his tongue slipped into my mouth. I leaned into his touch. But he tutted, gently pushing away.

"I'm a greedy man, little wife, and I always get my due."

The words were a whisper, but they hung

in the air between us.

My breasts rose and fell faster as I breathed, the fabric of my clothing rough on my sensitive skin.

He offered me something I thought I lost forever - a chance to experience desire without fear.

It was time to take what I wanted.

People took away my power before. But this moment belonged to me. He was setting a challenge, and I was eager to partake.

I bit my lip before hooking my fingers in the collar of my dress and opening it slowly. I stopped right above my cleavage.

He wasn't the only one who could tease.

His fists were clenched by his sides as he followed the movement of my hands.

I cocked my head. "What do you want from me?"

Doran smiled and swayed forward, his lips just centimeters away from mine. "This is your chance, Aleyna. You can surrender to me and be rewarded with pleasure beyond imagining. Or you can deny me and be left with nothing. Only emptiness."

I shivered, my body trembling from the intensity of his gaze. "I'm not the one begging."

My voice was soft as I stepped closer. "You are."

He brushed his lips against mine. "No, you are not. But that doesn't mean you can't be rewarded for taking a risk."

My core clenched. "Show me it's worth it," I said, my breath growing shallow as he leaned in closer.

"I will."

He captured my lips in a hungry kiss. The warmth of his body wrapped around me, and I melted into him.

I knew I was taking a risk, but it felt right. How could this be wrong when it felt so good?

His tongue moved against mine, and I gasped, feeling a primal need rising inside me.

It was time to surrender.

No.

I was done surrendering - this time I would be the one in control. The pleasure, the power, and the freedom were mine to take.

I placed my hands on either side of his face and kissed him deeply, my heart pounding against my chest. My hands roamed over his body, taking in every inch, as the heat rose between us.

This time, I wouldn't surrender - I would

conquer.

He pulled back and smiled, my name on his lips as if it were a benediction. "Aleyna."

I looked up into his eyes. The desire was still there, but there was something else as well. Warmth. Respect. And something else I couldn't define, but that I knew came from the depths of his heart.

Something I didn't want to ponder on, but I knew what it was. He lost himself in me.

At that moment, I knew my surrender was not a defeat. It was a victory. This was my chance to take what was rightfully mine - pleasure, power, and freedom. And I would take it all.

The game had only just begun.

He was still in the way only a Fae could be. A predator watching his prey.

I pressed closer. "That's not enough."

His hardness pressed against my stomach and it took everything in me not to take my dress off right now. The size of it made almost all rational thought go away.

The only thing that stopped me was the little game we were playing here.

Predator vs prey.

And in this game, both of us saw ourselves

as the predator.

I moved my hand lower down his body. My fingers grazed against his hardness, and Doran tensed.

Raising an eyebrow, I rubbed him slowly, feeling him thicken in my hands. Doran buried his face in the crook of my neck and groaned.

I swallowed hard. "I need more."

He was bigger than I imagined. Bigger than my previous lovers.

"I need more."

He chuckled and pressed his forehead to mine, our breaths mingling together. "Greed is a dangerous thing, my little wife."

I removed my hand, and he pressed against me.

"Perhaps." I licked his earlobe and his body tensed. "But if I'm going to surrender, it will be on my own terms."

He shut his eyes. "Maybe I was wrong about you," he drawled. "Perhaps you are a conqueror after all."

"Perhaps I am," I murmured, capturing his lips in a hungry kiss. "Or perhaps my husband is a Fae and has enchanted me with his words."

My stomach tightened with anticipation

as his lips grazed mine.

"The Fae do not enchant." His fingers twitched on my hips as he pressed me against the door. "We show you what you have been missing, and offer it to you for the taking."

When my hands ran along his chest, he lifted me up and pressed me against the door.

I placed my lips next to his pointed ear. "But only to those who are brave enough to accept them."

He raised an eyebrow as his pupils dilated. "And are you brave?"

I rested my forehead against his. "Aren't all conquerors?"

He chuckled and I couldn't help laughing along.

Maybe I was a conqueror. Or maybe, just maybe, my husband enchanted me with his beauty and power.

Doran's hands moved to my hips, holding me close. Flush against him, his muscles rippled beneath my touch. "Have you done this before?"

He licked my neck, and my legs trembled in response.

"Princesses aren't allowed to seek their pleasure. Royalty is expected to remain in control at all times."

His fingers trailed up my back. "And have you been in control?"

I shook my head and closed my eyes, reveling in the sensation of his touch. "I've never been a good girl, have I?"

He chuckled softly, his breath tickling my neck. "And I've never been a good king."

I smiled coyly. "Then perhaps we should both rebel."

He smiled back and brushed his lips against mine. "Rebellion has its rewards."

My core pulsed with desire. "Then what are we waiting for?" I asked, my voice barely more than a whisper now.

Doran paused, his gaze never wavering from mine. "What do you want?"

I wrapped my legs around his waist and giggled softly. "I don't beg," I said. "But I will take."

He pulled me closer, his lips dangerously close to mine. "All of it."

And with that, he kissed me - and I let myself be taken away. The world spun around me as his tongue delved into my mouth. I groaned as I melted into him, my body surrendering to his touch.

Freedom. That was what he offered me.

Freedom to take my pleasure. Freedom to be me. Freedom from the expectations of a princess.

To someone in a gilded cage, the taste of freedom was intoxicating.

He ruined me. I would never be the same.

Once you have the taste of freedom, of pleasure, you never want to go back.

His lips trailed down my neck, and goosebumps appeared. "I want to taste you, little wife."

As his cock pressed against my core, I arched my back and moaned. "You've tasted me plenty of times."

He placed a kiss on the swell of my breast, and my heart thudded in response.

He looked up, and his lips were curved into a devilish grin. "I want a different feast."

His words made me burn.

I still didn't trust him, but I knew I could trust myself.

His hand lowered, tracing circles on my waist. "Do you want more?" he asked, his breath tickling my ear.

"Give me all of you."

He walked to the bed and laid me on my back.

He pushed me onto the bed and crawled above me. His dark hair fell against my skin, and he looked larger than life before me. Against my stomach, his hardness strained.

My heart raced as his face lingered above my face, his dark eyes locked on mine.

He paused, and my breath hitched in anticipation.

"Are you sure?"

But I didn't want to wait any longer. I reached up and pushed his hair away from his face, my fingers threading through its thick, silky strands as he stared down at me.

I moaned as his hands finally pushed my dress up, his fingertips tracing circles around my legs.

Closer and closer, he moved until his thick fingers grazed my center.

He slowed his pace, watching my reaction. He caressed my folds, gently as he explored and teased.

I gasped as he placed a soft kiss on my clit. "So pretty. Perfect. And it's all for me."

"Stop teasing."

Doran looked up with a sly smile. "I intend to kiss you all over, little wife."

I bit my lip as he moved up and pressed his lips against mine, hard and demanding. My fear melted away as I surrendered to the heat between us.

He looked at me with an intensity that took my breath away.

A smile spread across his lips. "I want to be in you," he said, his voice low and husky. "First with my tongue, and then with my body."

I brushed my lips over velvety skin. "And if I deny your request?"

He grinned as his hands traced the outline of my face. "Then you'd deny me the pleasure of serving you, my queen." His thumb stroked my clit. "And that would be a crime I'm not prepared to commit. To deny you your pleasure would be to deny myself the exquisite pleasure of being inside you."

My core clenched as he pressed harder. I reached up and stole another kiss before pushing him away. "As your wife, I command you to pleasure me."

Doran smirked and removed his thumb as I moaned in protest.

He kneeled before me and looked up at me

with hooded eyes. "As you wish, my queen."

He bowed down and kissed my calves, his touch making me arch my back in pleasure. He then moved up, licking and caressing every inch of me as if I were the only thing that mattered.

How could a mortal resist a Fae's power?

How could I resist my husband?

I was a fool for thinking I could resist him.

Reflexively, I ran my fingers through his dark hair as he reached my knees. I could see the same desire that was burning through my veins in his dark eyes.

He gripped my flesh tightly as I pulled his head closer. "We are too overdressed for this."

He smirked in response, a hint of mischief lighting his gaze. "I can do something about that."

His hands glided up my thighs, and the feeling of his skin against mine made our clothes vanish.

Chapter 19

Consequences be damned

His tattoos shone in the fire's light as his muscles flexed against me. His gaze burned with intensity as his lips and tongue traced the curves of my body, setting fire to every inch of exposed skin.

I felt the heat of his breath as his lips touched my folds.

Finally.

My fingers tangled through his hair as he circled my clit.

His warmth was all around me as his tongue explored my body. He teased me with gentle caresses, taking me to dizzying heights before slowing down just enough to make me crave more.

My hands twisted the furs on the bed as my walls clenched. I swallowed my cry into the pillow as I reached my peak.

He grasped my waist, pulling me closer until our bodies were flush against each other. "I need to hear you this time. Can you do that for me?"

I nodded as I looked at him.

His ragged breath was sweet and earthy, like the forest outside my window. He teased my folds with just a tip before he pushed further.

I opened my mouth, letting his tongue explore.

His touch was gentle, yet powerful, and each thrust made me quiver with pleasure.

He raised my legs over his shoulders and entered me again.

The slapping sound of our bodies filled the room again as I clung to him.

My walls quivered, and I turned my face away from him, not wanting to let him see my vulnerability.

He cupped my chin and forced me to look into his eyes. "Feel, Aleyna."

I dug my fingers into his ass and pulled him tight against me. "You promised me pleasure and all I feel is bored."

He chuckled in my ear, as he harder and deeper, making me moan harder.

"You can lie to me, but I can feel the truth in your kiss," he murmured against my lips. "I can feel you clenching around me, darling. Begging for my seed. I will give you that and so much more."

I moaned as his words made my core throb with need.

His smile was, however, quickly removed when I wrapped my legs around his waist, and I turned us so that I was now on top.

I saw surprise in his eyes when he realized what I had done.

My hips moved slowly against his, my skin sizzling as I felt the heat of him. "It's my turn."

He tried to take control with a deep kiss, but I wouldn't let him.

I kept my lips just an inch away from his, teasing him as I occasionally pressed my lips against his jaw.

He cupped my chin, but I removed his hand and placed it on my breast, and allowed him to fondle my sensitive nipples.

"The bond goes both ways, Winter King. You can feel the intensity of my passion, but I can sense yours just as strongly." I clenched my core, and he groaned. "You should know I'm fully capable of seizing control when I decide to."

His eyes blazed with desire, and his hands tightened around my waist.

"Then take it," he whispered, as his hands moved up my body, exploring every inch of me.

My breath hitched as he placed his thumb on my clit. His soft strokes sent a wave of pleasure through me and I threw my head back, letting out a soft sigh.

I felt powerful and desired all at once. It was intoxicating. He was intoxicating.

My curls reached his chest, and I rode him harder and harder.

I wanted him in me forever.

His grip on me tightened before his body relaxed underneath mine.

A moan slipped from my lips as the pleasure rushed through me to an almost unbearable degree.

His grip on me tightened, his seed pumping deep in me before his body relaxed underneath mine. "Pretty little wife," he murmured. "Enchantress."

I let out a satisfied chuckle as I slipped next to him.

My mind was a whirlwind of conflicting emotions as I lay next to him.

On the one hand, I felt a deep sense of satisfaction in giving myself to him in such an intimate way.

But my conscience also nagged at me for betraying my own values. I never thought of myself as a person who could easily be swayed by emotions. Yet here I was. Distracted by a pretty face and lust.

I was no better than my father.

No matter what my mind told me, my body still ached with pleasure.

His arms tightened around me, and it lulled me into a deep slumber, my mind still clouded with conflicting feelings.

∞∞∞

The open window let in the morning light, waking me from my slumber.

I lay there for a while. My body was throbbing in a way I had never experienced before. Not even with my other conquests.

I shifted, and something inside me stirred. Deep contentment. But the feeling wasn't mine.

It was his.

I turned around as Doran gripped me tighter. He pressed his body against mine, his warmth comforting me in a way I hadn't expected.

I glanced up at him, his eyes still closed in sleep. A contented look crossed his face, making me feel both proud and guilty at the same time.

I did this to him.

I allowed myself a moment of indulgence, just lying in his arms and savoring the sensation.

"What are you thinking about?" his sleepy voice asked, and I couldn't help but smile.

My heart tightened as I looked into his eyes. His sharp gaze seemed to see right through me, and my cheeks flushed.

"Life," I finally replied, a wry smile playing on my lips.

He gave a small, gentle smile that spread across his face. "Philosophical," he said, and I laughed softly. "Truly. What were you thinking?"

I took a deep breath. "I'm glad I made this decision."

His eyes widened in surprise, and I knew

he understood the gravity of my words.

"Me too," he said with a smile, pressing his lips to mine.

His tongue moved around mine in a way that made me tingle all over, and I was filled with gratitude at that moment.

Gratitude for the pleasure, the exhilaration, and the warmth that I found in his embrace.

This was what it meant to be alive. I never wanted it to end.

Even princesses were allowed moments of selfishness.

"A story for a story?" his bare chest vibrated as he spoke, the tattoos on his skin in stark contrast to the softness of his voice.

"How about a painful truth for a beautiful moment?" I suggested, my fingers tracing the contours of his body. "Philosophy and pleasure, side by side."

He looked at the ceiling with a pensive expression as his hand curved around my waist. "Then let me tell you a story."

I settled in closer to him, ready for whatever he was about to say.

"Once upon a time, a fearless Winter King made a decision that changed his life forever.

He trusted the Summer King and invited him into his home. But he had been deceived, and his friend had betrayed him. The Summer King brought darkness into his life that would never leave; he took away the light of his world, his beloved wife."

My eyes widened.

His mother. He was talking about his mother.

I could feel the slight trembling of his hand as I took it in mine, pressing my lips to his forehead in a gesture of comfort.

He relaxed at my touch, and I heard a contented sigh as he leaned in.

"He murdered her?"

"Oh no, the Fae don't murder." His eyes glazed over and his jaw went slack, leaving his expression emotionless. "He hatched a plan. He led his allies, The Selwyn Family, into our kingdom, and they kidnapped her. I did not see again her."

I held his hand tightly in mine, my heart aching with sorrow.

How could someone be so cruel? And why?

"Once upon a time, he had been betrayed. But now, he knew everything would be okay. As his son swore to avenge them."

"Is that why you married me? The enemy of my enemy is my friend?"

He smiled in response. "Not exactly," he said. "But I would lie if I said it wasn't a factor."

I laughed, elated at his honesty. Here was a man who wouldn't shy away from being vulnerable, and I found that incredibly attractive.

"There were other reasons too," he said, his voice low and husky. "You are strong and passionate, and you have a fire in your soul that reminds me of my mother."

His magic left a faint, cool sensation on my skin. I shivered uncontrollably as I nestled into his body.

Doran closed his eyes, and it stopped. "I wanted someone who could bring light back into my life," he said. "And you are the one I chose."

He tightened his grip on me as I sighed.

"My turn." I smiled back, weakly. "Let me tell you a story," I said as he settled in closer. "Once upon a time, I thought I found a place to belong. But then, my world was shattered when a certain someone took away all of my power and control."

His gaze turned icy and unyielding. "The Selwyn."

I shook my head. "No. It was someone much closer to me." I paused, taking a deep breath before continuing. "He made me feel small and fragile. He wanted to own me, control me. He wanted to be the only one who could make me happy. I was lost in his eyes, and I was too scared to speak up. But eventually, I found my courage, and I fought back."

And I won.

He may have taken away my power, but he also taught me to fight for what I wanted. To never give up on me. I found the strength that I never knew I had. I was determined to keep it.

"Who?" Doran curled his lips in a snarl and hissed.

"My father," I whispered, my voice barely audible. "After my mother died, he wanted to make me dependent on him. He wanted to control me and I was too scared to fight back."

A painful truth, I thought. That was my story. But it was also a lesson. One which taught me to trust no one too easily and to always fight for my freedom.

And then, in that same moment, something shifted inside of me. A newfound strength that I never felt before.

"The web of power and control is strong, but so are you," he said softly. "Kings and queens may come and go, but you will always remain. You are the only one who has the power to choose your own destiny."

I nodded, feeling a tear roll down my cheek. I wiped it away. "Thank you, Doran," I said, my voice barely a whisper.

"Did he hurt you?" He asked, his voice trembling with emotion. I shook my head, and he pulled me closer to him.

"No, not physically or intentionally. But it doesn't matter, because I moved past it. And now, here I am."

"And she?"

My stepmother, the Selwyn Queen.

A rush of anger filled me.

She was the one who brought darkness into our lives, but I refused to let her ruin my happiness.

"It's easy to blame her, but I won't," I said softly. "My father is his own man. He made his own choices, and his mistakes will not define me. Instead, I will choose to focus on the good that has come from this experience."

He smiled, his eyes filled with understanding and compassion. He reached out and brushed away the tears that fell down my cheeks. "You are strong, and you have come so far. You will always have my support, no matter what."

His words were like a soothing balm to my soul.

I looked at the ceiling. "Yet I still want his approval."

He nodded. "We all want to be accepted and loved by those who matter the most. But you don't need to prove your worth to anyone. You are worthy and let no one convince you otherwise."

He was right. I didn't need anyone else's approval; I found my strength.

But deep down, I was still the scared little girl, and that was okay. I had come a long way, and I was proud of it.

The journey would be long, but every day I was healing.

"Thank you," I said, and then I leaned in, pressing my lips to his. "For understanding."

He smiled, and he pulled me closer. "Always."

Maybe we could make this an actual marriage?

I wasn't in love, but we could be great together.

Ruling together, fighting together.

Could we?

Would we?

Only time would tell. But it was a beautiful dream.

He was magnificent, and he gave me a new beginning.

I would never be the same because I knew now that I was capable of greatness.

"Let's do this," I said, wrapping my arms around him and leaning into his strength.

"Do what?" he asked, a soft smile on his face.

"Everything," I replied, with a mischievous twinkle in my eye. "Fae, mortal, Selwyn; we will conquer them all. Together."

"Consequences be damned." He laughed softly as he placed his head on my chest. "That's a very Fae thing to say."

I grinned and leaned in for a passionate kiss. "It is. Haven't I been crowned queen of Frosthome? I can do whatever I want."

He cradled my face in his hands, his gaze intense. "And I'm your king," he said, his voice steady. "I'll burn this world down before I let anyone take you away from me."

Chapter 20

Notes and banners

Shit.

Should I have asked for permission first?

He just stood there and stared at me, his gaze lingering for what felt like forever before he pinched his nose.

The Iron Sword bowed her head in deference as I looked at Doran.

Guilt bubbled in my stomach as I looked away. "I'm sorry. I shouldn't have gone into your studio without asking," I said, feeling even guiltier.

He gave a soft, wistful smile as he gazed off into the distance. "There's no need to apologize, don't worry. I'm pleased someone can appreciate my work."

When I looked up, I could hear my relieved exhale echoing in the air.

The portraits were beautiful, and the way Doran captured the beauty was astonishing. He had a way of bringing art alive.

The portrait of his mother was so beautiful that it deserved to be showcased in the throne room. Her gray eyes, so reminiscent of his, brought warmth to my heart.

At least when we were alone.

Outside of our chambers, he was strong, brave, and the leader our kingdom needed. But when we were alone, he didn't mind showing his soft side to me.

"You have a natural talent for art," I said as I stepped closer to him. "Your art should be celebrated and admired by everyone."

As I focused my attention back on his portraits, I was enamored by the lifelike features.

Doran's portraits were like living fairy tales. The paintings depicted stunning scenes from Frosthome; snow-covered forests, elegant fey creatures gliding through the night sky, and a majestic castle blanketed in winter snow.

Vivid colors and intricate details brought each painting to life as if they were actually alive.

The scenes contained a deep beauty that could only be experienced through Doran's magical touch.

No one else could bring these scenes to life the way he did.

I turned to look at him, a subtle smile on my face. "You should be proud of yourself. Your work is exquisite. I can't help but show it off."

The Iron Sword slipped away. She winked at me as she closed the door.

Doran chuckled, his eyes twinkling with amusement as he stared at her. "Thank you. It means a lot to me that someone like you appreciates my work."

"If your wife can't appreciate you, who will?"

"Who indeed?"

I slipped my arms around his neck as he closed his eyes. "All I want to do is ravish you right now."

I smiled brightly. "Does duty call?"

His face changed, and he took a step backward. "We need to leave."

I frowned as he took my hand and led me away. "What is going on?"

Doran stopped as I stumbled behind him.

"Your father is very ill, Aleyna."

I felt the tension in his grip, as if he was afraid to let me go.

He looked at me. His gaze was so intense and full of emotion.

I swallowed hard.

Father was sick?

"Come, we must hurry."

My body tensed. "Is it serious? Do you know what is wrong?"

Was he dead? My mind raced with questions as I followed Doran.

He turned to me, squeezing my hand in his. "Everything shall be alright. You will see your father soon."

My heart ached with anguish and fear, but I nodded my head in agreement. "I must make preparations. I need to pack a few things and-"

He stopped me mid-sentence. "Everything is taken care of. We will leave now."

I looked into his eyes for a long moment before I finally whispered, "Thank you, Doran."

A mirthless smile appeared on his face. "Anytime, little wife."

∞∞∞

The night was full of the crisp, cold air that was thick with a frozen dew, and we could see our breath.

The palace gates shimmered in the moonlight, their intricate design crafted from a shimmering gold and silver that evoked a sense of homesickness in me.

The palace itself was an awe-inspiring sight, its towers and domes rising high above the city like sentinels of glory. The walls were adorned with intricate carvings and mosaics depicting scenes from a far-off land.

It made my heart swell with nostalgia. I didn't know how much I missed it. Until now.

If only I hadn't returned in dire circumstances.

I turned my back and saw Ilanya spread over the hills like a blanket of stars.

Bright lanterns illuminated the city, casting a warm light over everything. The domed rooftops and terracotta-tiled streets gave the city its signature look.

The aromas of spices and fragrant oils filled the air, while the distant sound of laughter and music floated on the breeze.

It was a city of dreams and fantasies, where anything could be possible.

It was my home.

I missed it more than I could ever express.

The palace gates opened, and I stepped inside. The guards bowed as I passed. Doran followed me with a silent grace.

In the open courtyard, the air was filled with the sweet smell of flowers and the sight of tall, white marble statues and soft carpets of grass.

In the distance, I watched as Isra sprinted towards us, her hair flowing behind her.

She quickly embraced me, as if to make sure I was real and alive. "I am so glad you are here," she whispered.

I enveloped her in my tight embrace, breathing in her comforting scent. "What is going on?" I asked, my voice heavy with concern. "How did you know I was here?"

"I found a note from your husband tucked under a pillow in my room." I heard her sharp intake of breath as she looked at me fearfully. "The queen has requested your presence."

I turned, and Doran was gone.

I blinked, stunned by the sudden realization that he left without saying goodbye.

My throat tightened with emotion, and tears pricked my eyes. I tried to blink them back, but it was no use.

He left without telling me he was in Ilanya?

He left while my father was on his deathbed?

This was the time for action, not tears.

With a deep breath, I wiped away my tears and stood as straight as I could. "Is there anything you can tell me about the king? Who is presiding over the council?"

Isra looked away, her eyes misting with tears of her own. "He is ill... very ill," she whispered. "It was only a rumor, but it was enough to make people pause and take notice. The queen ensures that the king is kept far away from prying eyes."

My heart sank.

I had to get to my father, and fast. Who knew what was going on?

We made our way toward the palace. "Thank you, Isra. What has changed since I left?"

Isra looked ahead. "You will see."

Servants hurriedly rushed past us, their faces pale with worry.

The palace was in a state of chaos. That never happened before. Not even when my grandmother, the last ruling queen, died.

Goosebumps appeared on my skin as we turned the corner.

A few servants looked at me, but no one approached me. Instead, they looked downwards.

When we entered the main hall, I stopped. Red banners hung from the ceiling and gilded chairs stood lined up against the wall.

Everything was quiet, as if time itself stopped.

My fists clenched as I tried to swallow down the lump in my throat.

I was home, but it was not the home I left behind.

A world where my father's seat remained cold and empty.

A world where the blue banners of Ilanya disappeared.

What was going on?

I took a deep breath, steeling myself for the

task ahead. I needed to speak to my father.

Now.

As we walked through the corridors of the palace, my eyes were once again drawn to the servants, who moved silently in the shadows. They hurried down the corners with an unknown purpose.

My heart raced as I reached the antechamber of the queen's chambers.

Isra knocked on the doors, the sound reverberating through the hallway as she slowly opened them.

My stepmother slowly pivoted to face me, her movements deliberate. Her golden ringlets bounced around her head as she stood up. She looked at me with a polite yet uninviting expression.

The golden circlet ring on her finger glinted as she motioned for me to come closer.

Father's ring.

I had to speak up and make sure my voice was heard. I knew she was in control.

"Ah, my daughter," she said, the irony of her greeting not lost on me. "The guards informed me of your arrival. You have traveled a great distance and must feel weary. Please, take a seat and make yourself at home."

I bowed my head in respect. "Thank you, mother." I curtseyed and the silver hemline of my dress touched the ground. "But before I rest, I must ask; Is there any news on the king?"

She motioned for me to take a seat, and I did, my mind racing with questions.

She summoned the servants to bring us tea.

As we waited, she observed me with a keen expression.

I kept my face carefully neutral as the servants entered her chambers and placed the tea on the table.

No one reached for their cup.

"Your father is sick," she said eventually, her voice cold and flat. "I cannot give you any more information."

I nodded. I knew what she was really saying–that she wouldn't allow me to see him.

As I met her gaze, my eyes narrowed. I may not have my father's power, but I was still the heir.

"I understand." My voice was firm. "But I ask you, dear mother... Can you deny a daughter her father's love?"

"Daughter, I..." She paused for a moment,

and I saw her weighing her options. "With the king, I am afraid my hands are tied," she said eventually. "We can make no exceptions."

"Please, allow me the chance to look upon his face one last time, before I can no longer do so. Please, I'm begging you..."

Her expression melted, and a tinge of sadness filled her gaze. "My decision stands, but I will grant you one wish. A letter, till you meet him again."

I sat stiffly, my fingers clenched over the chair's metal arms. "Thank you, mother."

She stood up. "You are dismissed."

I bowed my head before leaving.

This was not the end. I wouldn't rest until I saw him again.

No matter the cost. No matter the danger. I would get to him somehow, someway.

For my father. For Ilanya.

Outside the queen's chamber, the vizier waited on me. He bowed his head as relief entered his eyes.

He placed his hands behind his back as he walked. "You are back."

I followed him. "Did you think I wouldn't keep my promise to return?

His bronze skin gleamed in the light as his gaze met mine. "There were rumors."

From the look in his eyes, I could tell things had changed since I left.

I clenched my fists as I looked forward. "At least that hasn't changed."

What exactly happened while I was gone?

The vizier led me to an alcove I had never visited before. Spiderwebs covered the entrance, and I peered inside.

There was a door hidden in the shadows. It was decrepit and creaked as the Vizier opened it.

The vizier stepped forward and opened the door, leading into a corridor. At the end of the passageway, I heard the faint echoes of dripping water as I entered the small chamber.

The center of the room was illuminated by a glowing pool of water, the blue light filling the air with a soft, calming energy.

We sat down on the edge of the pool, the dampness of the ground seeping through our clothes.

"Your father wanted you to have this. He left it for you as a parting gift."

He handed me a locket with a single snowflake engraved on it.

"A wedding gift. He said that it would help you remember him, as well as the love between you two."

I opened up the locket, and the sight of our smiling faces filled me with warmth.

I hugged the locket, feeling the intricate engravings on the metal.

The vizier placed a hand on my shoulder before standing up.

Vizier Aidamir Bey was my father's most trusted advisor, and I knew he could tell me what I needed to know.

I looked up at him. "What is going on?"

"Dark tidings, my lady," he said. "While you were gone, a great disturbance shook the world. You should know, your father...." He trailed off, letting the words hang in the air.

As I waited for him to say something, my heart stopped beating.

But he changed the topic instead. "Ilanya needs you." He placed his hand in the water. "Your father needs you. Soon court will be in session, and you must be prepared."

"Prepared for what?"

A faint smile appeared on his face. "The usual..."

I sighed. "Court doesn't wait for anyone."

He nodded in agreement before turning away, his back straight and strong. "The great sun will rise again."

Hearing the battle cry, I swallowed hard.

"And Ilanya will shine," I said, finishing his thought. "Bright and strong, like the star she is."

Chapter 21

Power Hungry

My eyes throbbed with the beginnings of a migraine, but I refused to succumb to it. I had a duty to fulfill and I would not shirk away from it.

Contracts were spread over my bed, and I signed them diligently. It may not have been the most glamorous of tasks, but it was necessary.

The door opened, just as I finished reading the proposed trading contract between Calan and Ilanya.

I signed the document before I picked up the blue ink and stamped the Han family crest on it. "You can put the documents on my desk."

"You're still awake."

Surprised, I looked up to see my husband

standing in the doorway. His dark hair shimmered in the light, as winter gray eyes met mine.

"I couldn't sleep," I said, gesturing to the paperwork. "So much to do. Why are you still awake?"

Doran stepped in and closed the door behind him. He took a seat on the edge of my bed and sighed.

"I couldn't sleep either," he said, his voice a gentle whisper. He looked up at me and smiled. "I was thinking about you."

"Oh, only good things I hope," I said, returning his smile.

My husband chuckled and shook his head in amusement. "Only the best."

He leaned back against the pillows as he placed my hand on his mouth. Gentle kisses were placed on my skin, as he looked up at me through his gray eyes.

A mischievous smile crossed his face as my breath caught in my throat, taken aback by the sudden gesture.

"I can help you with your paperwork if you desire," he said, his voice low and intimate.

I took a moment to collect my thoughts before I replied. "That sounds wonderful, but I believe I'm finished for tonight."

I pushed the papers aside and straightened my back.

He nodded and lightly kissed my hand again. "Duty calls," he said, a hint of amusement in his voice.

I nodded and leaned back on his chest. His warmth enveloped me and I felt at peace. "It does. Where have you been?"

We barely spend time together lately, I thought with a pang of sadness.

He smiled and lifted my chin so that our eyes met. "Taking care of business." He gave me a weary smile. "A king's job is never done."

I pressed a kiss against his cheek in understanding. "Does it get better?"

The workload was immense, and the days seemed to be filled with never-ending tasks. Knowing differed from experiencing it.

Would this be my life?

Doran sighed and shrugged his shoulders. "It can," he said slowly, "But for now, I'm here." He pulled me closer, wrapping his arms around me. "And so are you. That's enough for now."

His muscles tensed as he held me, and a wave of contentment washed over me. I wasn't sure if those were his emotions. *Or mine.*

"Now," he said, breaking the silence. "How was your day?"

I closed my eyes for a moment, the events of the day flashing through my mind. "My stepmother and brother made a mess of things," I said, my voice tired yet determined. "I've been in meetings the whole day. The noble houses are wary of any plan proposed by the crown."

"Absence makes the heart go fonder."

My absence only made the situation worse.

I wished they would be more cooperative, as their current attitude was not making the situation easier.

Doran nodded, his lips turning up into a gentle, reassuring smile. "Power comes with responsibility," he said, his voice a warm rumble. "We will sort it out soon."

I smiled and tucked my head into the crook of his neck.

He was right; I thought to myself. We would sort it out soon. Tomorrow would bring a new day and a new chance.

"I never expected them to make such a mess."

Disastrous decisions poured out of my stepmother's mouth. She made deals with other noble houses without consulting me and promised favors that would be impossible for the crown to fulfill.

Selfishness was a trait that had been passed down from her to my brother, who only wanted power and glory.

My brother spent more time drinking and carousing than actually attending matters of the state.

He canceled important meetings with our allies and even threatened to go to war with them. He couldn't stop spending on tournaments and parties.

Their decisions had the potential to destroy our kingdom and topple a millennium old dynasty.

Why didn't they use their brains for once?

One eats, another watches; that's how revolutions are born.

Artur received the same lessons as I did. How could he possibly be so foolish?

Doran's arm tightened around my waist as he pulled me closer. "We will find a solution," he said, his voice soft and reassuring.

I exhaled slowly, allowing myself to relax.

Thankfully, the Vizier canceled out some of their mistakes, but the damage had already been done.

Now it was my turn to fix it.

"It's in my hands now," I said, looking up at him.

He nodded his head in agreement.

I looked up at him and sighed. "It's a mess," I said. "But a manageable one."

The gold crown glinted in the dim light, a reminder of my duties.

He ran his hand through my braids and kissed me softly on the forehead. "Your room," he said, changing the topic. "It's not yours anymore?"

I narrowed my eyes. "The fire and frost damaged it too much."

The destruction of my room still felt fresh and vivid in my memory, even though the assassin's attempt on my life felt distant now. The knife, the flames, the smoke...

Someone in Ilanya wanted me dead, and I still didn't know why.

Liar.

My mind raced, but I pushed my thoughts away.

He squeezed my waist and sighed. "You will get another one." His voice was gentle and reassuring.

I let out a small laugh, shaking my head in disbelief. "Yes," I said, "And hopefully it won't be destroyed."

We shared a smile as his lips brushed against my neck.

"I'm sorry that you lost your belongings," he said, his voice a low whisper in the dark.

My heart was full of gratitude as I leaned into his embrace. I knew he would never understand the loss of something so important to me.

It was my mother's room.

But it meant a lot that he was trying.

"It's ok," I said, my voice muffled by his chest. I'm hoping for a restart, a do-over. I kept nothing of sentimental value in that place."

Nothing too valuable.

His ears twitched as a solemn look appeared on his face. "Was it truly that bad?"

Spies and plots, assassins and fire - it had been a harrowing few months. Even before I married him, I couldn't trust anyone.

Only Isra. But even I couldn't rely too much on her as the servants followed her every move.

"Yes," I said with a heavy sigh. "But this

room is more comfortable. And I have you."

I felt safe in his arms. But I knew that the political strife, the death and destruction, and my own ambitions wouldn't wait.

Tomorrow was a new day, and I had to be ready for it.

"I will destroy your enemies. I will spill their blood on the ground," he said, and I knew he meant it. "I'll make sure you are safe."

"You can't protect me. Not forever." I looked away, my voice so low it was almost inaudible.

He raised his eyebrows. "I can. What is a mortal to a Fae?"

I looked down at my wedding dagger. "This doesn't have to be your burden."

I should be able to protect myself.

He smiled and pressed his forehead against mine. "I'm your husband."

My lips curved into a smile. "My husband."

He kissed me and I melted into his embrace. His hand moved gently across my hips, his warm breath caressing my neck.

I sighed and leaned into him, feeling the safety of his embrace.

His hand gently moved around my waist,

and I knew he wanted more.

"Not here. Not now." I closed my eyes as his hand stroked my waist. There was nothing more I wanted than to give in, but it was impossible. "Nobody sleeps in the palace."

He paused for a moment before nodding his head in agreement. His lips brushed against my ear, sending a shiver down my spine. My patience is unparalleled, and my talents are known far and wide. Magical and otherwise."

"Save it for when we'll be together. When no one is watching us." I said, looking into his eyes.

He smiled and kissed my forehead. "You drive a hard bargain, Winter Queen."

He laid down on his side, and I followed shortly after. I snuggled into his chest and he kissed the top of my head, wrapping me up in a warm hug.

"What do you do for fun in this place?"

"Good princesses don't have fun," I smirked, and he laughed.

"Nothing? No books, no puzzles? No secret assassinations in the woods?"

I smiled and shook my head. "No secrets. Not here. They watch everything I do."

"Boring," he drawled, and I couldn't help

but giggle.

"I suppose it is," I admitted. "But outside of court, I am free to do what I please."

He raised an eyebrow. "And what would that be?"

I smiled and pushed myself up onto my elbow, looking down at him. "There are a few things that I can think of." I bit my lip. "There's a hidden gem outside the city walls that I visit sometimes."

His eyes twinkled in the darkness. "Tell me more?"

"It's a secret," I said with a mischievous grin. "But I can show you if you'd like."

He grinned and pulled me closer. "Show me."

Chapter 22

Winter Queen

As we entered the forest, we were met with a beautiful sight of tents of fine fabrics and colorful silks, illuminated by flickers of candlelight.

Underneath his cape, my husband held a large seashell, the currency of this place.

Tables were spread around the perimeter, with people laughing and talking. Food stalls sold delicacies of all kinds, and a large orchestra played music at the center of the dance floor. The flutes and drums filled the air, their enchanting melodies intertwining in beautiful harmony.

Doran grabbed my hand. "Dance with me," he whispered, pulling me closer.

I smiled and obeyed, spinning around in his arms to a secret melody playing only in my head.

Doran held me close and spun me around, his hands electric on my skin. Swaying in his arms, his red wig tickled my face.

I laughed.

He looked ridiculous in it. Still, the most handsome man I'd ever seen, but I preferred his dark hair.

I caught sight of a man in an orange robe, his eyes glassy and distant. He looked for something, perhaps someone.

A bookmaker, perhaps?

I hoped he wouldn't find the unlucky soul that owed him money.

He stepped back and disappeared into the crowd just as quickly as he appeared.

We watched as this strange man weaved through the people, his orange cape streaming behind him. His steps were careful and calculating, as if he was looking for something specific.

"One of your guards?" Doran asked, his voice low and filled with intrigue.

I shook my head. "Occasionally my father's guards try to follow me, but it's not one of them." I twirled around. "They wouldn't think of coming here."

The orange-robed man walked away, his figure becoming a silhouette in the night.

"Why not?" Doran asked, his voice laced with concern.

"The only people brave enough to enter this forsaken place were the rebels, the desperate, and the doomed."

Doran's grip on me tightened. "And which one are you?"

I raised my eyebrow. "What do you think?"

His chuckle echoed in my ears as his lips brushed my cheek in a sweet kiss. "I think you're the most fearless woman I know."

I gave him a playful grin. "Good answer."

The scene got livelier as more people arrived. A group of children ran around with sparklers in their hands, chasing each other around the tents.

A woman with a tambourine danced outside her tent, her colorful dress and long hair twisting around her body in rhythm with the music.

I grabbed Doran's hand and dragged him along, determined to make the most of our night.

Snake charmers and fortune tellers lined the streets, each offering their own form of entertainment.

My skirt twirled as I spun around. The blond wig I donned blended in with the other revelers.

Everyone was masked, their true identities hidden. I felt as if I could be anyone, do anything. No one here would know who I really was.

This is why I loved this place.

Tonight I wasn't Aleyna Han, but another mysterious customer.

"Why don't we try to win a prize?" I said, pointing towards a booth filled with stuffed animals.

Doran grinned and placed his shell into the hands of the booth's attendant. He smiled when a few seconds later, an enormous wolf stuffed animal appeared in his hand.

"For you," he said, and gently placed it in my hands.

I hugged the wolf close to me, feeling its soft fur and its beady eyes staring up at me. "Did you cheat?"

He laughed and shook his head. "No, little wife," he said. "Magical intuitiveness and a good eye, that's all it took."

"Liar." I smiled, leaning in to kiss him.

"The Fae don't lie." He smirked, his hands still tangled in mine. "They merely withhold the truth."

Despite his words, I felt a spark of excitement.

I knew that lying or not, Doran won me something special, and that meant a lot. He pulled away with a smile on his face as I leaned in to kiss him again.

I pouted.

Tease.

He pulled me towards the edge of the festivities. "Come."

As we made our way through the noise and the laughter, I couldn't help but think that this was exactly where I wanted to be.

Doran released his hold on me. He held out his hands and closed his eyes, whispering a few words under his breath.

A soft glow illuminated the surrounding air, and the smell of smoke filled the night. Doran's hands moved in swift and intricate gestures, creating a pale blue light that hovered above us.

He then reached into the glow and pulled out a handful of kebabs, the smell of roasted meat wafting through the air. The skewers were steaming hot and glistening with oil and spices.

He handed me one, and I bit into it, savoring the juicy flavors that filled my mouth.

The warmth of the evening seeped into my bones, and I relaxed more.

I took a bite of my skewer as the juice dripped down my chin. "I wish I had the ability to do that. I'd be the most powerful person in this court."

Doran shook his head and laughed. "No, Winter Queen. You're already the most powerful person here, even without magic."

I smiled at his words, but I couldn't help but disagree. "Maybe so. But magic helps too."

I reached out and wrapped my hand around his, letting the warmth of our connection fill me up.

"Besides," I added. "Who's to say that what I feel right now isn't just a little magical?"

Doran grinned, nodding his head in agreement. "I suppose you're right," he said, squeezing my hand. "But you have something much more valuable."

I bit my lip, not sure what he meant.

"Your strength, your courage, and your heart." He pulled me closer. "That's what makes you special."

The kebab skewer disappeared from my hand as he dragged me away to a fortune teller.

Red velvet curtains draped her tent, and the smell of incense filled the air. The fortune teller looked up from her cards. Her eyes twinkled.

"Welcome, stranger," she slurred. "I can see you're looking for answers."

Doran nodded, and I stepped forward, ready to learn more about my future.

The fortune teller laid out the cards in front of me. The cards showed a woman in a beautiful dress surrounded by animals and flowers.

"Interesting," she muttered.

I lifted my chin. "What is interesting?"

The fortune teller smiled. "This card tells me that your future is full of joy, love, and good luck. You will find yourself surrounded by friends, family, and allies. There will be obstacles in your life, but you will have many successes. The path to true happiness can be a long and winding one, but with patience and determination, you will reach your goals."

I thanked the fortune teller for her words, but I couldn't help but feel a little disappointed. There was nothing specific or meaningful about her words, just generic predictions.

Doran raised an eyebrow. "Tell me, charlatan, is this all the advice you can give us?"

The fortune teller chuckled. "No, my child. If you'll pay the price, I have more to tell."

Doran's eyes gleamed with curiosity as gold coins clinked in his hand.

The fortune teller studied the coins and then gave a satisfied nod.

She handed me a cup of coffee and I sipped on it.

When I was done drinking it, she drained the remaining liquid in the saucer before looking.

"I see darkness in your future. But there is also light." She paused and looked up at me. "You must be mindful of the choices you make. There will be times when you have to decide between right and easy."

On the inside, I scoffed at her words. But I nodded and thanked her for the advice, despite my doubts.

As we left the fortuneteller's tent, Doran's eyes met mine, and I knew he felt the same way.

"Mortals can't see the future," he said, looking out towards the horizon. "But what I know is that whatever road we take, you will be a light that guides us."

I looked back at the tent, as another customer entered it. "Are they all like that?"

Doran smiled and shook his head. "No, little wife. Some work with the spirits and others take your money."

"And this one?"

"The smell of alcohol wafted from her breath before she even spoke," he said, his voice low. "Enriching her wallet was her only goal."

I sighed and nodded, wishing we did more research before entering the tent.

"Magic would still be nice," I said playfully. "How much more would I get done with a few helpful tricks?"

He raised his hands, and a flurry of sparks erupted around us. Flowers and stars swirled in the air, and I laughed with delight.

Doran waved his hands again, extinguishing the sparks with a soft breath.

"My domain and powers are yours, my queen," he said, bowing his head. "I can teach you a few things if you'd like."

That was possible?

My heart raced with excitement as I nodded.

He placed his hand on my stomach, and the warmth of his touch radiated through me.

"Feel the magic, Winter Queen," His hands illuminated with a bright white light. "It will never betray you, and it will always be there when you need it the most."

I closed my eyes and exhaled, feeling the power of his words flow through me.

A strange sensation tickled my skin. Cold, slippery, and yet somehow comforting. It moved beneath my skin and I realized what it was.

Magic.

"Yes," I said, entranced. "I feel it."

As I opened my eyes and allowed myself to sink into the moment, the cold and slippery sensation inside me grew stronger and more vibrant.

It was like being engulfed in a blanket of snow, but with a warmth that soothed and healed.

I glanced at Doran, as a slow smile spread across his face. "How is this possible?"

"You are the queen of the Winter Court. The title, the power, it is yours to wield."

His hand tightened on my waist and he leaned down, his lips brushing against my ear.

"Winter Queen is not merely a title. I am the personification of Winter and my power is yours to command."

I shivered, despite myself. He leaned back and his eyes met mine, a knowing look in their depths.

My body trembled with excitement as the magnitude of his words sunk in.

I was the Winter Queen, and therefore I could control the power of winter.

"You feel my magic," he said, his voice gentle. "It has been passed down through generations and will come to you in the moments you need it most. Focus on it, let it fill your body, and you can do anything with it."

My eyes widened. "How?"

Doran chuckled softly and gave me a knowing look. "Anything is possible, Winter Queen. You just have to believe."

I obeyed his words and focused on the magic that now ran through my veins. It felt like a warm, protective cocoon I could wrap around myself when I felt vulnerable or scared.

Smiling, I opened my eyes, and snowflakes swirled around us, illuminated by the moonlight. The snowflakes danced in the air before they whirled around the tents.

The surrounding bystanders stopped and stared, awe in their eyes as they watched the snow twirl in the sky.

Doran's wig flipped in his eyes as he followed the movements of the snowflakes. "What do you feel, Aleyna?"

I laughed, feeling my cheeks flush with warmth. "It feels like I have the power of a thousand snowflakes. I can do anything with it."

He grinned, tucking a strand of hair behind my ear. "And you will. To be deemed worthy of such power is an honor, Aleyna. It's a gift that you must use with great care and respect."

I placed my hand on my chest, and the snowflakes tumbled down on the tents. "Why did you choose me?" I asked, my voice barely a whisper. "The power of Winter is vast and all-encompassing. Why entrust it to me?"

He stepped closer and touched my cheek with his fingertips. "You have earned it," he said. "You have a strength that transcends the world of mortals."

My stomach flip-flopped and I swallowed hard. "I've done nothing to deserve this."

He licked his lips. "If you were unworthy, you would be dead. Only the worthy are allowed entrance into my domain. You have passed the test and are now forever linked to me."

I raised an eyebrow. "The worthy? Am I not the only one you made this deal with?"

"You mortals are greedy. You are the last one in a long line of women offering their firstborn." He took a step back and placed his hands behind his back. "If Frosthome deems you unworthy, you perish on sight. My domain is for the strong and brave. Malicious beings are turned away. And those who wish to use my power for evil will be destroyed."

"And what do you deem evil?"

He raised an eyebrow. "Winter encompasses more than me."

I leaned forward and lowered my chin. "It's summer, is it not?"

"Summer is an enemy of Winter, a false warmth that must be extinguished."

I frowned, my brow furrowing in confusion. "But isn't the balance of Winter and Summer needed?"

How did the Summer King enter Frosthome? Unless an invitation nullified that.

He cocked his head. "Yes, but each must be kept in check. Too much of one or the other will bring destruction upon us all."

"But..."

"Tonight is a night for pleasure and not philosophy," he interrupted me. "Let's take the plunge and gamble. The night is young. Let's see what rewards await us."

I chuckled. "Baccarat or Go?"

"Let's start with Go."

I bit my lip and smiled. "And if I win, what will you owe me?"

His eyes burned, and he took a step forward. "Anything your heart desires."

"I will warn you. Gambling is my specialty."

His eyes met mine, and amusement danced in their depths. "Can princesses gamble?"

"Proper princesses don't gamble. The bad news for you, however, is that I am the reigning champion."

"That's a shame," he drawled as he looked at me.

I raised an eyebrow. "Why is that?"

He leaned forward and placed his hand on my stomach. "My plan was to bury my face between your thighs and feast."

My core clenched and a flush rose in my cheeks.

I turned away, trying to hide my reaction.

It was a struggle to keep my composure around this man. He seemed to have the power to make me lose all sense of reason.

I looked back at him.

His eyes darkened. "I like to win. And there's nothing I want more than to claim you as my own."

I took a step forward and placed my hand on his chest. "I'm feeling magnanimous today. When I win, I will allow you to feast to your heart's desire."

"Challenge accepted."

Chapter 23

Nimret

A hand clapped over my mouth, muffling the scream that threatened to burst forth.

I pushed back, trying to break free, but it was no use - a powerful arm had me in an iron grip and it pulled me into the shadows.

My heart raced as I tried to elbow my captor in the ribs.

He only held me tighter, his grip unrelenting.

Glancing down at my dress, the glint of my wedding dagger caught my eye. It was the only weapon I had on me, but to use it now would mean losing my only advantage.

My captor loosened his grip. "Do not be

afraid, Aleyna, it's only me."

Grabbing the dagger, I turned around, placing the dagger against his throat.

His gray eyes flicked up to me and he gave me a sly smile as he leaned against the wall. He lifted his chin, and I dug the dagger even harder against his throat.

Bastard.

"What is wrong with you?"

A warm smile spread across his face.

He calmly took the dagger out of my hand. "This brings back fond memories."

He placed the dagger back in its sheath before carefully placing it back around my neck.

I turned away and glared at him. "I'd rather not be reminded of the day you met my family."

He laughed, pulling me close and kissing my forehead. "Ah, but that's when I knew you would be mine forever. You were brave, standing up to them."

I rolled my eyes, but a smile pulled up the corner of my mouth.

He was such a bastard.

He pressed his lips on my collarbone, and my heart beat faster. I lifted my face to look at him. A sly smile appeared on his face.

"You scared me half to death."

He grinned, tracing the outline of my jaw. "No one can hurt you as long as I'm here."

"Princess Aleyna." A voice called out, breaking us apart.

Doran dragged me further into the shadows, his gaze smoldering. He slowly raised a hand to my chin and tilted it upwards.

I licked his neck, making his eyes flutter shut. His hand moved to my lower back, pressing me against him while his lips moved to my ear. His breath was hot on my skin, making me shudder with anticipation.

"What are you up to?" he asked, a hint of amusement in his voice.

I grinned, pushing my hair behind my ear. "Just thinking about what trouble I could cause."

He leaned in, his breath warm against my skin. "Enchantress," he said, before capturing my lips.

His tongue explored my mouth, and I gasped in surprise before giving in to the pleasure.

Letting out a satisfied sigh, I pulled away with a raised eyebrow. "Surely, you didn't scare me to death to kiss me."

He chuckled, shaking his head. "The reward was worth the effort. Come, let's cause some mischief."

"What sort of trouble?" I asked, as his hand slowly slipped away from mine.

He winked at me, a smile playing on his lips. "The kind that will keep your stepmother and the court on their toes. I found a way for you to visit your father."

How did he pull *that* off?

The queen made sure that no one could visit my father.

Not Artur. Not me. And definitely not someone else.

He could not pull that off.

"How?" I breathed. "Magic?"

A satisfied smile appeared on his face as he drew near. "Money. Everything can be purchased at the right price."

My eyes widened before I started laughing. "That is so like you. Always finding a way to make something happen. Just because you can."

My heart fluttered as I looked into his eyes. He did this for me. He defied the queen and found a way for me to see my father.

I cleared my throat. "Thank you. Without

you, I wouldn't be able to see him at all."

"Husbands don't need thanks, Aleyna. They spoil their wives," he said, his voice low and husky.

Not the men I knew. They were headaches for their poor wives.

My cheeks burned as I looked away. "Well, let's get going and test your theory."

He reached for my hand, lacing his fingers with mine. "Anything for you, my Aleyna."

Together, we stepped out of the shadows.

In the hallway, servants and courtiers scattered at our approach as Doran dragged me through a series of corridors and passageways.

We eventually stopped in front of an ornate door covered in carvings depicting scenes from when we swiftly conquered the lands East until our people reached the island of Ilanya.

Doran pulled out a key, unlocked the door, and ushered me inside. The room was dark and musty, smelling of old books and forgotten secrets.

On the far wall was a mosaic mural of my ancestor, Nimet the first. A haughty expression graced her face as she looked down at us. She was the one that murdered her brother and stole the throne of Ilanya.

I shivered. No matter how many times I saw her, it still sent a chill down my spine.

Doran walked to the mural and pressed on the snake medallion on her chest. A rumble followed and a crack in the wall slowly opened, revealing a secret passageway.

I raised an eyebrow in surprise.

He turned to me, his expression one of sly satisfaction. "My lady, your adventure awaits."

He bowed slightly and offered his arm.

"It seems I have to thank you."

He bit his lip. "I can think of a few ways you can thank me."

I rolled my eyes before I took his arm and stepped into the unknown.

We walked for what felt like hours through the cobweb-filled halls, the only sounds, our steps, echoed against the walls. Eventually, we reached a brick wall at the end of a corridor.

Doran knocked three times on the door and it swung open. The bright sunshine blinded me for a second before my eyes adjusted.

I swallowed hard.

We were in the private courtyard of my father. The one next to his chambers.

The tall apple tree in the center of the

garden was in full bloom, its branches swaying gently with the breeze. I used to play underneath its shade as a child, and it felt surreal to be here again.

The colorful flowers around the courtyard filled the air with their sweet scent as I glanced at Doran. "How did you find this place?"

He smiled, putting his hands in his pockets. "I have my sources," he said, amused. "Right now, we need to make sure you can spend time with your father. We need to leave before anyone notices we are here."

I shook my head. "Impossible. His guards are like hawks."

"Ah, I have solutions for that, too." He tapped the side of his nose. "This is why you need me."

I walked past him. "More like tolerate."

He grinned and placed his fist on his heart.

"So, how are we doing this?"

"Right about now," he drawled, as a servant rushed into the garden. "Our escort arrives."

The servant bowed before us. The blue ribbon on his chest showed he was part of my father's private staff.

"Winter King, the king awaits you."

His voice trembled as he looked downward.

I looked at Doran suspiciously. "Money?"

"Little wife," he said, his voice full of mirth. "Wolves do not always have to howl in the night. Sometimes they make a song of it."

"Beware of the wolf in sheep's clothing, for it is a dangerous beast that will lull you into a false sense of security before striking," I answered carefully, my mind whirling.

A wild grin appeared on his face. "Precisely, Winter Queen." He rubbed his hands together. "The Selwyns have never been ones to be trifled with. The Fae can do more powerful things. We can change the rules."

"Beware the Fae who bends the rules," I murmured, my stomach fluttering. "Danger abounds when the rules of the game are altered."

"Yes indeed. But if you are willing to risk it..." He held out his hand, and I took it. "Songs can be sung."

"Ballads or lullabies?" I asked, curiosity getting the better of me.

He grinned, a glint in his eye. "Howls, of course. The kind that will shake the ground beneath you and make the heavens tremble."

The underlying danger of his words hung

heavy in the air, but I found myself strangely drawn to it.

I smiled at Doran. "Let us try for something more harmonious instead. Something that will make our enemies rise, but not in fear." I looked him straight in the eye. "Let us create a melody that will make them stand in awe."

He laughed and nodded, releasing my hand. "Agreed. I like the way you think, little wife. War ballads are powerful, but a melody of peace can be just as effective."

Chapter 24

Father

The stench of death hung heavy in the air, permeating every corner of the room.

My father lay on his bed, his face gaunt and pinched with pain. His skin was a pale gray, and his once bright eyes now held only sadness. In just a few months, he aged decades.

What disease could do this? How did the healers not notice it? I almost didn't recognize him.

I moved closer, sitting beside him and wrapping a blanket around his shoulders.

He looked at me with weary eyes, the corners of his mouth twitching to smile. His hand reached out for mine, the coldness of his skin startling me.

"Did you finally decide to visit your old, dying father?" he said in a voice that was barely above a whisper.

I closed my eyes. "The queen thought it was unwise for me to visit."

And as I looked at him, I didn't blame her. It wasn't maliciousness, but common sense. He was too weak.

And weakness was deadly when you were king.

He smiled fondly. "Dear Genna visits me every day."

I looked at Doran, who stared outside the window to give us an illusion of privacy. "Her kind heart does her credit."

Frost appeared on the window as Doran clenched his fists.

A hand grabbed my elbow, and I turned to my father. His hand shook as bloodshot eyes stared at me.

"It's not too late to make amends."

I grabbed his hand and kissed his palm. "No, father," I whispered. "It's never too late."

He smiled, his eyes finally holding some warmth. "My dutiful daughter." He squeezed my hand gently. "I know I haven't been the father you've deserved, but I'm so proud of the Winter Queen you've become."

I squeezed his hand in return, unable to find the words to return

"But you have disappointed me beyond measure," he said, his voice suddenly stern. "Your actions have brought shame and dishonor to our family's name."

My heart sank at his words, and I bowed my head.

How did I dishonor the family name? I hadn't been presented with evidence of my wrongdoing, and I had no way of defending myself against his accusations.

"But," he continued softly. "You can redeem yourself. With the help of your husband, you can reclaim our family honor."

I looked up at him, my eyes wide.

"I'm not sure what you mean, father. What can I do?"

My father smiled, the wrinkles around his eyes deepening. "You must make your mother and Artur proud," he said. "It is time for you to sacrifice for your Ilanya."

The reality of what he was asking me to do, hit me like a ton of bricks. I knew my father always favored my brother over me. His precious son. The one he always wanted.

But never in my wildest dream did I expect him to ask me to sacrifice myself for his sake.

Did he hate me that much? Was I unworthy?

The sadness in his eyes answered all my questions.

"Father," I began, my voice wavering. "What sacrifice do you ask of me?"

His gaze grew more intense, and he leaned in closer, his voice low and conspiratorial. "You must prove yourself worthy of the Han family name," he said. "Show me you can prioritize the needs of the family above your own."

I swallowed hard, my heart pounding in my chest. He was asking me to do something I didn't think I was capable of.

But, as I looked into his eyes, I could tell he believed in me.

"What do you suggest I do?"

My father let out a deep sigh, as if he had been expecting this all along. "Give up your claim to the throne," he said. "Your brother can rise to power and you will have done your part to protect our family name."

I looked away, unable to meet his gaze.

How could a father ask his daughter what he would not ask of his son? Was I that worthless?

Doran placed his arms over his chest. The look on his face was unreadable. My husband knew what my father was asking of me, just as he knew all along. He knew right from the start.

My father's words broke the silence. "You must make a decision. One that will keep our family name alive."

I saw pride in my father's eyes despite the sadness.

"Think about it, my daughter," he said. "It's time for you to make a decision that will affect not only you, but your family as well."

Fury burned inside me, hotter and brighter than any flame. My jaw clenched and my fists balled up as I thought of the injustice of it all. How could a father ask his daughter to do something he would not demand from his son? Didn't he realize my worth?

I was a queen. Not some pawn to be moved around the board at his whim. I earned my place with hard work.

"Do you think I would be unfit to rule?" I hissed, my voice barely audible.

My father stared at me for a long moment.

"No. You are capable of being a great queen. But there are other considerations to think about. This is your choice and you must make it for yourself."

My eyes narrowed. "Why?"

My father turned his face away from me. "You can use your gifts to make a difference. That is something a true ruler would do."

The curls of his hair were stark against the moonlight, and I saw a spark of life in his eyes.

"What powers do you speak of?"

He smiled and patted my hand with a knowing look. "You are married to a powerful king. Together, you can make a difference. Do not be afraid to use your gifts and follow your heart. A young woman can do great things."

All I could do was stare at my father in disbelief, unable to process his words. My marriage to a Fae king was what he spoke of. Not anything I did on my own.

I closed my eyes and took a deep breath.

I had a purpose. A chance to fight for what I believed in. And he told me to give up everything for my family.

My hands shook.

How dare he ask me to sacrifice myself?

"Promise me one thing." He placed his hands over mine. "Make your mother and Artur proud. Promise me that."

Grey spots littered his face and I could barely recognize the man in front of me. A man who only wanted what was best for his daughter.

I looked behind him at Doran.

Doran lifted his chin, a silent understanding between us.

My heart clenched as I remembered his words that were imprinted in my brain *"Allow yourself to want and to take what you desire. You deserve to be queen, not only because you fear what your brother might do, but because you are more than capable of ruling."*

I nodded slowly. "I promise that…"

Doran crossed his arms tightly. He was watching me intently, as if he was daring me to defy my father. His face was stern, his eyes never leaving mine for a moment.

"That I will make my mother and Artur proud."

There was a pause, as if the entire world had stopped spinning. As I spoke those words, I knew I was making a tremendous sacrifice.

One I didn't want to make.

"On my honor as the queen of the Winter Court Fae, I promise they will want for nothing and that I shall do my utmost to bring honor and glory to my family."

Honor and glory.

Two words that held so much promise and potential. And two things Artur was incapable of.

"I promise I will make Ilanya proud."

My father smiled, his eyes glistening with tears. He pulled me in for a hug and I clung to him, knowing that this would be our last embrace.

He hurt me; he asked me to do something against my will. But at that moment, all I wanted was for him to be proud of me.

My father pulled away and looked at me with a knowing smile. "I believe in you, Aleyna. You will do great things."

If only he believed in me. If only he saw my worth.

Doran stepped closer, placing a hand on my shoulder. His icy touch sent warmth through my veins and I felt a newfound strength.

I looked up at him, realizing that he had been there for me every step of the way. He never left my side, even when I pushed him away.

His gaze met mine, and he smiled, a genuine, understanding smile. I couldn't help but feel relieved that no matter what happened, I had my loyal protector and husband to stand by my side.

My father coughed, his whole body shaking. He looked at me with a sad, yet proud expression and gave a single nod of approval. "My dependable Aleyna," he said, his voice thick with emotion. "Your mother missed you when you were gone, and she will be proud of you."

He placed his hands on mine.

My stomach churned, and I nodded, my throat too tight to speak.

They will be proud of me.

This is something I could do.

My family needed a leader, and I could be that leader.

My father's face softened, and I saw the faint traces of a smile as he drifted off into slumber. His hands still rested on mine. A warmth emanated from his touch.

I stayed there for a moment, watching over him until he was fast asleep. Then, gently, I extricated myself from his grasp and stood up.

I turned to Doran, who watched me with a stoic expression.

Tears pricked my eyes as I looked him in the eye. "Help me make him proud."

Doran nodded, solemnly. "We will, Aleyna. We will."

I fell into his arms and wept. The tears flowed freely down my cheeks.

My heart ached as the reality of my father's illness sunk in. The tears were those of sorrow, but also those of grief. A heavy weight was lifted off my shoulders with each tear. I knew I had to grieve in order to accept this moment.

Doran held me close and stroked my hair as I sobbed into his chest. He whispered words of comfort.

"Why does he not see what I can do?" I asked, my voice muffled by his chest. "Why does he not see me?"

"His failure to do so," he whispered, stroking my hair. "It's not your fault."

I clung to him, trying to believe his words. My father failed me. Failed to see the potential I had, and all that I could do.

"Thank you," I said, my voice barely audible.

He nodded and kissed my forehead. "He's not worth the dirt on your shoes. You're worth more than he ever gave you credit for, Aleyna.

Remember that."

I managed a weak smile. "You are my husband, Doran. You have to believe in me."

"I believe in you, Aleyna. Always." He smiled and held me tighter. "I see you and I love you."

My heart raced as his words lingered in the air.

I never expected him to say something like this, not after our marriage had been arranged for the sake of power and convenience.

But, as I looked into his eyes, something stirred within me. Something that I never felt before.

My mind raced and my chest tightened as I tried to process my own feelings. All this time, I had been telling myself that this marriage was only for show, not for love. But here I was, feeling something more than just convenience. Not love, but something.

I quickly stepped away from him, my cheeks flushed with embarrassment.

"I'm sorry. I didn't mean to make you uncomfortable," Doran said, gazing me.

"No, it's alright," I replied softly. "I just need some time to process all this."

A gentle smile appeared on his lips, and

he nodded. "You don't have to return the sentiment," he said softly. "Just know that I'm here."

I nodded, too overwhelmed to find the right words.

He couldn't possibly love me. It was impossible.

But as I looked into his eyes, I knew that what he said was true. He was here for me, and that alone meant more than anything.

I nodded. "Thank you," I whispered.

"Tears of sorrow will turn into tears of joy. Take control of your destiny. Own it and embrace it. It's time to put your own dreams into motion and make them a reality."

Chapter 25

Schemes and lies

Doran tilted his head down, his lips close to my ear. "Scheming suits you, little wife," he murmured, his breath tickling my skin.

I smiled, not bothering to hide my pleasure. "A woman must protect her interests. I was not born a queen, but I like to think I learned quickly."

He twirled me around. "A woman who is too ambitious is at risk."

"You believe that a woman shouldn't strive for greatness?" I asked, my eyes searching his face.

Doran chuckled softly. "No, I believe no one should strive for greatness unless they are prepared to risk it all." He spun me around once more before drawing me close, his eyes twinkling with amusement.

The silk of my dress swirled around us as we moved around the dance floor.

I smiled and settled into his embrace. "Then let them come." Arching an eyebrow, I grinned. "I am ready and willing to risk it all."

Doran's lips curled into a sly smirk before he leaned in and brushed his lips against my forehead. "Your brother might not approve of your ambition, but I'm proud to call you Winter Queen."

My feet moved faster and faster, keeping time with the music. I spun and twirled as my body swayed back and forth, dipping and gliding across the floor.

"He will learn to accept my ambition," I said, looking up at Doran. "In time."

He trailed a finger along my jaw before spinning me out and back in. The pearl-studded choker glimmered in the light of the fire.

"One eats, another watches; that's how revolutions are born. We must be careful," Doran said cryptically, his gaze sweeping over the crowd. "Do you think mortals are the only ones prone to disobedience?"

The laughter died in my throat. I didn't have an answer for his warning, but this seemed to amuse him more.

"Are you using my words against me?" I asked, trying to lighten the mood.

He stroked my back with his thumb and smiled down at me. "No, I'm merely reminding you that even you need to be cautious."

I nodded, not allowing my eyes to leave the room. Behind the golden curtains and velvet walls, a storm was brewing. It was time to prove that I was more than a pretty face.

The Selwyns were gossiping in the corner, their voices laced with spite and envy. The Valtinovi brothers were gambling nearby, their loud laughter ringing through the air. And in the corner were my targets - a small group of ambassadors, who were quietly discussing a new alliance.

Doran swayed us closer, his calm presence grounding me. "Ambassadors can be treacherous... But they can also bring glorious rewards if handled correctly."

I threw my head back and laughed. There was nothing to lose and everything to gain.

"Headaches await, but so do opportunities. Trade wars, secret alliances, even the fall of a kingdom. Anything is possible with the right pieces in place."

He twirled me one last time before the

music changed into something more somber. "Ruling was never meant to be easy." He bowed his head and stepped away. "But it can be done if you're brave enough. Are you ready?"

I lifted my chin. "I think I have been since the day we met."

He placed his hand on my lower back and guided me away from the dance floor.

Courtiers stepped aside as we passed, watching us with a mix of respect and curiosity.

Doran followed a few steps behind me, his eyes never leaving my back. His gaze was like a warm caress as we strode through the crowd.

His aura of power filled the room, yet I knew it was all an illusion. My husband's presence was powerful, but his actions lacked purpose.

At least tonight.

He leaned towards me, his lips close to my ear. "An interesting crowd, isn't it?" he said in a low voice. "Can you see the fear in their eyes?"

I turned to him, my eyes twinkling with amusement. "The fear is not in their eyes," I said. "It is in their hearts. Your reputation has preceded you."

Doran raised an eyebrow, his lips curving into a smirk. "That is good to know. I suppose I should make an impression then."

Icicles formed on the walls of the room as a chill descended. The temperature plummeted and an icy aura surrounded the air, making it harder to breathe.

Snow-white teeth flashed in his smile and the room seemed to go still.

Show off.

He stepped behind me, his hands on my shoulders as we faced the group of ambassadors.

What did they see when they saw us? A formidable force or just a foolish young girl in the arms of a Fae king?

It didn't matter.

Perceptions could be manipulated, but actual power came from within.

"Dear ambassadors, how are you tonight?" I asked, my voice a purr of politeness.

The room went quiet as I looked at them. The ambassadors shifted uneasily, their eyes darting around the room.

"Have you met my husband?" I asked, gesturing to Doran. "The Winter King."

The air seemed to freeze as the words left my lips. I played my hand, and it was time for them to fold.

"The rumors are true," one of them said, his voice trembling with fear. "You married *him* and sold your soul to his realm."

I smiled, my lips stretching into a satisfied grin. "Half-truths," I said. "It makes a lasting impression. How about we make a deal?"

They glanced at each other, and I knew I had them.

It was time to make my move.

∞∞∞

"Interesting power play," a voice said from the shadows.

Startled, I spun around to see Artur standing behind me. His face was unreadable as he looked at me.

Doran tensed beside me and then stepped forward. "Are you here to join the negotiations?" he asked.

Artur ignored him, his gaze locked on mine. "You have a remarkable knack for negotiation. It's been an honor watching you work."

"Thank you, brother. Your words warm me more than I can say," I said, taken aback by his compliment.

"Care for a dance, sister?" he asked, his voice steady.

I hesitated for a moment before accepting his outstretched arm.

We walked to the center of the room, and Doran stepped away as Artur pulled me close. He placed his hand on my back. We moved across the floor as if we had done this a thousand times before.

This was the first time I danced with my brother.

Ever.

We ignored the stares of the court as we spun and twirled, his movements precise and controlled.

"You know," he said, his eyes never leaving mine. "No matter how hard you try, I will always be your brother. Not your puppet."

"You are my brother. Do you think I take pleasure in trying to control you?" I said, releasing a sigh.

"No," he replied. "But you must understand that I don't want to be controlled."

I looked away. The sentiment felt familiar, and I could sense the same struggle within myself.

"I understand," I said at last. "We are both strong-willed people, and we will clash."

He smiled as he spun me around the room. "Our parents ruined us."

The anger in his voice was palpable, and I knew he was right. We were both a product of our upbringing.

"But we can make the best of it," I said, looking up at him. "We can be a team. It doesn't have to be this way."

He smiled again, a bitter smile this time, and nodded. "This time you need to listen to me. You turned into our mother. Scheming, plotting, and manipulating others to get what you want."

My ambitions clouded my judgment, and it was time to face the consequences.

"You're right," I said, my voice quiet. "Scheming and plotting may have gotten me here, but it won't get me out."

Queens are not made by taking risks, I reminded myself. They are forged through strength and determination. Scheming and plotting will only get you so far, and it's best to rely on yourself for the rest.

Artur twirled me around. His feet moved with ease as his eyes looked into mine.

"And I turned into our father," he said, his voice laced with bitterness. "Power-hungry and arrogant. The life of the party, but taking no responsibility for his actions." He shook his head, and his arm tightened around my waist. "Always expecting others to do the work for him."

I could feel Artur's anger radiating off of him, and I suddenly felt a wave of sympathy for him.

"It doesn't have to be this way," I said softly. "We can make our own path and find our own way."

He pressed his forehead against mine. "You're right," he said. "We can be different from our parents if we choose to." He pulled away and smiled at me, and for a moment, everything felt right. "And despite everything that has occurred in our past, I love you."

His words moved through me like a wave. Fear and excitement all rolled into one.

"I love you too, brother," I said, and for the first time in a long time, I felt truly content. "Remember how our lives were before they ruined us? We could go back to that if we wanted."

He squeezed my hand. "Running to your

chambers, playing in the gardens, calling each other names, and laughing until our sides hurt? Those were good days."

I smiled up at him. "And they can be again. We just have to try."

Artur nodded and then spun me around. "We are too old for that now."

"Family is never too old to laugh and love," I said, my voice resolute. "No matter our age or station in life. We can always come back to that."

And with that, the music ended, and Artur bowed before me. "Dance with me one last time, sister."

I smiled and accepted his offered hand. "Yes, Artur."

We danced as if nothing else mattered, spinning and twirling around the room. The beat of the music and the sound of our laughter echoed off the walls, reminding us both that life was more than just politics and power.

"Does your husband make you happy?"

"He does." I smiled. "He's the best thing that has ever happened to me. He reminds me of what it means to be a person and not a pawn."

Artur gave me a wry smile. "Even monsters can love."

I couldn't help but laugh, though I knew he

wasn't joking. "Yes, even monsters can love. His reputation is not the same as his heart."

"Then you have done something remarkable, sister." Artur kissed my forehead. "But remember, a man like that can never be tamed. His enemies can never be trusted, and his heart can never be truly conquered."

I nodded, taking the words to heart. "I know that," I said. "If you fight for something, it will eventually be yours."

"Death and destruction are not always the answer," Artur said.

"No, they're not," I agreed. "But fighting for what you believe is not always wrong, either."

"Very true." Artur contemplated me and then nodded. "But you married the personification of death and destruction and you seem happy, despite it all."

"He has a heart of gold buried beneath his gruff exterior." I twirled around Artur. "He's my strength when I feel weak, and my courage when I'm scared."

"He can turn on you. The Fae are not known for their loyalty."

Artur was saying something, but I couldn't quite put my finger on it. Was he trying to warn me of something? Was he trying to tell me that my husband could turn on me, or was he saying that nobody can truly be trusted?

Despite my confusion, I kept my gaze focused on Artur. He seemed to study me, as if trying to gauge my reaction.

"Speak, brother," I said finally. "What are you trying to tell me?"

Artur sighed, and he looked away for a moment before turning back to me. "Just be careful," he said. "Remember that loyalty is scarce in this world, and you should never take it for granted. Never forget that people can be unpredictable."

I nodded, understanding the hidden meaning behind his words. In our station in life, loyalty was a rare thing indeed—a thing that had to be earned and not taken lightly.

"Don't forget who you are," Artur said softly. "No matter what happens, never forget who you are. You are the Maiden, for you bring life to everything around you, while he is the Death, for he brings destruction to all that stands in his way. It's a dangerous balance, but it's one you must remember."

My heart pounded as I realized Artur was right. We were two sides of the same coin —two pieces of the same puzzle. It was a dangerous game. And affection and loyalty could be fleeting. Danger lurked in the shadow and we had to be ever vigilant.

I swallowed hard. "Do you know something I don't, Artur?"

He gripped my hands tightly as we both looked into each other's eyes. "I'm feeling poetic this evening," he said with a slight smile. "But remember, my sister. The Fae are unpredictable. Darkness can never be trusted."

I nodded, understanding what he was trying to tell me—that it was important to keep my guard up, even with those I trusted the most.

But my husband never ceased to surprise me. Despite his reputation, he had a good heart, and I knew deep down that he would do nothing to harm me. He loved me.

But how did the Fae love? Was it even possible for them to love?

I shook my head, pushing the thoughts away. I had to stay focused and not let myself get swept away in these thoughts.

Artur glanced around the room and then back at me, a faint smile on his face. "He's watching you."

"A husband's prerogative." My lips curled into an amused smile. "But I know he would do nothing to hurt me. He loves me."

Admitting it out loud made me feel

vulnerable, but I knew it was true.

He gripped my hands tightly and looked into my eyes. "Be careful, little sister," he whispered, before pulling me in for a hug. "You never know when the darkness will come calling."

I hugged him tightly. His curly hair tickled my nose, and I felt safe in the embrace. His eyes still had a glint in them after he pulled away. He wanted me to be careful, and I vowed to myself that I would.

"Did you have a pleasant talk with your brother?" my husband asked as Artur stepped away.

I looked up at him and smiled. "Yes, I did," I said. "And I feel all the wiser for it. We finally understand each other better."

My husband nodded, his face unreadable. "A wolf never changes his pack." His tone was light and playful, but I could tell that he was serious. "Its true nature is always the same."

Who was he talking about? My brother or himself? I wasn't sure, but I knew it was a warning.

Was something happening that I didn't know about? Was there darkness lurking in the shadows, waiting to strike? My brother's words echoed in my head as I looked around the room.

Doran pulled me tighter as he drew me close to him. We slowly turned around on the dance floor, and I surveyed the crowd.

It seemed like a typical ballroom scene: servants in colorful liveries carrying trays of drinks and food, music playing in the background, and couples dancing in time.

It all seemed normal. I couldn't shake the feeling that something was amiss.

Suddenly, my eye caught a familiar figure in the corner of the room. It was my brother, Artur. He was watching us with an unreadable expression on his face.

Next to him, a servant with a blue ribbon on his chest stood, eyes straight ahead.

I narrowed my eyes, trying to get a better look. Suddenly, the light from a nearby chandelier caught on something metal in Artur's hand—a dagger. The blade glinted in the light, sending a chill down my spine.

It was then that I knew he wasn't just protecting me—he was preparing for battle.

The music came to an abrupt halt, and I looked up at my husband.

He raised an eyebrow, and I forced a smile. "It seems like the evening is drawing to a close."

"Don't worry, little wife," my husband

drawled, his voice deep and resonant. "I would slay a thousand foes to keep you safe. No one can take what is mine."

The doors of the ballroom were thrown open with a loud crash. I jumped, my heart pounding in my chest as a figure strode into the room.

It was the head of guards, his face stern and his dark eyes scanning the crowd.

Everyone seemed to stop what they were doing, all eyes turning to him as he marched closer.

He stopped in the center of the room. "The king is dead. Long live the queen."

His head was cut off with a single stroke.

Chapter 26

Winter King

My husband's eyes narrowed as his hands shimmered with ice. Whirling winds gathered around him. Frosty tendrils of snow circled my feet and the surrounding air crackled with energy.

"You all have forgotten who you are serving," he said firmly. "You serve the queen now. She is your ruler, and she is mine." He leveled a gaze around the room, his voice full of authority and power. "Anyone who dares to oppose me will be met with consequences."

The room shrunk on its own. The silence was oppressive and heavy. No one dared move an inch.

My husband stepped forward. He raised his arms, and the winds howled around us. "Now, bow before your queen."

Swords were drawn, but none dared to move.

I strolled up to him, my steps echoing in the stillness.

My husband let out an eerie laugh. The sound echoed through the room like a clap of distant thunder. His eyes glowed with a fierce intensity and his arms dropped to his sides.

"This is Aleyna Han," he said, his voice booming throughout the room. "She is your queen."

His dark cloak billowed around him, and his pale skin seemed almost luminous in the candlelight. Even in this moment of chaos and fear, he was as mesmerizing and beautiful as ever.

The courtiers bowed before me, their faces a mixture of shock and awe.

I met each of their eyes, nodding my head in acknowledgment.

One brave soul stepped forward, sword held high.

My husband simply raised one hand and a wall of ice emerged from the ground, freezing the man in place.

The other guards quickly followed suit.

Loyal to a fault.

As soon as their swords were within reach, a blizzard of snow and ice rose from the ground. It encased the guards in a thick layer of frost, making any movement impossible.

A wind roared through the chamber as my husband unleashed another wave of power. The snow and ice responded to his command and swirled around the guards, binding them in a magical prison.

My husband turned to me, his eyes still glowing with the same intensity. "Do not fear," he said softly. "No one will touch you while I am here."

I felt a sudden chill, my breath catching in my throat as I was confronted with his power. My heart raced and the hairs on the back of my neck stood on end.

How much strength and control did he possess? He vanquished the guards with a single glance, his icy gaze freezing them in place.

Their screams filled the room as their bodies slowly froze, their flesh turning blue and brittle. Finally, they stopped struggling, and the chamber fell silent, save for the sound of melting ice.

Their screams will haunt me for the rest of my life.

At that moment, I realized how dangerous he truly was and why people were afraid of him. He was right. No one could hurt me while he was around.

I heard pounding footsteps and saw my brother sprinting towards me, brandishing a sword in his hand. His face was twisted with rage and his eyes were glassy with hatred. He was coming for me, determined to take my life.

No, Artur, I thought desperately to myself. Don't do this!

But it was too late.

My husband stepped forward, and the winds howled around us once again. A swirling vortex of white and blue engulfed my brother, freezing him in place.

He opened his mouth to scream, but no sound escaped.

My husband smiled coldly and waved his hand. The ice shattered and my brother lay at our feet, shivering and broken.

Doran stepped forward, putting his foot firmly on my brother's chest. He leaned down close to Artur's face and whispered something into his ear. Artur's face changed, his rage melting away as he listened to my husband's words.

Artur's expression changed, and he looked up at me. He held my gaze for a few seconds before averting his eyes.

Doran turned around to face me, his icy gaze mere inches away from my own. He held me in that intense gaze for several moments before finally tearing away, his expression unreadable.

My husband was a powerful figure, and he seemed to control even the most chaotic situations.

He contained my brother without a single word and enforce his will simply through the power of his glance.

I realized then that I underestimated him and his abilities.

He knew.

He knew Artur wanted me dead, but he said nothing.

He wanted to control the situation, and that scared me the most.

His hands glowed with power as he stood tall and proud, his gray eyes flashing.

"For your crimes against the crown, I sentence you to death," he said calmly. "Let this be a lesson to all who come after you, that justice will not be taken lightly."

His words were bitter and calculated, each syllable reverberating throughout the chamber. There was a finality in his tone that made me shudder.

"Release him," I whispered, my voice barely audible.

Doran glanced at me dismissively. "Release him? That is not an option," he said in a voice that carried the same icy edge as his gaze. "He tried to kill my wife, and he must face the consequences."

His words were tinged with a controlled rage, as if he was struggling to contain his anger.

My brother's eyes widened in fear, and he pleaded for mercy.

I swallowed hard. "I am the queen, Doran," I said firmly. "I can pardon him."

He glanced at me, and his expression softened a fraction.

"Rationality and mercy can exist together," I continued. "I implore you to consider his fate with a more equitable lens."

My husband stared at me. He waved his hand, and my brother was released from the icy grasp of his magical grip.

He looked relieved yet shaken.

"You may be queen, but rationality and mercy are my domain," Doran said to me, his voice softening. "This animal tried to take your life, and for that he deserves punishment. But I will listen to you, my love, and be merciful."

He looked at my brother as he turned away. He stepped forward and Artur's screams echoed through the chamber as he pressed his feet down on my brother's chest.

"Your punishment is death," Doran said finally. "But I will be merciful and grant you a swift and honorable end."

Artur gasped for breath as he pressed down harder.

I rushed forward, grabbing his arm. "Please, Doran! Don't do this!"

Doran turned back to me and smiled sadly as he brushed a lock of hair from my face. "This is what must be done," he said firmly, his voice low and gentle.

He raised his hands, gathering the surrounding winds. The winds swirled around Artur. His body trembled as he was lifted off the ground and into the air. He encased him in a cocoon of ice that froze him in place.

Nobody moved or said anything as he slowly dissipated into the air, leaving us all in shock.

The silence that filled the chamber was suddenly broken by a loud scream. It took me a moment to realize it was my own.

I dropped to my knees, pain radiating through my body.

Doran kneeled beside me and gently brushed away the tears from my face. "This is why they fear me," he murmured, his voice thick with emotion. "I am a man of justice and mercy."

Rage built up inside me. "Justice is not justice if it causes pain," I shouted, my voice icy cold. "This is not mercy, this is revenge!"

Doran's face softened, and he stepped closer to me. "It may feel like revenge," he said softly. "But I assure you, my love, that it is not."

He reached out and touched my cheek, his hand warm and gentle. "This is justice," he whispered, his voice gentle yet firm. "It is a hard truth that we must all face. One that I will never forget."

"Who made you the judge of justice and mercy?" I asked, my voice trembling with emotion.

"Winter Queen, life has made me the judge," he answered, his voice still calm and composed. "Love isn't always enough, and even though I love you, I must still demand justice. That is the way of this world."

He stepped back and looked down at me, his gray eyes intense and unyielding.

I shook my head, his words ringing in my ears. "That is not love." I stood up. "Love is much more than justice and punishment. It's about understanding, forgiveness, and mercy."

He chuckled softly and brushed a strand of hair from my face. "Maybe not... But it's something."

I stared up at him, my body trembling with rage. "You are a monster," I hissed through gritted teeth. "Who are you to decide who deserves justice and mercy? Who gave you the right?"

Doran's face remained unreadable as he looked down at me.

My knuckles cracked against his hard chest. "Who gave you the right?"

He grabbed my wrists and pulled me close to him, his eyes blazing as he looked down at me.

"A monster I may be," he said, his voice calm yet powerful. "But I am your monster and will do as you command–even if that means slaying and murdering in your name."

I tried to break free, but he wouldn't let go.

He paused for a moment, his face softening slightly. "They fear me," he whispered, his voice barely audible. "Because I do not take life lightly."

I swallowed hard and looked away, my heart pounding in my chest.

I knew he was right—even if it was hard to accept. In my name, he did what was necessary. His twisted mind and frozen heart had seen justice served.

He let go of my wrists and stepped back, his gaze never leaving mine.

I pulled away from him and stood tall, my gaze meeting his. "You cannot control me," I said firmly, my voice strong and unwavering. "You cannot sacrifice lives for that, *husband*."

Doran stepped forward and grabbed my shoulders, his grip vice-like. "I am your husband," he said firmly. "And I will protect you with my life, whatever the cost may be. My plan was never to control you, but to protect you from harm."

"A puppet queen." I looked away. "I'm nothing more than a puppet queen."

Doran's grip softened, and he pulled me close to him, his lips brushing against my temple. "You are a queen who cares about justice, who stands for what is right," he murmured. "You are a queen of mercy and wisdom."

I looked up at him. "A queen without

power is nothing," I said, my voice echoing through the room. "A queen is only powerful when she has an army behind her."

And Doran was an army of his own—a force to be reckoned with.

I stepped away from him and straightened my spine, my gaze meeting his. "Without an army, I'm nothing more than a figurehead."

A glamorous figure, but powerless.

He shook his head slowly. "No, Aleyna," he said softly. "You are not powerless. We are equals, and together we can be a force to be reckoned with."

I smiled sadly and shook my head. "You used me." I closed my eyes. "Your power-hungry ambitions have cost me everything. My father and brother are dead. You used me in your war against the Selwyns."

Doran nodded slowly and stepped forward, his eyes never leaving mine. "I could have taken the easy way out," he hissed. "Believe what you will, little wife. Make me your villain if you must. All I know is that sometimes we have to make hard choices, and this is one of them. I'd rather be the villain than risk your life."

My anger rose inside of me like wildfire, fueled by a mixture of frustration and betrayal.

My breath quickened and my fists clenched

as I stepped away from him.

"You think you can control me?" I spat, my voice shaking. "You think you can make all the decisions and I just have to obey. But I won't be controlled. I won't be your figurehead."

I took a deep breath, my anger still simmering in the pit of my stomach.

"Get out now. And don't you ever come back."

He stared at me for a moment, his eyes wide with shock. "I love you, no matter what you believe," he said, his voice a dark and menacing echo in the silence of the room.

I could feel his presence like a heavyweight in the air, a smell of something dark and dangerous that made my skin crawl.

"Leave. Don't come back," I repeated, my voice trembling slightly.

He took a step towards me, and I backed away instinctively.

He sighed heavily and shook his head, his shoulders slumped in defeat. "This isn't over. Not by a long shot."

And then he was gone, fading away like a fleeting dream, leaving me with nothing but the bitter taste of anger and betrayal in my mouth.

Chapter 27

A mother's love

Ash covered my face and clothes as I walked through the city streets. Citizens formed a bucket brigade, and they were desperately trying to put out the flames.

My heart clenched in my chest as I passed by the destruction, knowing that it was all because of Artur's actions.

He did this. He sacrificed innocent lives for his own gain.

The heat from the fire was intense, and I felt as if I was about to buckle under its weight. But something inside of me kept pushing forward, and I soldiered on, determined to make a difference.

Wagons full of supplies plodded by. The surrounding people looked grateful as they loaded up food and medical supplies. Children cried and hugged their parents, clinging to them for safety.

Now I was standing in the ashes, surrounded by the destruction of my ambition.

I kept walking until I reached the palace gates. The guards were gone, and a heavy blanket of silence shrouded the air. Inside, violence simmered, waiting to be unleashed.

The once-great palace was a charred ruin, and my heart ached at the sight. My stepmother's last present to me. Power came at a price.

But in the silence, something stirred inside me. It was a small flame of hope, one that promised to never be extinguished.

If I was going to make a difference, I needed to confront her.

I entered my chamber, and then I saw it—the stuffed wolf *he* won for me. It was a reminder of happier times when my father and brother were still alive.

I took a deep breath and vowed to never be controlled by anyone again.

I picked it up and cradled it for a moment. The scent of my husband still lingered on it, and I closed my eyes in remembrance.

I threw the wolf into the raging fire,

watching as it burned to ashes in moments.

Goodbye Winter King, goodbye.

I turned away as the flames died.

Isra waited outside the door, her face a mix of understanding and sorrow.

"Come," she said. "We have much to do."

"Have they found her yet?" I asked her, my voice heavy with dread.

"She's in the holding cells, my queen."

∞∞∞

My stepmother's cold eyes peered out from behind the iron bars. Her face, once graceful, was now distorted with hatred and malice. Her long, wiry hair hung crazily around her face, making her look unkempt and wild.

"Do you know why I'm here?" I asked her, my voice shaking only a little. "You thought you could get away with it, didn't you?"

"Get away with what?" she replied, feigning innocence.

Despite everything she'd done, I felt a

certain pity for her; to fall so far from grace must have been devastating. I saw it in her eyes—the fear of being forgotten, erased from history.

The elegant queen I once knew was now an empty shell of a woman, consumed by her own hatred.

I sat down across from her, my chin held high.

"You have a choice," I said firmly. "Either you accept defeat and surrender to me, or I will put you to death. There is no other way."

My stepmother glared at me for a long moment, before pressing her lips together in a thin line. "Yes."

"Trying to assassinate me and overthrow my kingdom was a foolish mistake," I said. "But why did you involve Artur?"

She sighed heavily and looked away, a thousand memories flashing before her eyes. "He wanted power," she said at last. "He wanted to be king."

My heart sank as I realized the full extent of her treachery.

"So that's what this was all about," I said. "You wanted to control the kingdom through him. But you failed."

"He's my son," my stepmother said quietly.

"I'd do anything to keep him safe."

I nodded, understanding her emotion, if not her actions.

"You poisoned him," I said. "You killed him with your own hands. You brought this tragedy upon yourself."

My stepmother's face crumpled in grief, her body trembling with sorrow. "I'm sorry," she said, her voice barely audible. "I'm so sorry..."

I took a deep breath and looked her in the eye. "It's too late for apologies," I said coldly. "The death of my brother resulted from your treachery. That's all they will remember you for."

A cold fury replaced the sadness in her eyes, and I saw she was ready to fight back. But she knew it was futile; I had the upper hand this time.

As I looked into my stepmother's eyes, I couldn't help but feel as if I was staring into a reflection of my own life. It seemed as if fate laid down a cruel hand for me, and no matter how hard I tried or who I became, tragedy followed me wherever I went.

The poets had long said that tragedy resulted from hubris and ambition. But what of those of us who did nothing to merit such misfortune? What about those who simply tried to survive?

Did my hubris and ambition really deserve such a cruel punishment? I would never know.

All I could do was accept the consequences of my stepmother's actions and carry on, no matter the cost.

My stepmother retreated into the shadows, her eyes never leaving mine.

This was the last time we would ever speak to each other. Relief and sadness coursed through my body in equal measure.

"It would have worked if not for your husband."

Her voice croaked out, the resignation in her tone unmistakable.

"Yes," I replied softly. "I know."

"He was the one who stopped me."

I smiled sadly, knowing she was right.

"If he hadn't interfered, I would have succeeded!" she snarled. "My son is dead! All my plans have gone up in smoke!"

My eyes narrowed. "Blaming another won't bring him back."

My stepmother stared at me for a few seconds, her eyes blazing with hatred, before turning away. Her green dress was tattered and stained, a stark contrast to the vibrant gown she used to wear.

She trudged to the barred window and gazed out. The sun was setting, painting the sky a deep orange hue, and she tilted her face toward the warmth that it provided.

"Don't let your husband's power overwhelm you. Don't underestimate him," she warned me. "He's a dangerous man."

She turned to face me, her eyes glinting in the fading light.

I met her gaze steadily, my chin held high. "What do you know about danger?" I asked her, a hint of challenge in my voice.

"The Fae are dangerous. He butchered my son and destroyed my plans. The Butcher of Calan has no mercy. He destroyed our city and left it in ruins. Beware of him."

And the Selwyns murdered his mother.

I sighed. Despite all she had done, I couldn't help but feel a twinge of sorrow for her loss.

"I will never forget what he did," I said. "But I will never forget what you tried to do, either. You will hurt no one again."

My stepmother's lips curled into a sneer, her eyes darkening with malice. "Your father will regret the day you married that man," she hissed.

"He does not know what he's gotten himself into. Mark my words, you will be the downfall of our family."

My heart pounded in my chest, her words hitting me like a punch to the gut. I wanted to scream at her, tell her she was wrong, but I held my tongue.

Instead, I just nodded my head slowly in acknowledgment. "Father is dead."

She turned away, her shoulders slumped in defeat. "I murdered him."

I remained silent, my jaw clenched tightly as I fought back the tears that threatened to spill from my eyes.

"Did you even love him?"

My voice broke on the last word.

She shook her head slowly and then sank to the ground in defeat. Her hair spilled around her, framing her face.

"I loved the power," she said finally. "I thought I could have it all."

She fell silent, lost in thought as the sun set.

My stepmother suddenly looked up at me, her eyes softening. "You have much of your father in you," she hissed. "You have his charm, but you have my cunning." She paused for a moment before continuing. "Use it to your advantage, my dear. Don't let anyone take away your power."

I looked into her eyes, understanding the weight of her words. I didn't want to think of myself in that way, but I couldn't deny the truth.

A manipulator taught me how to manipulate, and I would never forget her lessons.

"When you married the Winter King, you saw an opportunity to gain power, and you seized it. You risked your own happiness for a chance to gain control."

I stood rigidly, my hands clenched tightly at my sides as I struggled to contain my discomfort. "You forced me into a corner and I had no choice."

My stepmother nodded and rose, her expression solemn. "I know. You still fell in love with him, despite all his manipulations. That's what makes you so like your father."

The realization hit me like a wave, crashing over me and stealing my breath away. I fought it for so long, denying the truth, but it was undeniable. I loved him - even if it was against my better judgment.

Monsters can be loved, even if they don't deserve it.

My stepmother suddenly reached out and slipped her hand into mine. She gave me a tender smile and squeezed my hand lightly.

I stepped away from her grasp and took a deep breath.

"You were just a pawn in a game, my dear," she said softly. "But you can be queen if you want to be."

"Isn't it too late to act like a mother?" I asked, my voice unsteady.

My stepmother shook her head and smiled sadly. "It isn't too late for anything. It's never too late to start again, my dear."

She stepped away from me and tilted her head towards the sky; her face bathed in the light of the setting sun.

"You have your father's heart. And you can be a leader if you choose to be. Just remember...you don't have to do it alone."

My breath caught in my throat.

Did she imply I needed to forgive the man who killed my brother? Her own son?

"That baby will be your chance to start anew," she said softly. "You have the power to make something beautiful out of this."

I stared at her in shock, and my mouth

opened slightly.

"What baby?" I finally whispered.

My stepmother smiled sadly. "Your baby. The healers have been checking on you regularly to make sure you were not pregnant." She paused for a moment, her eyes searching mine. "You are pregnant, my dear."

The world seemed to stand still for a moment as the realization of what she was saying sunk in.

It was impossible, yet here I was. I was pregnant with his child, despite the odds.

I looked up at my stepmother, my heart racing. She looked so proud, yet so sad at the same time.

My throat tightened as tears brimmed in her eyes. "But how?"

She gestured to the wedding dagger hanging from my neck. "You are married to the Winter King now and have tied yourself to him. You will bear his child, no matter what."

She reached out and cupped my cheek with her hand. "But you don't have to do it alone," she said. "You can be the queen you were always meant to be, and I will be here to guide you."

Anger swelled within me as I realized my

stepmother was trying to manipulate me. She used her words as weapons and now she was trying to use my pregnancy against me.

"I will handle this on my own," I said firmly, stepping away from her.

I walked away, but a hand on my arm held me in place.

"My dear, I only want what's best for you." Her grip tightened. "I care about you, and I will do anything to protect you."

I turned to her. "Your punishment will be a reminder of the consequences of your actions. You will rot in that cell, and you will never see the light of day again. You have brought this fate upon yourself, and now you must live with it. Goodbye Genna," I said coldly. "May the death of your son haunt you for eternity - just as it will haunt me."

With that, I turned and walked away.

The sound of her sobbing echoed behind me.

Chapter 28

Crowns and promises

"The crown suits you," Doran said, his voice low as he stepped into the throne room. Clad in a fur-lined cloak and a silver crown, I looked up at him in surprise.

How did he breach the castle's security?

Doran had a certain air about him that made the hairs on the back of my neck stand up. He was too confident. Too sure of himself.

I felt like he had my life in his hands and I was completely powerless to stop him.

I sat up a little straighter, my eyes meeting his gaze. "What do you want?" I asked coldly.

His face was unreadable as he slowly approached the throne. "I wanted to talk about your stepmother's words," he said, his voice soft yet firm. "She was trying to manipulate you. But I only want what's best for you."

I swallowed and looked away. When I was a naive girl, I believed everyone had the best intentions. But now...

I looked up at Doran. His dark hair framed his face and his eyes shone like the stars in the night sky.

"You have every right to be angry." He stood tall and proud, like a king should, but his tone was gentle. "But I hope you realize I was only trying to help. You are a leader of your people. Just remember...you don't have to do it alone."

In his eyes, I saw sincerity and compassion. But that didn't mean I will forgive him. His protection wasn't worth the price of my freedom.

"I only wanted to protect you."

My anger simmered, but I couldn't deny the truth in his words. I looked away from Doran, unable to meet his gaze any longer.

His presence filled the room, and I reminded myself that this was my kingdom and he was a guest there.

"I believe you," I said finally, my voice barely louder than a whisper. "Your intentions were good. But your methods were wrong."

Weakness and anger suddenly flooded through me, but I held on to my composure.

Doran nodded, a hint of a smile playing on his lips. "My apologies." He paused for a moment before continuing. "I will not repeat that mistake again."

"Do you even know what you did wrong?" I said, my voice rising in anger.

"Yes," Doran replied calmly. "I underestimated your capabilities and tried to do too much for you. I should have trusted in your strength and allowed you to find your way."

He reached for my hand, but I pulled it away.

I lifted my chin in defiance. "How about a truth for a painful moment?"

Doran's eyes locked with mine, and he nodded. "Agreed."

"You turned into your enemy when you tried to control me. How does it feel being a Selwyn? You might as well bear their name. You act like them."

Doran was silent, his face expressionless. But his eyes betrayed the hurt I inflicted. He bowed slightly and stepped back, away from the throne.

"You're right, and I accept your rebuke," he said. "It was wrong of me to control you." He looked away, his words heavy with sadness. "Being compared to *that family* hurts, but please understand, I didn't want you to become a kin slayer. Killing your brother would wreck you."

"I pleaded with you to not murder my brother," I said, the words spilling out of my mouth. "But you wouldn't listen. You can't ever be trusted again."

The moment hung between us, heavy with emotion.

Doran's face softened, and he took another step back. "You are right, and I understand why you feel this way." His throat bobbled up and down. "Now it's my turn to say something important. Please remember that despite my mistakes, I still love you."

His eyes were sad but sincere. I looked away, unable to face the truth of his words.

His love was something I could never deny. But it didn't mean I forgave him.

His love was a cruel reminder of the power he had over me. No matter how much I wanted to be, I could never be completely free of him.

I was trapped in a prison of my making, and he held the key to my freedom.

I could never trust Doran again.

"Do you even know I'm here?" I asked, my voice trembling with barely contained rage.

Doran's expression was unreadable as he stared at me. "I know why you are here," he said, his voice a deep rumble. "And I understand why you are so angry."

He stepped closer to me, his eyes burning with intensity. "But while she wanted to keep you in chains, I never wanted to control you. I only wanted to guide and protect you. I failed to do that, and I am sorry."

His words echoed in my mind like thunder. I wanted to deny his apology, but at that moment, I felt something else. Sadness. He didn't deserve my forgiveness, but he deserved my understanding.

"I wanted to keep you safe, but in my hubris, I failed to see what was right in front of me. I will never become a tyrant like the Selwyns, I promise you that."

He reached out to brush my cheek, and I felt a surge of warmth. I looked up into his gray eyes and saw the truth of his words.

"Doran," I said, my voice soft. "I appreciate your promise and your sincerity. But it's too late. You've already broken my trust, and I cannot forget that."

He looked away for a moment before returning his gaze to me. "I understand," he said, his face filled with sorrow. "It is your choice to make, and I will respect it."

He stepped back and bowed his head.

"Wait," I called after him.

He stopped and looked back, a questioning look in his eyes.

"I have not forgiven you, but I'm not an oath breaker. A firstborn for a throne. That was our deal."

He arched his eyebrow as his gaze lingered on my stomach. "I absolve you."

I placed my hand on my belly, rubbing it lightly. "Your child needs their father. What you did was wrong, but they need you."

He was silent for a while, then nodded. "My precious child. I will not fail them."

He stepped closer and kissed my forehead, his lips lingering for a moment longer than necessary.

"How much did you hear?" I asked, already knowing the answer.

His eyes never left mine. "Everything," he said, his voice barely above a whisper. "How can I protect you if I don't know what you face?"

He looked away as he stepped away.

"Will you let me prove my love to you? I need you to trust me again."

I stared at him, my heart pounding in my chest.

"It's impossible to forget what you did," I said, my voice shaking. "Your actions have consequences."

He smiled a sad smile. "But I can still try to earn your trust back. I promise you, I will never let you down again. Meet me tomorrow at dawn, and I will show you."

"How can I trust you?"

"You can trust me because I love you," he said, his gaze never leaving mine. "The Fae can't lie, and my words are true."

"The Fae can omit the truth," I said, my voice still filled with doubt.

Doran smiled and stepped closer to me. "That is true," he said, looking into my eyes. "But I give you my word that I will never omit the truth from you ever again."

He brushed a strand of hair away from my face before pulling his hand away. "A truth for a truth?"

"A truth for a truth."

We both looked away, the moment suspended in time.

"Will you come to me tomorrow?" he asked, his voice barely audible.

I nodded, my heart pounding in anticipation. "Yes," I said, finally finding my voice. "I will meet you tomorrow."

And with that, he turned and walked away into the night.

Fools never knew when to stop loving. I was no different; despite my doubts, I still found myself drawn to him like a moth to a flame.

My brother was dead, and I was now a mother-to-be. I needed to protect my child, no matter what it cost me.

So I took a chance - on Doran, and on his promise that he would never break my trust again.

My child needed a protector and a father. I could only hope that Doran would be the one to provide them with both.

Only time would tell.

Chapter 29

Frostspire

The fairy ring glowed brightly in the darkness.

I stepped inside and the energy surged through me as my surroundings changed.

The darkness stretched around me, smothering all light.

The walls of the cave were cold and damp, reflecting the pale light that streamed through the entrance.

Doran placed a fur coat around my shoulders. "It's cold."

The brown fur was soft against my skin.

He stepped closer to me, his face illuminated by the pale light. "I won't let you down," he said, his voice low and steady.

He led me out of the cave and my mouth dropped open as I saw what lay before us.

High walls of snow and ice stood tall, surrounding the mountaintop like a fortress. The turrets were adorned with intricate icicles, glistening in the morning light.

A winding staircase of ice led up to the entrance, shimmering with a silver hue.

It was breathtaking.

"Welcome to Frostspire," Doran said, gesturing to the mountain. "My people lived here for generations."

I stepped closer and noticed a small fire burning in the center of the courtyard.

Doran walked over and picked up a burning branch, then handed it to me.

I looked at the palace. "Why did you stop living here?"

"A terrible war broke out." he sighed. "Generations before I was born. The place was destroyed. Horrible tales were told of what happened here, and no one outside of the royal family wanted to return. Until now."

The fire in his eyes was brighter than ever as he smiled.

"And this is how you want to prove your

love for me?" I asked, my voice full of disbelief.

"Yes," he said, his voice full of conviction. "I want to prove to you that my promises are true."

He stepped closer to me and took my hands in his.

A gentle chill ran down my spine.

We stood in the courtyard for a few moments, just looking at each other in silence.

"I wanted you to visit this place. The only place I knew would make you understand how much I love you."

I raised an eyebrow. "And what's so special about it?"

He brushed his lips softly against my knuckles, and as I tried to pull away, he held on a little tighter.

"I will show you something here that only I have seen," he said, his voice low and intense. "My love for you is like this mountain: strong, unyielding, and everlasting."

He gestured towards the palace.

"Come," he said, his voice barely a whisper.

We climbed the steep, winding staircase that led to the top of the castle.

When we finally reached the top, we

stepped into a vast chamber. Ancient stones lined the walls, and the air was cold and damp.

There were no windows. Only two iron doors that served as the only entrance and exit.

In the center of the room was a circular pit filled with rickety wooden cells.

My breath caught in my throat as I saw my brother locked inside one of them.

He looked frail and pale in the dark.

He looked up at me with a gentle, sad smile.

I rushed over to him and kneeled, tears streaming down my face. I couldn't believe my eyes.

"Doran," I gasped. "You didn't kill him?"

Doran stepped forward and put a hand on my shoulder. "You asked me to spare him, and I did. I would have gladly ended his life, but your pleas were so strong I couldn't deny them."

How was he capable of this act of compassion and mercy? Doran, who seemed so cold-blooded before, saved Artur.

Why didn't he tell me the truth?

Doran smiled at me, his eyes full of understanding.

"I knew that if I could just bring you here

and show you this, you would understand how much I love you."

I wouldn't have believed him otherwise.

He took a step back and gestured to the ancient cells. "I can't release him. He's too dangerous and I can't take that risk. But this is the only place I know of where he's safe, and it will stay our secret."

He looked away, then back at me.

I stared into his eyes, and for a moment, I felt like I could see into his soul before he closed our bond. He loved me - truly, deeply, and forever.

Doran stepped back and nodded. "I will leave you alone with your brother for a moment," he said, his voice gentle and full of understanding. "We can talk later if you like."

He gave me a reassuring smile and stepped out of the room, leaving me alone with my brother.

I peered into the darkness.

My brother looked up at me with wide eyes, and I saw the relief in his expression as he saw it was me.

My brother reached for my hand and I squeezed it, giving him a small smile.

He smiled sadly. "I tried to murder you.

Why am I still alive?"

I shook my head. "My husband saved you because I asked him to."

"You tamed the Winter King. A man who seemed so cold, and yet he loves you more than anything else in this world." My brother looked away, tears welling up in his eyes. "Why am I alive when so many others aren't?"

I put my hand on his shoulder. "Maybe it's because you are worth saving, my brother. Maybe it's because you can be redeemed." I lied.

He scoffed. The curls of his lips tugged downward. "Redemption is a fool's hope. You aren't a fool, Aleyna. So why are you latching onto something that won't work?"

I looked down and sighed. "You're right," I said softly. "You are wretched, and I'm sure you've done more terrible things in your life, but maybe there is still some good left in you. Maybe you can still be saved."

I looked up at him, my gaze firm.

"Foolish sister." A smile tugged at the corner of his lips. "You do not know how much it means to me. You still care."

"I don't forgive you." My eyes were sharp. "But I understand why you did it. Our parents ruined us, and we were both broken." I paused, taking a deep breath. "Desperateness can make us do things we wouldn't normally do. I understand that, and it makes me want to help you."

"Your kind heart will ruin you." He smiled sadly and shook his head.

I gave him a sad smile in return. "It's not kindness, but selfishness. You will be locked up here forever..."

My brother looked up at me, his eyes wide in disbelief.

For a moment, it seemed like he was going to cry.

"No matter what you think of yourself, Aleyna, you are still kind and compassionate. Never forget that."

He pulled me in for a hug.

I hugged him back, my heart heavy with emotions I couldn't explain.

We stayed like that for what felt like an eternity, but eventually, my brother pulled away and nodded.

"I won't forget."

Even though this was far from an ideal situation, it was still a step in the right direction.

"Thank you."

"Tell me the truth," my brother whispered.

"How much of this is you trying to save me, and how much of it is because you still love me?"

I looked away. "A bit of both, I think. I'm a fool for loving my brother, but I can't help it."

A bitter smile crossed his face, but it was a smile nonetheless. "I'd like to believe that there's still hope for us," he said quietly. "How is mother?"

"Rotting away in the dungeons," I replied. "She lost her mind."

He closed his eyes and nodded. Then, he opened them again and looked at me with a fury and determination in his eyes that I hadn't seen before.

"Perhaps one day, I can be the one to save her." His voice was resolute, but I could tell that he was still scared.

Bitter tears stung my eyes, but I smiled and nodded. "You will."

Chapter 30

Monsters

Towering bookshelves lined the walls, all overflowing with ancient texts and stories from another time. An enormous stone fireplace crackled and heated the room, while two plush couches created an inviting atmosphere for visitors to relax and explore.

I sat in one seat, while Doran sat in the other.

"Why him?" He looked up. "Why can you forgive your brother when you haven't been able to forgive me for the same mistakes?"

I sighed, my heart aching. "I don't trust my brother. Neither have I forgiven him. On the surface, we had an idyllic childhood, but in reality, we were both living through our kind of hell."

Childhood memories flooded my mind - being overlooked and ignored, being hurt for no reason.

"I understand his desperation in a way that you never will."

His eyes softened, and he nodded in understanding.

"That's why I'll never give up on him," I added softly, my gaze falling to the fire. "I don't think I'll visit him again... but deep down, I still care about him."

The flames danced in the darkness, painting the room with a warm, golden hue. The winter chill dissipated and the tension between us seemed to fade away.

My brother was right; forgiving him and helping him doesn't make me weak. It only strengthened me.

We sat in comfortable silence for a few moments until finally Doran spoke up. "I'm here for you too," he said, his voice low and gentle. "Whatever you need."

I smiled at him gratefully and nodded. "Thank you. But that's not what you want to tell me, is it? You wonder why you are not deserving of my forgiveness yet."

I looked into his eyes and saw the truth - he

was scared. He wanted to prove himself and not make a mistake.

I stood up and embraced him tightly, feeling his body trembling against mine. "You are worthy of forgiveness," I whispered into his ear. "And don't forget it."

He pulled away, searching my face. "Being worthy of forgiveness doesn't mean I'm forgiven," he said, his voice low and sad. "You cannot let go of the past."

I sighed and looked away. I wanted to tell him it was because I was scared - scared of getting hurt again. But I couldn't bring myself to say it.

"I know the past won't always stay in the past," I finally said. "But I believe that if we both stay vigilant, the future will be brighter."

His lips twitched as he nodded and looked away.

In the background, the fire continued to crackle. The wood hissed and popped in a comforting rhythm.

"Because he's family, my sense of boundaries is wrecked." I looked at my hands. "Even if I wanted to, I couldn't let him go. How undeserving he is of my kindness, or how complicated the situation becomes between us. It doesn't matter - he's still my brother. And you are my husband…"

Doran looked at me, his eyes searching mine. "Do you believe you are incapable of being loved?"

His voice was gentle, yet laced with a hint of fear.

I paused, my throat tightening as I considered his question.

Family was always the most complicated thing to navigate, but I learned that for a relationship to survive and grow, it was important to open up and be vulnerable.

Doran deserved that.

"You claim to love me." I looked at the bookshelves. "And I don't understand why, but I'm willing to accept it. I want to believe that love can exist."

Doran stood up, towering over me as he looked down with a determined expression. He then got onto his knees and took my hands in his. His palms were warm and calloused, his skin smooth to the touch.

"You are everything." He gently caressed my cheek with the back of his hand. "You are perfection and grace. You are the light that guides me home in the darkness. You are the sun that never sets, the moon that never hides."

He looked at me with an intensity that made my heart skip a beat as he cupped my face.

"I'm a monster that worships your perfection, and I strive to love you in the way that you deserve."

The intensity of his words was almost too much. I wanted so badly to believe him, but I was still afraid.

But then he leaned in, slowly brushing his lips against mine. Everything made sense at that point.

My doubts melted away, replaced by the warmth of his embrace. I closed my eyes and allowed myself to surrender to him.

My body tensed up as his tongue brushed against mine, a stark reminder that the wounds of my past were still fresh and tender.

I pulled away from him instinctively, my heart racing as I tried to process the feelings of fear and insecurity that suddenly overwhelmed me.

Doran stepped back, his eyes wide with shock and confusion. "I'm sorry," he whispered, his voice strained with emotion.

He slowly reached out to touch me again, but I pulled away. I was too scared to let him in, but I wanted to.

"It's ok," I said, my voice trembling. "I know you won't hurt me."

Doran nodded slowly and looked away.

I knew he understood. That he would never push me too far, and that he would be there to protect me if I ever needed him.

"I don't know if I can trust you completely," I admitted. "But I know you care for me, and that's enough."

Doran smiled sadly and leaned in, pressing his forehead against my kneecaps. I ran my fingers through his hair and kissed the top of his head, allowing myself to feel the warmth of his embrace one last time before he stepped away.

We looked into each other's eyes for a few moments before he stepped away.

"It's okay to be scared," he said. "My mistakes have hurt you, and I can never take them back. Your fear is justified, and I understand that. But I want you to know that my love for you is true. No matter what, it will never fail."

His gaze was intense and unyielding, filled with a love that could not be denied.

"I'm in awe of your strength and courage. I am forever humbled by your spirit and in awe of how much you have endured."

The words hung in the air between us, like a promise of a future together. His love was a blessing and a burden at once. It soothed the hurt and doubt that was festering inside me.

It would take time to trust him again, but maybe there was still hope.

I shook my head. "You idolize me, and I don't understand why. You have created this vision of me I can never live up to, but I'm so desperate to try."

"You don't need to live up to any expectations," he said, taking my hands in his. "You have already given me more than I could ever ask for, and I am thankful every day that you are in my life."

He touched my chin, gently lifting it up so that our eyes met again. His gentle gaze searched my face.

"You are beautiful," he said softly. "In all your imperfections, you are perfect. I adore you for who you are. I will always strive to love you in the way that you deserve. I will never give up on us."

I nodded, taking a deep breath. "We should be perfect, but we're not," I said, my voice barely above a whisper. "But maybe that's alright. Maybe perfection isn't what matters most."

"You want to know the painful truth?" His

lips quirked up as he smiled at me. "I resented you for not trusting me, for fearing me. But now I understand why. You have been hurt before and, understandably, you are scared to trust again. I could never stay mad at you for that."

"I resented you too," I replied, my voice barely above a whisper. "For making me feel weak that night. I had weapons and magic, but I felt powerless against you. It made me feel helpless and exposed, like I was a child again. I didn't even think about using anything. I just froze in fear."

Doran's eyes darkened. "How could you be weak when so much was happening? Your brother tried to commit a coup. When that failed, he tried to murder you. You just heard your father passed away, and you became queen. You are strong, Aleyna—you have faced impossible odds and survived."

He paused for a moment before continuing.

"I only wish someone was there for me when I became king. Someone who would have been with me and helped guide me through the transition." He narrowed his eyes and looked away. "But I didn't, and instead I figured it all out on my own."

He sighed, his gaze returning to me.

"Is that why you initially kept me at arm's length?" I asked, my voice barely above a whisper.

Doran nodded slowly. "Yes," he said. "I am a controlling bastard, and I wanted to make sure that you would be safe. But," he added, his voice softening. "It was also one of the reasons I intervened that night and didn't say a thing. I wanted to make sure you were safe, and I knew no one else could do that better than me."

He smiled sadly and brushed a strand of hair out of my face.

"I was scared, Aleyna. I was scared that I couldn't save you, that something would happen to you if I didn't intervene."

That changed everything. He had been scared, just like me. He didn't do it out of spite or control—he did it because he cared about me.

"I'm glad you stood up for yourself and fought for your kingdom," he said, his voice full of admiration. "You are a strong woman, and I am proud to have you as my queen."

"Broken people don't have to stay broken forever," I whispered. "We can pick up the pieces and rebuild ourselves in whatever way we want."

"Yes," Doran said, his voice barely above a whisper. "We can."

Chapter 31

Goblins and healers

Cold sweat prickled my skin as hands glided over my stomach, mapping out the baby's movements.

Healer Anida asked me routine questions, and I barely concentrated on her words. All my attention was on the Goblin druid, the one with the eerily bright eyes and color-shifting aura.

Doran held my hand, his thumb tracing circles on the back of my palm. He smiled at me reassuringly, but I saw the unease in his eyes.

The Goblin druid petted my arm. "I'm here to make sure your baby is healthy. You have nothing to be afraid of."

His words did little to ease my fears, but I nodded anyway.

Healer Anida prodded my stomach and listened to the baby's heartbeat with a stethoscope.

The Goblin druid hummed an ancient tune that filled the room with a calming energy.

After what seemed like an eternity, Healer Anida declared everything good and bid us farewell with a bow.

The Goblin druid. "You humans always move too quickly."

He shook his head, and I swear a glimmer of amusement flashed across his face.

"Is something wrong?" I asked.

"No, Winter Queen." His mouth turned up in an imitation of a smile, and sharp black teeth revealed themselves to me. "You have a beautiful baby growing inside you."

I exhaled in relief. "It's not every day a Fae child is conceived."

"No, I suppose not. But don't worry, I'm here to make sure your baby is healthy and that you're taken care of."

I smiled brightly at him.

The Goblin druid flinched slightly, his eyes widening as he looked at me. From the way he looked at me, he found me just as interesting as he found him.

He quickly composed himself, however, shooting me a polite smile before turning away and murmuring something I couldn't make out.

I could feel the tension in the room and the awkwardness between us, but I appreciated his efforts to be polite, regardless. It made me feel a little less uncomfortable.

"Thank you," I said, my voice soft and kind.

He looked at me with surprise, as if he hadn't expected me to be so understanding. He nodded in response, and I could see a hint of gratitude on his face before he bowed.

Doran turned to the Goblin druid and asked a barrage of questions about the baby's health and what we should expect during the pregnancy.

The Goblin druid smiled, clearly amused by Doran's protectiveness. He patiently answered each question and even offered additional advice on how to keep the baby safe.

"The next twelve months are going to be the most important in your baby's development," he said. "Take care of yourself, and your little one will thrive."

I stared at the Goblin druid, my eyes wide and my mouth hanging open. His words took me aback—that was seven more months than I expected.

I swallowed hard. "Twelve months?"

The Goblin druid smiled and nodded. "This is not a mortal pregnancy, Winter Queen. Fae pregnancies take longer, and the process is more complicated. Ailments that are common in human pregnancies don't apply to you. You must take care of your body and mind for the baby."

Doran squeezed my hand, and I smiled at him. "I will be with her the entire way."

The Goblin druid nodded. "You can help her with whatever she needs, but it is important to remember that does not mean there are no dangers," The Goblin druid said, his voice low and steady. "For your own and baby's safety, take whatever precautions you can. Fluxes in magical energy, sudden shifts in temperature, and the possibility of your baby becoming entwined with a spirit are all dangers you must consider."

I glanced at Doran, who nodded in agreement. We would do our best to keep myself safe for the rest of my pregnancy.

"What do you mean by entwined with a spirit?" I asked, a chill running down my spine.

The Goblin druid nodded sagely. "It is rare. But there is the chance that your baby could become connected to an otherworldly being. If that happens, it is important to be aware of the potential consequences."

Frost crept up my spine as I listened to the Goblin druid's words. This was not the pregnancy check-up I expected, but I was determined to take his advice and do whatever it takes to ensure the safety of my baby.

I glanced over at Doran. A faint shimmer of blue light glowed around him. His power was emerging, and through our bond, I felt his fear and desperation to protect me and the baby.

I smiled at him, feeling a warmth spread through me. Whatever happened in the coming months, I knew Doran and I would make it through. He would fight anyone or anything that threatened us.

He pulled me close, and his warmth spread throughout my body like a blanket. "Don't be scared," he whispered. "Fear mongering does no good. Winter triumphs over fear."

"Thank you for this advice," I said, turning my gaze to the Goblin druid.

He smiled and bowed his head in a sign of respect. "It is my pleasure, Winter Queen."

With another bow, the Goblin druid bid us farewell.

Doran helped me up from the exam chair. He turned around as I adjusted my clothes, and I caught sight of the blue light once again.

"Are those your tattoos?"

He smiled and let out a soft laugh; the light flickered around him like stars in the night sky. "They are conductors of my power and a reminder of who I am. The goblin overstepped his bounds, so I showed him who was in charge."

A knot twisted in my stomach as I realized the gravity of our situation. "What information do I need to know? I feel like I'm walking into this blind."

"We'll figure it out together," he said, meeting my eyes with a reassuring look. He held out his hand, and I took it. His grip was steady, and the surrounding light pulsed with his magic.

"We'll get through this," he said, squeezing my hand ever so slightly. "I promise."

He slowly reached his hand to put it on my belly. His touch felt gentle and comforting, like a cool breeze in the middle of a hot summer's day.

I slowly reached out and put my hand on top of his, interlacing our fingers together. He let out a content sigh and smiled wider.

"You will be an amazing mother, Aleyna," he whispered, pressing his hand more firmly against my belly.

I glanced away. "You think so?"

He nodded. "I know so."

He removed his hand and took a step back. The blue light slowly faded away.

"I shall leave you be so that you can get some work done."

"Wait," I said, stopping him mid-stride. "Will you be okay?"

He smiled and nodded. "It's alright, little wife," he said. "I'm here for you, no matter what comes our way."

He took a few steps back.

I exhaled and sighed. I promised myself I would try to give our relationship a chance, and Doran proved he was willing to help me. The courage to take the leap was what I needed.

"Doran... can you help me with something?"

He paused and nodded. "Of course."

"The ambassador from Beronisa is coming in a few days, and I need to prepare for her arrival. I have to finish other tasks as well. Could you please look over the military expenditures for me? I know you have an eye for detail and can spot any discrepancies quickly."

He smiled, understanding the gravity of the situation. "I can do that," he replied. "Tell me what you need, and I will take care of it."

My heart fluttered with apprehension. I wanted to trust him, but I was wary of letting someone else take control over an important decision that could affect our family's future. But then I remembered my promise to give our relationship a chance.

I took a deep breath and nodded in agreement. "Alright," I said, my voice wavering slightly. "I trust you. The documents are in the study."

He gave me a warm smile and bowed slightly. "I will take care of it," he said. "Consider it done."

With a last nod, frost swirled around Doran's feet. Suddenly, a gust of cold air swept through the room and he vanished, leaving only a trail of snowflakes in his wake.

I stared at the empty spot where he once stood and shivered, feeling a chill run down my spine. It was as if he took the winter night with him when he left, leaving behind a cold and empty void.

The cold air lingered for a few moments before vanishing, leaving me alone in the hallway again.

"I hope you won't let me down," I whispered. "Winter storms can be treacherous, and I'm trusting you to keep me safe."

Chapter 32

Truths and comforts

Late at night, after the sun set and the sky turned an inky black, I found myself holed up in my chambers, pouring over the documents.

I wanted to make sure that no discrepancies existed in the military expenditures.

The only sound in the room was the occasional scratch of my quill on parchment.

My eyes drooped with fatigue. "I must be nearly done," I muttered, rubbing my eyes as I quickly scanned over the last few documents.

"Are you almost finished, little wife?"

I jumped and turned around, startled.

Standing in the shadows was Doran, his

black hair shining in the dim light. He stepped forward, his gray eyes glinting with something I couldn't quite place.

"Yes," I said, my voice barely above a whisper. "I need to check the last few documents."

He nodded and stepped closer, gently taking the parchment from my hands. He read it silently before handing it back to me.

"You don't have to do this alone, you know," he said, his voice kind yet firm.

My cheeks flushed, embarrassed that he caught me.

But instead of reprimanding me, he simply smiled. "Rulers must always ensure that their people are safe. The smallest of mistakes can cause a ripple effect and put people in danger. So it's important to double-check the work, no matter how tedious it may be."

He put a hand on my shoulder, and my heart fluttered. Even though he saw me at my weakest moment, his words were gentle and reassuring.

"You're not mad at me?"

"No," he replied, his voice softening even more. "You should never be afraid to ask for help. You are a powerful leader, and I am here to support you. But that doesn't mean you should trust blindly. Make sure that everything is in order by doing your own research. That is the price of leadership."

I sat and leaned back in my chair.

Doran lay down on the ottoman in front of my desk and his clothes shifted, revealing the firm muscles beneath. His posture was relaxed, and he looked completely at ease despite the formality of our meeting.

The firelight danced along his features, drawing out the rich tones of his skin and the defined curve of his jaw.

His lips were slightly parted, almost as if he was ready to say something, but instead, he just closed his eyes and breathed in the scent of the burning wood.

I couldn't help but admire him, even if I knew better than to be distracted.

His strength and self-assurance radiated from him, even in repose. He was a man who knew his own worth, and his comfort in his own skin was a captivating sight.

I cleared my throat, trying to focus my attention back on the task at hand.

I collected the documents and placed them neatly on my desk. "Let's make sure that everything is as it should be."

Doran opened his eyes and smiled at me as if to say that he knew I had been admiring him.

"You are right," he said, pushing off the ottoman and standing. "The details matter. We need to be vigilant if we are to protect our people."

He reached forward and tucked a loose strand of my hair behind my ear, his fingers lingering against my skin.

I swallowed, my heart racing.

Even after all these months together, the proximity of his body still made me feel alive.

"Can I ask you anything I want?" I whispered, my voice barely above a whisper.

Doran chuckled and stepped back, his hand dropping to his side. "Yes," he replied, his voice deep and sure. "You can ask me anything you want."

"How can I trust you?"

Doran looked thoughtful for a moment, as if contemplating his answer.

The question didn't seem to bother him. If I were him, I would be pissed.

"You can never be certain of anyone's intentions," he said eventually. "But you can trust that I will always act in the best interests of our people." He paused, his gaze steady and sure. "And I can trust that you will always strive to do the same."

He smiled and stepped back, the intensity of the moment fading away.

"Romantically speaking, I think we both know what the answer is," he said. "We can never be certain, but if we open our hearts to each other and move forward with caution, then I believe that trust will come in time."

I nodded, his words resonating with me. He was right; trust takes time to build. I couldn't help but think that the answer was already there.

"It's a risk," I said finally.

"It is." He arched his eyebrows. "But it's a risk that can bring substantial rewards." He reached out and took my hand in his. "Do you trust me?"

He asked with a smile, but the intensity of his gaze was undeniable.

I took a deep breath and nodded, my heart beating faster with anticipation. "No." I looked away, my voice trembling slightly. "But I believe in you."

Doran smiled and stepped closer, brushing his lips against my forehead. "My turn to ask a question."

"What is it?"

Doran looked down at me and smiled, his eyes twinkling in the firelight. "Do you believe there is beauty in life, even in the midst of pain?"

The question surprised me.

"Even though we are going through something hard, I believe that beauty can be found in small moments. It's a reminder that joy can still exist despite our circumstances."

Doran nodded, a look of understanding passing over his face. "There is beauty in the smallest moments." He paused, his gaze never leaving mine. "That is something worth fighting for. Your trust is worth fighting for."

Flustered, I stepped back, feeling my skin flush.

Doran smiled and reached for my hand again, his fingers curling around mine.

"Another truth for a truth?" he said, his eyes alight with mischief.

I smiled and looked down at our intertwined hands. "What do you want to know?"

Doran considered for a moment, his gaze thoughtful. "What do you hold dear?" he asked finally. "The slight comforts, the moments of joy, the things that make life worth living?"

The daily moments of joy, the sunsets, and the laughter shared with friends. The long days spent working on a project, rewarding myself afterward with a treat.

"The things that make life worth living for me are the small moments of comfort, like a warm cup of tea in the morning and cuddling up with a good book in the evening."

I smiled brightly.

"I enjoy making something with my hands, whether it's needlework or weaving, and savoring the simple pleasure of a hearty meal. And most of all, I treasure the moments spent with others, enjoying each other's company and catching up on all of life's little adventures."

"Those are the things that truly make life worth living."

I smiled, remembering all the moments that made my life so special.

"Yes," I said softly. "Those are the things that make life worth living. How about you? Painting?"

He smiled, his gaze far away. "My moments of joy come from spending time in nature," he drawled. "Being surrounded by the beauty of the world, whether it's a breathtaking vista or a simple meadow. Taking in the silence and being still in the moment, allowing my mind to wander and be free."

I nodded, understanding the solace he found in those moments. "It sounds like a beautiful way to spend time."

He looked into my eyes, his gaze full of warmth. "It is," he replied. "And I can't think of a better way to spend time with someone."

My heart fluttered and my cheeks flushed, but I smiled back, squeezing his hand in response.

"So tomorrow I wish to cordially invite you on a journey," Doran said, his tone light and playful.

"Oh? Where to?" I asked, intrigued.

"That will be a surprise," he said, eyes twinkling. "But I can tell you this - it will be a combination of both of our desires."

I shook my head in amusement. "You're not giving much away, are you?"

"I'm teasing," he said with a grin. "But bring comfortable shoes, because our adventure will include plenty of walking."

My heart raced, and I felt a thrill of anticipation.

I knew it would be an adventure.

"Sounds perfect," I said, smiling up at him.

He returned my smile, his face illuminated with joy. "It will be."

He nodded once more as if to confirm my thought and then stepped back.

"Now," he said, his voice laced with amusement. "I believe you have some documents to review."

I smiled and looked down at my desk, ready to take on the task.

"Yes," I said. "I do."

I took a deep breath and turned to the task at hand.

What could he possibly be planning for tomorrow?

Chapter 33

Miray

Sheeps blotted the meadow, their white wool reflecting in the setting sun. The distant mountains loomed large and purple against an endless sky.

I couldn't help but smile as I watched Doran take in the view with a wide grin. He looked so content and peaceful, standing there beside me.

He turned to me then, his eyes shining with joy. "Ready?" he asked, offering his hand.

"We are in Ilanya?" I raised my eyebrow in surprise. "Why did you bring me here?"

Frosthome was a veritable wonderland, full of magical creatures and mysterious sights. Ilanya couldn't compare to the beauty I found there.

But, as I looked out over the rolling hills and valleys, my heart felt full. What Ilanya lacked in wonders was made up for in peace and contentment.

Did Doran feel it too? I could only hope so.

Doran smiled and gestured to the meadow. "The mortal world has its own beauty," he said, his voice full of admiration. "The way the light falls on the landscape, turning it into an ever-changing canvas of colors and shapes. It's a beauty that never grows old, no matter how many times you witness it."

Doran had a painter's eye for beauty. He looked at the world and saw its depths in ways that I hadn't imagined.

Here, in the mortal world, he appreciated its subtle nuances and complexities.

He saw more than just a meadow of sheep and a setting sun - he saw the potential for an infinite amount of beauty.

My heart swelled with love for this man, and I squeezed his hand in gratitude.

We stood there, just watching the world as it changed before us.

He paused for a moment, his gaze distant and thoughtful.

"If there is one thing I have learned in my

life," he said, looking at me with his intense gray eyes. "It's that beauty is everywhere. We just have to open our eyes and look for it."

I couldn't help but agree with him. Even if we couldn't see it, the world was beautiful. We only had to open our eyes and search for them.

"Walk with me?" Doran asked, offering his arm.

I smiled and looped my arm through his. Together, we walked across the meadow, our steps light and sure.

The grass beneath our feet melted away, replaced by gray cobblestone walkways. The sheep were replaced with people, their conversations and laughter creating a pleasant hum. And before us was a village nestled in the alpine foothills.

The buildings were made of warm, cream-colored stone and had colorful shutters that opened up to reveal windows with vivid flower boxes.

The air was filled with the scent of freshly baked bread and wood smoke, and I could hear a bubbling stream in the background.

A few locals chatted on their doorsteps, and there were small clusters of colorful wildflowers growing here and there.

Doran smiled as he took it all in. He

lingered at the edges of the village, admiring every detail and drinking in the beauty of it all.

We continued our walking tour in peaceful silence, as he led me to the edge of the village, where a farm was nestled in the foothills.

The land was overgrown with wildflowers, and the buildings were made of faded wood. It was obvious that it had been abandoned for a while. Yet Doran seemed undeterred by its state.

He gazed at the farm with a look of admiration, his eyes twinkling in the sunlight. "Come," he said, his voice full of anticipation. "I want to show you something special."

Doran reached out and gently helped me over the crumbling stone wall that surrounded the farm. He clasped my hand firmly, his gaze never leaving mine, as he smiled reassuringly.

Stones crumbled beneath our feet as we stepped into the field, and I could feel the freshness of the air around us.

The wildflowers were in full bloom, and dew still covered the grass.

My hat flew off in the wind and I laughed as I retrieved it. The wildflowers caressed my cheeks, and the sun kissed my skin.

Doran picked a wildflower and handed it to me with a smile. "This is for you," he said, his voice soft.

I accepted the flower with a thankful smile. As I tucked the flower into my hair, I looked at him and saw his admiration.

"Your beauty is timeless and captivating." He gently brushed a strand of hair away from my face, his fingertips grazing my cheek.

His touch was like a spark of electricity that ran through me, and I felt my heart flutter.

We stood there in the middle of that wildflower field. The world faded as we looked at each other.

He shook his head, his eyes still locked on mine. "No," he whispered. "Enchantress, you distract me from my purpose, but in the best way possible. I want to show you a place that will forever be here in my heart, and I hope it etches itself into yours too."

He turned and gestured towards the farm. "Come," he said in a husky voice, beckoning me with a wave of his hand.

I smiled at him and nodded, my heart pounding in anticipation as I followed him into the forgotten farm.

He led me to a small pond at the edge of the farm, where an old pear tree grew. Its trunk was twisted and gnarled, its branches reaching out in all directions.

Doran pointed to the low-hanging branch, and I saw, etched into its surface in bold handwriting, the name of my mother.

Miray, daughter of Aleyna and Mirza.

He looked up at me and smiled, his eyes twinkling in the bright sunlight.

"Your mother carved her name here when she was a young girl on a visit to the farm, and it has been here ever since."

My heart raced as I read the inscription and remembered my mother, who died when I was 9 years old.

Doran smiled sadly, placing his hand on the trunk of the pear tree. I watched as he closed his eyes and took a deep breath.

Suddenly, the air around us sparkled with a gentle silver light. His lips moved silently, and as he finished speaking, I felt a tingle of energy that seemed to escape from his fingertips.

The pear tree bloomed with fragrant white pear blossoms, and I gasped in wonder as the air sparkled around us.

Doran opened his eyes and smiled, his gaze never leaving mine.

"Your mother's memory will always be here," he said. "Your great-grandparents used to live here." His gaze was distant and thoughtful as he looked around the farm. "Your mother spent many summers here as a child, and this tree holds many fond memories for her. It's your legacy, and a reminder of how special she was."

"I wanted to give you this, a piece of your family so that you could feel connected to them, even when you're far away."

My family history was so deeply rooted in this place, and I didn't even know it.

As I stood there, the sun setting in the distance, I traced the letters of my mother's name with the tip of my finger. My family was here, and I could feel it.

I looked up at Doran and smiled, my heart swelling with love for him. He had given me a piece of my past, and I felt so humbled by his gesture.

"Thank you", I said, placing a kiss on his palm and intertwining my fingers with his.

He smiled and nodded, pressing a gentle kiss to my forehead before turning towards the farm.

"The stories of this place will stay in your heart and in the stories you tell our children. I wanted to give you something of lasting love."

He brought me here to make sure my family's stories would live on.

I marveled at his thoughtfulness and kindness, and I knew that I was blessed to have such a wonderful man in my life.

My heart fluttered. "What have you discovered? Tell me, husband."

Doran smiled, his eyes twinkling in the fading light of the day.

He took my hand in his and explained how he had asked around the village and found out more about my mother's family.

He told me stories of my great-grandparents, who had been married for over seventy years, and of my mother's childhood spent playing in the meadows near their farm.

I knew none of these things about my mother's family, as my father had never spoken of them. But Doran, with his gentle and generous spirit, found a way to give me a connection to my family's past.

He had given me a gift, and I was so grateful that he had taken the time to search for it.

We stepped closer to the pond, and I let go of Doran's hand as we slipped off our sandals and dipped our feet into the cool water. Fish darted between our toes, and I smiled as the sun sank behind the hills.

I felt a gentle tickle on my nose and, looking up, saw a small ladybug perched there. Its shiny black wings were tipped with a bright red border, and its tiny black eyes seemed to twinkle in the fading light.

Doran placed his finger on it, gently lifting it off and setting it free. I watched as the ladybug fluttered away, its wings shimmering in the sunshine.

His black hair blew in the wind, and I smiled as I looked up at him. "A truth for a beautiful moment?"

He leaned forward, a mischievous glint in his eye. "A secret to keep forever between us?"

A smile tugged at the corner of my lips. "Secrets are always better when shared, but today, I think I want to share something with you that is true and beautiful. Something that I want to keep between us, now and always."

I heard the distant sound of sheep in the rolling hills, their gentle bleating a peaceful melody that lulled me into a sense of serenity.

"I want you to know that I will always be here for you," I said, taking his hand in mine. "No matter what life brings us, I am yours and you are mine. And that will never change."

Doran took my hands in his and pressed them to his lips. I felt the warmth of his breath on my skin and the gentle caress of his lips.

His eyes sparkled like tiny stars, and I felt a thrill of excitement course through me.

Then he moved one hand to his mouth and blew on it, making a soft whistling sound.

Suddenly, an icy chill traveled up my arm and slowly spread throughout my body.

I looked down and gasped in surprise, for my hands were now covered in tiny snowflakes, glittering like diamonds in the fading light.

Doran smiled softly and brought his hands to mine. He cupped them in his palms; the snowflakes dusting our fingertips.

"If we're not telling secrets, I have a gift to share with you," he said in a gentle voice.

He brushed his thumb across the snowflakes, and they swirled around our hands like tiny stars.

"You have already given me the greatest gift," I interrupted him, my voice shaking with emotion. "You gave me back my mother, even if it's only through stories and memories. You've shown me that love and history can live on, even when the people we love are no longer here."

He would never truly understand how much this gift had meant to me. All traces of her family had been erased. But with Doran's help, I could still feel connected to her.

"No gift could ever compare to what you have given me."

Doran smiled and looked down at me lovingly. "I believe husbands should spoil their wives," he said softly. "And that's why I want to give you this special gift. It will remind you that you are special and loved every single day."

I chuckled as my feet sunk slightly into the mud. "That's a lovely sentiment, but I'm sure my husband is quite busy enough without taking on extra duties."

"Never too busy for you, my Aleyna," he murmured and brushed a strand of hair away from my face. "You don't need to fully understand it, Aleyna. All you need to know is that this is the most important gift I can give you: my name. In Frosthome, we don't give our names to just anyone. We select those worthy of knowing us for who we truly are, and I have chosen you."

He smiled and took my hand in his, our fingers intertwined.

Names had power among the Fae, and I knew that too well. Knowing someone's name gave you power over them.

It was a gift too grave for me to accept, as Doran was not only giving me his name, but also a part of himself that he never shared before.

My throat tightened with emotion.

He would hand me something that would make me his equal and, with it, a sense of control over our relationship.

Not his equal, but his partner.

Doran opened his mouth, but I placed my fingers on his mouth, and he looked into my eyes.

I saw the longing in his gaze, but I just smiled softly and shook my head.

"You cannot give me something so precious. I could never accept it. That you trust me with your name is more than enough."

Doran wrapped his arms around my waist and buried his face in my hair. I felt his heartbeat against mine, and everything around us melted away.

"Little wife, what is a name to a love like ours? You are my wife, and no name can ever give you the power I have given you."

His fingers threaded through my hair, and he looked into my eyes with such intensity that it made my skin prickle.

"My beloved, I give you all that I have: my name, my love, my kingdom, and everything in between. They are all yours, and all I ask is one look of love in return."

He smiled that knowing smile, as shudders of electricity ran through my body. Doran was the first to break away, his gaze still locked with mine.

His lips brushed against my throat, sending shivers down my spine. Although it was a chaste kiss, it felt so much more intimate and meaningful.

"To control another being's name is a power that should never be taken lightly. I don't need your name, Doran. I have something far greater than a name can give me: your love."

Doran's eyes darkened with a mix of hunger and greed, his throat bobbing as he swallowed hard.

The intensity of his stare left me feeling breathless and captivated.

He devoured me with his gaze, as if my very presence was a feast he could not resist.

"My love for you is so great that I need to give you something that will last forever." He slowly pulled away, his eyes never leaving mine. "My name is yours to keep, Aleyna. Take my name and keep it close, so that you may have a piece of me with you always."

"How could I ever forget you?"

Doran chuckled, his eyes twinkling. "Oh,

my Aleyna," he whispered and pressed a tender kiss to my forehead. "Slaying dragons and conquering kingdoms is nothing compared to loving you."

"Doran," I whispered, smiling up at him. "You don't need to give me your name or slay dragons. You have already conquered my heart."

Doran's lips crashed against mine with a fierce intensity, as if he was desperate to drink in my love. His tongue explored my mouth, tasting me as if I was the sweetest nectar he had ever encountered.

His hands gripped my waist as if he could not possibly get close enough.

"Daihanon." Doran pulled away slightly, a satisfied smile on his face. "My little queen," he murmured. "My name is yours to keep."

The air around us seemed to freeze as the power of his words took hold.

Daihanon.

The name echoed in my heart and soul.

"Daihanon," I murmured, savoring the syllables.

Doran smiled, his gaze darkened. "Yes, little one. Daihanon. That is my name, and it belongs to you now."

"Daihanon the ever-lasting, my husband."

Chapter 34

Daihanon

"My nipples have turned blue, Doran!"

Doran's eyes lit up with excitement as he looked at me. He ran his hands over my growing belly, feeling the baby kick inside. "It's a girl," he said, his voice full of awe and admiration. "A strong little queen who will one day rule the realm, just like her mother."

He smiled, and I could see the love and pride radiating from his face.

"She will be a fierce warrior. In the face of adversity, she will never back down. She will have your courage and tenacity, Aleyna."

"Blue nipples mean a girl?" I said teasingly.

"Yes," he replied, his eyes twinkling with

amusement. "And I know she will be the perfect ruler for Frosthome. The realm will never face a stronger queen."

I smiled and nuzzled against him, feeling the safety and security of his embrace. "I'm convinced it's a son," I said. "He will be as strong and stubborn as his father, but I know he will also have your heart and compassion. He will have a good head on his shoulders and will know how to balance justice with mercy."

I paused, a content expression on my face.

"He will be a wonderful king, Doran."

Doran smiled and pressed his lips to my forehead. "With your help, I'm sure he will be." His gaze suddenly grew serious. "Either way, we'll be ready," he replied, a smile playing on his lips. "Boy or girl, they will both be incredible rulers, just like their mother. And as contriving as their father."

I laughed, and Doran joined me. We stayed like that for a while, just enjoying the moment and the warmth of one another's embrace.

There was a lot to do, but there was no rush. We had all the time in the world.

"What are you thinking about?" Doran asked, his voice gentle.

I sighed. "I was just thinking about Ambassador Börek and his endless visits," I replied, my voice full of exasperation. "He drags out every conversation and every decision. It's maddening."

Doran chuckled and shook his head. He rolled onto his back and pulled the covers up to his waist, revealing his beautifully sculpted muscles.

His chest was strong and firm, and I could feel a warmth radiating from him as he looked up at me with a wry smile. "At least you don't have to deal with the Summer Court's trade deal. They are so haughty, always trying to weasel out of their obligations. It's infuriating."

"That doesn't sound so bad," I said, unable to hide the teasing tone in my voice.

He laughed again and pulled me close. "It's not," he replied. "A glare and a few choice words can be all it takes to move things forward." He paused and kissed my forehead. "But I'm glad I have you by my side to help me through it all."

I smiled and snuggled against him. "Me too," I said. "No matter what, we'll make it."

Doran nodded, his expression full of certainty and confidence.

He was right. We would make it, no matter what challenges lay in our path. Together, we were powerful, and nothing could stop us.

I laughed and said, "Or we could always

just stop being king and queen and let someone else take on the hard job. Wouldn't that be nice?"

Doran smiled and shook his head. He touched my face tenderly, and his eyes twinkled with humor. "That's not an option," he said, his voice gentle yet firm. "If I have to face these arduous tasks and challenges, then so do you."

"You could also stop being so noble and just let me take a break," I said, trying to lighten the mood.

He laughed softly and kissed my forehead. "I'll let you take a break," he said. "But just today."

I rolled around in the bed, trying to get comfortable, but my ever-growing baby bump made it difficult.

I smiled as I felt the little kicks and movements of my unborn child. I was sure that no matter what, this little one would grow up to be strong and powerful, just like their mother and father.

"You're right," I said to Doran, my voice full of affection. "We will make it. Together."

Doran slowly stood up, the fabric of his nightclothes quietly rustling around him. He stretched and then took a few moments to admire himself in the full-length mirror. His toned physique was accentuated by the soft glow of the candlelight, and I couldn't help but ogle him.

I raised an eyebrow, amused. "You are so vain."

Doran chuckled and flexed his arms. "I can't help it," he replied, winking at me. "When you wake up next to a goddess, you can't help but admire the view."

I chuckled.

He grabbed his robe from the side of the bed and carefully wrapped it around himself. His movements were graceful and confident, as if he was always aware of the effect his presence had on me.

I sat up in bed to get a better look. My gaze lingered over the contours of his body. He flashed me a roguish grin before he pulled the blanket up and over my shoulders.

"Sleep tight, little wife," he said, before turning to leave the bedroom.

As I watched him leave, a thought came to my mind - horny pregnancy hormones were real, even in a Fae baby. I smiled and shook my head at the absurdity of it all.

My body was changing in so many ways, and yet here I was, lusting after my husband like a lovesick teenager. But I couldn't help it - he was just so amazing and I was completely smitten.

I sighed and snuggled into the blankets, my thoughts heavy with longing for my husband. Maybe I could surprise him in his office? I thought to myself.

Yes, that's definitely something I should do...

∞∞∞

I quietly opened the door to Doran's office and stepped inside.

He was sitting at his desk, eyes focused on a large map that was spread out in front of him. His brow was furrowed with concentration, and I could see the wheels turning in his head as he plotted out his next move.

The room was dimly lit, but I could make out the various bookshelves and ornate furniture around the room. He had made this place his sanctuary, a refuge away from the hustle and bustle of court life.

"How did your meeting go today?" I asked, breaking the silence.

Startled, Doran looked up from his map and smiled when he saw me. "Well, it went better than expected," he said. "We discussed a few key points that will help us with our mission."

A smile tugged my lips. "And how many Summer court Fae did you scare off in the process?"

Doran laughed and shook his head. "Not as many as you'd think," he said, standing up from his desk.

He walked towards me, and my heart raced as he drew closer.

"But enough about court business," he said, his voice low and inviting. "What brings you to my office?"

I offered him an innocent smile and stepped closer.

I wrapped my arms around his neck and looked up into his eyes. "I'm here because I wanted to surprise you," I said, pressing myself against him.

Doran raised an eyebrow and grinned. He leaned down and kissed me, his lips lingering on mine for a few moments, before he pulled away.

"Well," he said, looking into my eyes. "I can definitely say that this was a pleasant surprise. But what exactly were you hoping to accomplish?"

I blushed and looked away. "Oh, nothing," I said, trying to play it cool. "I just wanted to show you how much I love you."

Crave you. Desire you.

Doran smiled and ran his fingers through my hair.

He leaned down and kissed me again, this time with more intensity. My body heated as his lips moved against mine, and I knew he felt the same way.

After a few moments, we both pulled away and smiled at each other. I rested my head against his chest and felt the steady beat of his heart.

"Thank you for coming here," Doran whispered, tightening his arms around me. "It means a lot to me."

I smiled and closed my eyes, thankful for this moment of peace. I rested my head against his chest and savored the moment.

I was nervous as I spoke, my words almost caught in my throat. "Doran," I whispered, trying to steady my racing heart. "There's something I've been wanting to ask you for some time now, but I haven't had the courage."

"Little wife, you can ask me anything," he said, his voice low and comforting.

I took a deep breath and closed my eyes, feeling the warmth of his arms around me. I opened my eyes and looked up at him, steeling myself for whatever reaction he might have.

"I want us to open our wedding bond," I said softly. "It's been closed since the beginning of our marriage, and it feels like there's a hole in my heart. After all this time, I feel like it's right that we do this."

Doran was silent for a few moments as he looked into my eyes. His expression was unreadable, and I held my breath in anticipation.

Finally, he smiled and pulled me closer, pressing a gentle kiss to my forehead. "Yes," he breathed. "I agree."

Tears sprang to my eyes as relief flooded through me.

As I closed my eyes and felt Doran's arms around me, I could sense a warmth spreading through my body.

His emotions filled my own, flooding into me like a river rushing over its banks.

A wave of joy and love surged through me as the bond was opened, filling every corner of my being with emotions so powerful it was almost overwhelming.

His arms tightened around me, and I opened my eyes to look into his.

His expression was full of love and joy, and

I could feel the same emotion flowing from him into me. We stayed like that for a few moments, our hearts connected through the bond we had just formed.

"What do you feel?" Doran whispered, his voice full of emotion.

I smiled and snuggled closer to his chest. "I feel so much love," I said, my voice barely above a whisper. "You fill every crevice of my heart."

Doran smiled and kissed the top of my head. I closed my eyes and stayed in his embrace, reveling in the warmth and love that surrounded us.

"I feel our child growing strong between us," Doran said, his voice full of wonder. "Our bond is a beautiful thing."

I nodded in agreement.

Doran smiled and ran his fingers through my hair. "You should have told me you were aching for me. I would have opened this bond sooner just to make you feel better," he said, his voice full of innuendo. "My tongue is at your service."

I blushed and smacked his arm lightly. "Oh, Doran," I said with a laugh.

His pupils dilated, and his lips curled up into a mischievous smile. "Oh, Aleyna," he said in a low voice, pressing a kiss to my neck.

I shivered as his lips made their way to my earlobe. "You're going to make me forget all about the bond," I said, my voice barely audible.

Doran laughed and nuzzled my neck, his breath tickling my skin.

"Is anyone listening in?" I asked with a giggle.

Doran pulled away and looked into my eyes, his gaze filled with love and desire. "No one but us."

"Daihanon," I whispered his true name, letting its syllables wash over me.

Doran smiled and pulled me closer, planting a gentle kiss on my forehead.

"How about we make a deal?" he said, his voice husky. "If I can make you scream my true name, then I'm allowed to make all your dreams come true."

"No deal, you are already making all my dreams come true," I said, pressing a kiss to his lips.

As he pulled away, his eyes twinkled with amusement. "You drive a hard bargain, little wife."

"The Winter King taught me well."

Thanks you so much for reading!

Can't get enough of the Winter King and his little wife? Don't worry, I got you...

A secret bonus chapter is waiting for you! One that takes place after the book ends... from his point of view.

The Winter King is most eager to share his secrets with you. Are you ready for it?

Thank you so much for reading my work! I hope you enjoyed it. If you could take a moment to leave a review, it would mean the world to me.

As an independent author, reviews are essential in helping new readers discover my books.

Thank you again and happy reading!

If you are interested in my work, you can also follow me on tiktok: @silyabarakatbooks

xoxo

Silya Barakat

About The Author

Silya Barakat

Silya Barakat Silya Barakat is a fantasy romance writer, whose fantasy-loving spirit has been alive since early childhood. As she grew older, Silya found new ways to escape into her fantasy worlds. Writing about fantasy realms filled with strong and complex heroines, magic, and a bit of romance became her latest passion.

When she's not busy writing, Silya enjoys spending time with her family and friends, discovering new music and films, or curled up with a good book.

Books By This Author

Bride Of The Gilded Prince

When the elves come looking for a bride, you do whatever it takes to protect the ones you love. Even if that means marrying the coldest and most dangerous of them all.

Thimsal's life was perfect until she became a bargaining chip for her people. When they come to find a bride for their ruthless prince, she volunteers to save the only person who she's ever thought of as a sister.

Now, she's embroiled in a snake pit of court politics which might be more treacherous than any battlefield. Thimsal may start out as a naive outsider, but if she doesn't become the princess she needs to be, she'll find that there are worse endings than death in the elvish courts.

As if that weren't enough, Prince Maedras, her betrothed, is a man with secrets of his own. She's always known him as a monster, a creature set to end her people's very existence, but as their courtship continues, she'll find that there may be more to him than meets the eye.

When your people's lives are stake, do you trust your head or your heart? And in a world where everyone commits atrocities, how do you choose a side?

There is only one thing that matters in her world now: power. Maybe she belongs here more than she ever knew...

This slow burn romantic fantasy with a touch of spice is perfect for readers looking for an immersive, unique world.

Author's note: This is book 1 in a series and ends on a cliff. Book 1 is not the standard for the heat of the romance and each book gets spicier.

PS: This is a romantic fantasy.

Printed in Great Britain
by Amazon